CHASING *the* AVATAR

DESCENT BOOK I

JOVAN JONES

DESTINY IMAGE® PUBLISHERS, INC.

P.O. Box 310, Shippensburg, PA 17257-0310

"Speaking to the Purposes of God for This Generation and for the Generations to Come."

This book and all other Destiny Image, Revival Press, MercyPlace, Fresh Bread, Destiny Image Fiction, and Treasure House books are available at Christian bookstores and distributors worldwide.

For a U.S. bookstore nearest you, call **1-800-722-6774.**

For more information on foreign distributors, call **717-532-3040.**

Or reach us on the Internet: **www.destinyimage.com**

ISBN 10: 0-7684-2824-6

ISBN 13: 978-0-7684-2824-7

For Worldwide Distribution, Printed in the U.S.A.

1 2 3 4 5 6 7 8 9 10 11 / 13 12 11 10 09

DEDICATION

THIS book is dedicated first and foremost to my Lord and Savior, Jesus Christ—my Everything. Thank You for coming and retrieving me when I was so far gone and as good as dead. Thank You for restoring me. I am well aware that any good thing found in me is Your doing. You are, and always will be, my Knight in Shining Armor.

Second, I dedicate this book to my parents, Ryven and Brenda Jones. If it were not for your steadfast, unfailing prayers, and your constant support and love even when I acted *supremely* unlovable, I am sure I would have died a long time ago. I am honored to be called your daughter.

And third, I dedicate this book to my son, Isaiah. I owe you so much. Thank you for being my son.

ACKNOWLEDGMENTS

TIFFANY DAHLMAN, you are a shining example of an incredible woman of God. In going to Cambodia and Burma on mission trips and then in adopting an African-American boy, a Filipino boy, and now a baby Ethiopian girl, you truly walk the walk of the Christian heart. By your example of courageous love and action, I have found the inspiration to see this book through to its completion. Thank you for encouraging me to write this book, for reading it, and for offering helpful feedback.

Thank you, La'Quanda McGeachy, for encouraging me to write this book over the years even when I faltered. Thank you for reading it and giving me your generation's perspective. You have always been one of my biggest cheerleaders.

Tamara Shove, you slogged through the manuscript when it was still really rough and picked it apart for me. I love your critical eye and your honesty. You have no idea how I enjoyed our conversations on things philosophical and intellectual.

Thank you, Aris Wells, for being an awesome friend and for loving God so fiercely. You are truly my sister in the Lord's dance.

And last but definitely not least, a special heartfelt thank you to those of you who were my students at Westover Middle School (and Max Abbott, back in the day). My, how you inspired me! Thank you for urging almost every day, "Ms. Jones, tell us a story!" and "Ms. Jones, you gotta write a book! You just have to!" Well, I have. So, here's to you guys! Thank you!

TABLE OF CONTENTS

FOREWORD

T HIS book answers the question asked by every human being past, present, and future. Pilate spoke it when Jesus stood before him: "What is truth?" (John 18:38). People around the world are searching for the answer. They seek it in different religions, in relationships, in titles, in material and financial acquisition, in accomplishments, and in achievements. Still, they come up empty and frustrated.

Jovan's search led her to the reality of truth—the one answer that revolutionized her life forever. As you read this book and its sequels, you will follow a journey that will make you laugh, cry, and rejoice. Every page will stir your heart as you follow the adventure and discover the greatest treasure of all. You will be fascinated; you won't be able to wait to finish one page so you can get to the next page.

It's time to begin your search for truth. At the end, you will discover the answer to your life's quest.

I have personally seen the amazing difference this truth has made in Jovan's life. She has peace, joy, and fulfillment. She is impacting a generation. If you want to make a difference with your life, you have picked up the right book.

Dr. James A. Brice Jr.
Senior Pastor
Covenant Love Family Church
Fayetteville, North Carolina

INTRODUCTION

Dear Reader,

MY deepest prayer is that you (and as many people as possible) will be touched by this book and will truly be set free—or at least set on the road to freedom through Christ. I pray that people will come to see that He is intensely alive. He is vibrant and passionate. He knows us through and through and constantly watches over us.

I wrote this book for many reasons. One, I wrote it for myself. The process of writing has been profoundly and irrefutably cathartic. It has proven to be an excellent vehicle through which I have been able to purge my past—the memories, the guilt, the sting—from my heart and mind.

Two, I wrote this book for all the people I met while I was in the midst of "it." They are the myriad faces and characters found in this book—all the ones left behind, all the ones struggling in darkness, so accustomed to it that they do not even know they are in it. This book is for all the people who, when they read this book, might be touched. I pray that it will delve deeply into their souls and cause them to examine their relationship with the One True God and His inconceivably beautiful Son, Jesus.

Finally, and most importantly, this book is my offering to God. It is my story laid bare for the world to see the wondrous journey He allowed me to take, an account of what He has done and continues to do in and with my life. It is my hope that He is pleased with what I have written.

As you read, you will want to consult the glossary in the back of the book. By the nature of the subject matter, this story is filled with terminology that will be unfamiliar to many readers, and I trust that my explanations in the glossary will help you.

For the record, although I call this series a work of fiction, it is based upon my life—a fictionalized autobiography. It is a true account from my memory and from that of my parents of what happened over the two-year period in which I lived in India and traveled throughout India and the United States with the guru. I would say that 90 percent of the events in this book are true. I have written this book from my memory and according to my own perceptions and interpretation. I mean no offense or harm to any person and I have changed the names of the characters and the location of the events out of respect for the people and to protect their identities. I loved them then and I still do love them. I miss them even now. They were vibrant, colorful personalities, beautiful in their idiosyncrasies. If my story has any purpose, it is that I may see them in Heaven one day.

This is my story, the only thing I can give God along with my life. It is for Jesus that I write—simply because He saved me when I was beyond being saved and because He was then and is now my Everything.

Enjoy!

OF VISIONS
AND ARCHANA

Maya

Poona, India

SILENCE. Utter silence. I was on a high cliff, standing to the right of a waterfall that fell down, down, and farther down. The grass was vibrant green, lush. The water was crystalline, clear, intensely alive. I was wearing white robes and holding a big, golden bowl.

A voice told me, "You must leap to surrender. Do or die. Make a choice." Either I could stay on the edge and let what I was wanting pass me by or I could jump—jump and surrender. Implicit in the jumping was the surrender, true surrender even to the point of death. I looked up. I saw Swami approaching. In that moment he represented god to me. He was everything god ever meant to me. He was striking—long hair, keen Indian features, beautiful, almond-shaped eyes that peered enigmatically into the unknown. Flaming orange robes. He was speaking, but he was not moving his lips.

"Choose. Choose now!" he ordered emphatically, eyes boring through me, searching my innermost being.

I peered down the waterfall. I looked at him. I poured the water in the bowl over the edge of the cliff. I let go of the bowl and it fell gracefully behind the water, beside a waterfall so vast it appeared suspended. I gazed into the sky, blue, empty…and stared…not hesitating, not waiting, I spread my arms and leaped…over the edge. I felt myself falling, headfirst, spread-eagle…falling. No fear, no sensation. Suspended.

Whoop! Chaos! Jolted out of meditation. Vision shattered. Camera flashes going off. I was blinded. Noise, noise, and more noise. Loud music. People chanting—no, screaming, at the top of their lungs. Blaring voices in the loudspeakers. An Indian woman plopped down on top of me! Literally. *Man! I hate when they do that!* I pushed her over, but we were so crowded on the women's side that there was really nowhere to push her. She had managed to squeeze her body into the two inches of space between me and the woman on my right. I was forced to tolerate her.

I ventured an angry glance at her, although a person in deep meditation was not supposed to have "negative" emotions. We believed that in higher spiritual states (as indicated by deep trances and meditations), one was supposed to have mastered one's self and not be gripped by lower emotions. I would have to say I was not angry. No, not at all. But, aggro? Yes, definitely aggro. "Aggro" was a word we had coined in the ashram when we felt *beyond* angry or mad. It was not a momentary sensation, but rather a feeling that smoldered and festered like an ugly infection, oozing negativity—a feeling in excess of the causal event.

I glanced sidelong at her, not wanting anyone to see that I was "out" of my deep meditation. Dark, dark skin. She was grinning, missing one of her incisors. Her head was bobbling from side to side (a strange caricature of a bobblehead doll) in that way that only Indians can bobble their heads. Her face was weathered and beaten. Perhaps years ago it had carried a trace of beauty. Now, she was just a weathered remnant of a woman. Probably not too old—being poor, especially in India, has a way of aging people beyond their years. Skinny. Stomach to ribs. Her worn, faded, tie-dyed sari was hanging off her body in the manner of many shudra women. The long edge wrapped around her shoulders, barely, out of religious respect.

Ohhhh! Bearings…bearings…gotta get my bearings. I pulled myself from my thoughts, in which I had been entirely lost. *Ah! We're in Poona doing archana. Wow! So powerful!* I loved participating in the hour-long archana, which was a call-and-response Sanskritic chant of the thousand names of Devi, the Divine Mother. It was so spiritually powerful; sometimes I could get incredibly blasted. This was one of those times.

I finally noticed my body. My right arm was still suspended halfway between myself and the ghee lamp sitting between me and three, now four (including the "new" lady) others. *I must've been "out" in meditation.* I was still sitting cross-legged, lotus position. My back rigid, straight. *What are these photographers doing here, so many of them, taking pictures? Hmmm. Can't worry about it right now. Get back in, get back in. Stay in the meditation. Don't let anything pull me out. Lady, there, crashing beside me almost pulled me out….* The chanting snatched me back from my own wandering mind.

"*Om sheevuh shukteeyaykay roopinyay nawmuhhuh!*" I screamed the refrain at the top of my lungs along with all the other people. The refrain, "Om shiva shaktyaikya rupinyai namaha," was the mantra of the union of Shiva and Shakti.

"Om para shaktyai namaha." The lead chanter was Narayana, a brahmachari (a Hindu monk) who was belting out the words at the top of his lungs. He was wearing the yellow robes of sannyasa, which meant that he had taken a formal vow of lifelong celibacy and service to the guru. He was beautiful—all the brahmacharis were, for that matter. He was tall, a couple inches over six feet, and slim, very slim. His face was exquisite—aquiline nose, full lips, big, liquid, expressive eyes set in caramel-colored skin. Yes, he was outrageously beautiful. And he was very off-limits.

Our interactions with each other were chaotic and unstable. Passionate and upsetting. Everything about him confused me. Even his eyes confused me! Sometimes he peered straight through me as if I were a letter written on glass—he refused to see me although I could be standing directly in front of him. Sometimes he looked at me in anger for no reason at all. He would shoot out of the temple—one glance at me and his liquid eyes would flash and spark like lightning on a wet summer's evening. Inevitably, following the glance, a series of words would roll off his tongue that would scorch me to my heart.

And then sometimes, and these were the times my friends always seemed to notice for me, they would tap me during meditation or singing bhajans and gesture toward him. I would look. There he would be on the stage sitting beside the singers, sitting on the temple floor with the other brahmacharis, or standing by himself staring at me with the most inexplicable expression. His eyes filled with a myriad of emotions—desire, wonder, bewilderment, fear—caught in the act of betraying him and his every emotion. In those moments, I knew how he felt about me. So did everyone else and they loved to tease me about it. Those moments did not last long before his usual mood would overtake him and I would wonder if I (or anyone) had really seen his heart at all—unless it was bitter and cold and mean. Ah! Narayana, my heart! And there he was on the stage leading us through archana.

In between screaming the responses, I ventured a veiled look to the stage. Maybe I could watch him unawares—I loved observing him with his eyes closed, focused upon meditation or engrossed in leading archana. But, no! His eyes were open and he was looking at me. A dazed, faraway, focused look—*was that even possible?!*—in his eyes. Immediately he shut them. I looked away, now intensely focused on my offering of flower petals. *Could he have been looking at me?* I wondered as I continued in the chanting, although I knew he had been.

"Om sheevuh shukteeyaykay roopinyay nawmuhhuh!" we all thundered the response. The crowd in the temple had grown to over a thousand, nearing a couple thousand more than likely. We surely exceeded the fire code—*if* there was a fire code. I could not say that I had ever seen a fire code posted on any edifice in India and definitely not in a temple. People were piled upon each other, particularly in the women's section.

I looked outside of the temple. People were seated around palm leaf plates everywhere. Ordered chaos. We were in northern India, Poona—a suburb of sorts of Bombay (Mumbai). We were suffering through the dry period. The air was hot and oppressive. The ground was reddish brown, hard-packed. Everything was dusty, including us. Flies swarmed around us but somehow one grew used to the flies after a while. Strangely enough they became tolerable. I and everyone around me had ceased to fan them from our sweaty, stained faces. And so we sat, with them climbing all over us.

By far the greatest nuisance was early-morning mosquitoes that swarmed in thick black clouds around us and feasted upon any exposed flesh. They had an intuitive ability to find human flesh through layers of thin clothing. At sunrise we had to be swaddled thickly in order to avoid being horribly chewed up by the "morning mosquitoes."

Luckily for us, it was not early morning anymore. We were careening through the fifth, the last archana of the day, which meant it was late afternoon.

Focus! Focus! I chided myself.

"Om maha kalyai namaha," Narayana intoned.

"Om sheevuh shukteeyaykay roopinyay nawmuhhuh!" we chanted (shouted) back to him in homage to the Divine Mother.

The archana was nearing its end. Narayana was "handling" us well—drawing us deeper and deeper, further and further into the Divine Mother. His voice, blaring through the loudspeakers, was answered by our screaming. The chanting was at a feverish pitch. Our hands worked faster and faster, picking up flower petals from the palm leaf in front of us (if any petals remained) and throwing them as offerings into the fire. Tears streamed out of some peoples' eyes. Other people were convulsing through kriyas—their bodies jerking, eyes rolling in their heads—movements and behaviors caused by the kundalini energy moving up and down their spines. This was the part I loved. Could the chanting and screaming get any more feverish?

"Om chamundayai namaha!" Narayana chanted. His huge almond eyes were at half-mast as he was deep into the chanting, thoroughly absorbed.

"Om sheevuh shukteeyaykay roopinyay nawmuhhuh!" we screamed back.

"Om shiva shaktyaikya rupinyai namaha!" Narayana said it so fast and forcefully that it really sounded like a long, *"Sheeeyoooblaaat!"* We loved it. He could lead an archana to a phenomenally intense finale.

"*Om sheevuh shukteeyaykay roopinyay nawmuhhuh!!*" we responded even louder.

"Om shiva shaktyaikya rupinyai namaha!"

"*Om sheevuh shukteeyaykay roopinyay nawmuhhuh!!*"

The third, the final, cry. The climax, "Om shiva shaktyaikya rupinyai namaha!"

"*Om sheevuh shukteeyaykay roopinyay nawmuhhuh!!!*"

And then...

Silence.

Silence.

Silence, although the very air was undulating with the vibration of the words, the intensity. Again, as in all the archanas, I felt that "feeling" and wondered if I could take it—the intensity. The last archana of the day was the most intense, the most powerful. The power of the words was almost tangible, "touchable." In fact, the force of the words over the course of the day had stirred the air, stirred the atmosphere, had stirred invisible "beings" to move and to act. I could feel them. I could feel the power, the stirring. I was being called...pulled...I closed my eyes and dropped off into meditation. *So...easy...to...meditate.* Not for long. I felt the woman who had decided to sit on top of me pushing even more against me as she made herself comfortable. Clearly, we were done. I was reeling inside. The meditation, the vision, the chanting, the archana, fasting. I had been fasting for three days in order to take full advantage of the power of the archanas.

Time to back up a bit and give some background. At the time of this archana, I had been living in India for over ten months. I and many others were traveling through India with a guru named Chamunda Ma as she visited the many temples that were dedicated to her. People came from great distances to see her and receive her darshan when she came to one of her temples in a city. During the time of our visit, we would chant archana five times a day for five days.

What was archana? Archana was a practice in which we recited a specific set of Sanskritic chants to our favorite god or goddess. In this case, we chanted the thousand names of Devi, the Divine Mother. It was said to purify the air, purify our hearts, and make us more like the deity for whom and to whom we were chanting. It was believed to burn our karma so that we could move more rapidly toward, and finally attain, freedom from the cycle of reincarnation, also called enlightenment. Hindus called such freedom *moksha*.

Who was this Cha Ma? Most Hindus believed she was a guru and a saint. Many, however, believed her to be more, much more than a saint, guru, or even a satguru. Many believed she was an actual incarnation of Devi—an avatar. Yes! Those of us who lived with her and knew her personally were convinced that she was an avatar—the physical incarnation of the goddess Kali—a most malevolent and destructive being. We believed that Kali had decided to take on a human body and live on the earth as Cha Ma.

I remember the first time I saw her…

But that takes me all the way back to the beginning. By the time of Poona, I was in deep, too deep….

CHA MA
AND MA! MAN

Maya
Boston, Massachusetts

BOSTON. Many years ago. I was in graduate school at Harvard. Political science. German politics, more specifically. I was in my fourth year of working toward my doctorate. I was teaching a couple of lower level undergraduate courses and advising undergraduates in our department. I had a very promising future.

And yet I was unfulfilled. Insanely unfulfilled. I was searching, searching like a mad woman for the answers to life. However, the harder I searched, the emptier I found myself. The more questions I asked, the more questions I stumbled upon that needed to be asked. Nothing satisfied me. Nothing drew me and kept me interested. Furthermore, I was a thrill-seeker—anything that could give me a great high I was willing to try. I had started delving into other religions— Voodoo, Santeria, Yoruba—and over a circuitous route through New Ageism, I had found myself standing on the edge of the

Eastern religions. Curiosity and the thrill of the unknown snagged my attention. I knew a little and I wanted to know more. Combine the desperately unsatisfied searcher with the risk-thirsty thrill-seeker and you had a woman ready to go anywhere, at any moment, for any reason—that was where I was when I stumbled upon Cha Ma.

Cha Ma was holding a public program at a hall in a Boston suburb. I did not know her then. A friend, Manjula, an older black woman with unusually thick, long dreadlocks (they hung so far that when she sat down she had to fling them out of the way or she would sit on them) suggested that I go see her. "Girl, you need to check out Cha Ma. She's the real thing. She gives great darshan." We were hanging out in the kitchen at Manjula's house talking about things spiritual. She knew so much about so much!

"Darshan?" I asked, puzzled. "What's that?"

Even five minutes with Manjula was like living in a foreign country. She was deep into Hinduism, every sentence peppered with several unintelligible words. She seemed so certain and knowledgeable, so secure and confident. I wanted to be like her.

"In Hinduism, darshan is the 'seeing' of a divine being…"

"A divine being?"

"A divine being is anyone of a high spiritual state—a god or goddess, a guru, satguru, or an avatar."

"Huh?" I asked eloquently.

Manjula walked to the stove and stirred up the pot of chai—how I loved her chai! I breathed in deeply the aroma of freshly crushed ginger, peppermint, cloves, and cardamom. She had learned how to make it from a real Hindu guru—her guru. "Okay, I'm going to explain it in a roundabout way. Do you understand the concept of reincarnation?"

"Being reborn over and over again, lifetime after lifetime?"

"Yes!" Manjula nodded, peering at me over her wire-rimmed glasses. "Exactly." She pursed her lips and flung her dreads behind her as she poured the chai into cups. "People are reborn over and over again for eons. They start out as the most primitive of life forms and gradually they progress through demon lokas…"

"Lokas?" I inserted.

"Lokas are worlds…realms…"

"Realms?" I asked. I knew I was making it difficult for her, asking so many questions, but I wanted to understand.

"Yes, realms. Sometimes we call lokas realms because they are not always of this dimension. They may be in an entirely different, *other*, dimension. The Puranas state that there are seven lokas." Her forehead wrinkled in thought. "I've also heard of nine…"

I nodded although I knew I would have to ponder her words.

She continued. "People progress through demon lokas—realms— as evil beings and through angelic lokas as loving beings. This goes on for many lifetimes of the being. Finally, a being is blessed with a human birth, because it is only in the human realm that a person can reach enlightenment." She paused and set our cups on the table with a container of honey. "As people evolve into a higher and higher con-sciousness, and move closer to enlightenment…moksha…"

"Moksha?" I asked, spooning honey into my chai.

"Moksha is enlightenment, the state where one has been set free from samsara."

"Samsara?"

"The cycle of rebirth, reincarnation. We are held in this cycle of being born over and over because of the karma we accumulate, whether good or bad. We must exhaust, or burn off, our karma before we can be free." She sat down in her chair, tossing her locks out of the way before she sat on them. She spooned honey into her chai, stirred it, and then took a couple of sips. I sat in silence, watching her and thinking.

"See…people, over thousands of years, move closer and closer to the end of their karmic cycle. When they are on the verge of being set free, they will begin to meet 'divine beings'—'enlightened ones'—who are already free from samsara, the cycle of reincarnation. These divine beings can come in the form of a guru, a satguru, or an avatar." She took another sip of her chai. I sipped too, my mind whirring at lightning speed to digest all she was saying.

"According to Hinduism," she continued, "only a few people will ever be blessed to receive darshan from such a being." She paused as she thought. "To *see* such a being, darshan, is considered auspicious…"

"Auspicious?"

"Yes, a very good thing. It's considered a blessing to *see* a divine being—one that only a very few people on the face of this earth will get as they progress toward the end of all their cycles. To *touch* such a being is considered a *great* blessing. To actually *live*…"

"To live with a divine being? Is it even possible?" I could barely believe it possible.

"Oh, yes! To live in constant contact with one is considered the *greatest* of blessings. It's believed that to have such close contact with such a being is a key indicator that moksha…"

"Moksha…" I attempted to recall what she had just told me about moksha. *All these words, all these concepts—it's a lot to remember.* I drained the rest of my chai. "Moksha means…"

"Freedom." She finished my sentence for me. "Being set free from the cycle of reincarnation." Manjula cast an odd look in my direction as she sipped her chai. "To not have to be reincarnated again…" She sighed and stared at the wall. Finally, she stood up, "More?" she asked, indicating my empty cup.

"Yes, thank you." *Her chai is heaven!*

She explained as she poured, "To live with such a being is a huge clue that a person is about to be set free."

"Oh," I responded intelligently. I was in over my head. I did not understand half her words. Nevertheless, something inside of me stirred, quickened. My heart speeded up expectantly. What to do in such a moment? Had I known how pivotal a moment it was, I would have done something different…said something deep and profound. Instead, I cleverly said, "Oh."

Manjula set our refilled cups on the table. "So as I was saying…" she continued as she spooned honey into her chai and stirred. *She loves her chai with honey, that's for sure.* "this guru, Cha Ma, gives great darshan."

"Yeah? What do you mean?" I asked, stirring my chai and then taking a sip. *Good!*

"Well, being that darshan means to see a divine being, hers goes a step further. She actually hugs people. Most divine beings don't like to touch people because our karma and lower natures burn their higher consciousnesses. Like my teacher—she doesn't like to touch people because it burns her. However, Cha Ma does."

I heard what Manjula was saying, but I did not think too hard about seeing this Cha Ma. I already had a guru, and I did not need another. *Although I really don't like my guru.* I did not like her personality. Not that she was a "bad" guru. It was just that my personality was louder, flashier, noisier than hers. I felt I annoyed her sometimes. She was just so…quiet and petite. And I was so loud and noisy. And now, all that Manjula was saying struck a chord within me—*Is my guru the correct one? Can she, will she, get me to enlightenment? Is it even my time?*

"Girl, you need to check her out!" Manjula urged as she took another sip of chai. "She's the real thing. She lives in India and comes to the States only once a year. You need to take advantage of her coming."

"We'll see," I answered noncommittally. I had already decided I was not going to see Cha Ma.

It was a beautiful, balmy summer evening, the type peculiar to Boston. I had not been planning to go to this...*Cha Ma's*...darshan, but at the last minute I caught one of the city buses to her program. I had just finished working out at one of the campus gyms and I felt alive. I had no desire to go home. I wanted to do something. Get into something.

Without giving it much thought, I climbed onto a bus in Harvard Yard that was heading toward a nearby suburb. At my request, the driver promised to let me know where to get off. True to his word, when he stopped the bus, he pointed down a neat, ordered suburban street. "Heah's yah stop! That's the place dahn theah," he said, a Boston accent heavy in his voice.

"Thank you!" I responded as I clambered down the steps.

I looked around as I walked the short distance. In that odd light of an early evening in late summer, the neatly cut grass of every house seemed unusually well-ordered, even for Boston. *Definitely too suburban.* In the fading light, the tall, New Englander houses glowed luminously white, stately, and old.

Strange. I wouldn't think a guru would be here. Actually, I had no idea where in Boston I would see an Indian guru. I walked the few blocks to the hall thinking, *What will she be like? Is it wrong to go see her when I have a guru? Man! I need to go home. I have so much work to do.* In spite of my many contrary thoughts, I did not turn around.

As I walked toward the steps of the building, I spotted this...guy. Tall, skinny, white guy. Goofy-looking. Balding, not that that was what made him goofy-looking. He was wearing high-water jeans, mix-match socks (one black, the other multi-colored striped), a ratty, holey white tee shirt underneath a red, faded, zip-up, hooded sweat jacket that was two sizes too small for his very slender frame. *Where'd he get that? His five-year-old sister?* I snorted to myself. Black "birth-control glasses" hung crookedly on his thin nose (BCGs—Army issue type, called birth control glasses by soldiers forced to wear them because of their acute ugliness—thick, black, unfashionable frames).

This guy was saying—no, screaming—"MA! MA! MA!" at the top of his lungs, at the same time threading a string of baby building blocks (you know the kind—wood, in pastel colors with a letter from the alphabet on them) as his rosary (in Hinduism called a japa mala). He walked over shouting "MA!" and attached himself to me.

"Hello...MA! MA!" he greeted me while nervously shoving the baby building blocks through his fingers. *"MA! MA!" must be his mantra. Weird. Someone needs to introduce him to something much, much smaller than a string of baby building blocks. If he can't find a small japa mala, he needs Catholic rosary beads or something! That's definitely not the easiest japa mala to handle.* I arrogantly snickered to myself as I eyed his load of blocks.

"Have you MA! MA! met Mother? MA!" he asked, interspersing his conversation with exclamations of "MA!"

His question snapped me out of my considerations of appropriate japa malas. "Uh, no. I…"

"MA! MA! MA! She's amazing. MA! MA! So you've never MA! had MA! one of her hugs? MA! MA!" He asked another question, not pausing long enough between hollering MA! to hear me answer his last one, all the while witlessly shoving (that is the only way to describe his japa mala technique) the gargantuan baby-block-japa-mala through his fingers. I tried to look around to see what else was happening, but I was transfixed by his long skinny fingers shoving the blocks of the mala around. "MA! MA!" he chanted as I opened my mouth to speak. Shifting his weight from his left leg to his right, he looked at me intensely, crazily, through his BCGs. He reminded me of a cat peering at a cockroach right before it was going to bat it around. He made me nervous—not the "I'm afraid of you" kind of nervous, but the "could you please be still for a second?" kind.

"I've…"

"Do you have a guru? MA! MA! MA!"

I was able to insert a nod.

"Yeah, well, when you see MA! Cha Ma, all that will change. MA! MA! She is a satguru, MA! *the* satguru of our time, the ultimate MA! guru! The guru MA! of MA! gurus. MA! MA! MA! The guru MA! you had up MA! until now was just preparation for Cha Ma, MA! MA! who is the satguru MA! and will take you to enlightenment. MA! MA!" He said all of this in one massive gush of spiritual verbosity.

I was feeling overwhelmed and a little resentful—overwhelmed by all the MA!-ing he was doing and resentful because *how dare he tell me what this Cha Ma was to me and what my guru was not!* I simply wanted to escape him, but he had deemed himself my tour guide *(guard?).*

He asked, "Do you MA! know Cha Ma's full name? MA!"

I shook my head. I did not trust myself to speak.

"Her full name is Shri Chamundamayi Ma," he responded without inserting an annoying MA!

"What's it mean?"

"Shri is a form of salutation. MA! MA! Like Ms., Mrs., or Mr. MA! MA! Chamunda is the name of Kali in her fiercest, wildest form."

My mind rifled through what I knew of the Hindu goddesses. *Kali.* At the name, an image sprang into my mind. Jet-black with dreadlock-like hair. Blood red tongue sticking out. Eyes rolling up in her head. Four or more arms…*Isn't it, the more arms the more malevolent?* In my mind's eye, I could see the arms brandishing different weapons—a machete, a sickle, a sword…a severed head and beneath the head a bowl with which to catch the blood.

He prattled on, oblivious to my mental digression, "MA! MA! *Mayi* means embodiment and *Ma* means mother. MA! MA! So, MA! when it's put MA! all together MA! MA!, her name says she is the embodiment of Chamunda Kali, which is her most ferocious form MA! MA!, and she is the Divine Mother. MA! MA!"

"Wow!" was all I could think to say. I had reached my information saturation point.

This entire exchange took place outside the building. When I approached, he had met me on the steps. Arrested by his exuberance, I had been unable to progress beyond the first step. Seeking relief and freedom, I surveyed the scene. He looked around, too, ostensibly to see what I was looking at.

Several people, all in white, were standing outside the hall talking. The women were wearing long white dresses, the fabric of which was wrapped around their bodies several times. I knew that these dresses were called saris. The men were wearing white pants or long white skirts and tee shirts. Many of them, men and women, were wearing shawls with unusual lettering—lettering, which in my spotty exploration of Eastern religions, I had come to learn was Sanskrit. *This is all very similar to my guru, except for the kooks! This Cha Ma must be a kook, too!* I thought superciliously.

"Do you want MA! MA! to go inside?" my tour guard asked me.

"Sure…" I answered reluctantly. *I might as well see what this hug is all about…since I'm already here.* I almost heard myself sigh with resignation.

We climbed the steps of the hall. I could smell the delicious aroma of incense from inside, wafting lightly upon the air. I breathed in deeply. *Ah! So relaxing.* "MA! Man"—my own personal moniker for him—was still beside me, talking, without stopping to catch his breath. *Ugh!*

"Do you MA! have a seat?" he asked as he pushed open the door.

I managed to shake my head no.

"MA! MA! Well, let's go in now. If we MA! MA! hurry we'll be able to MA! save some seats. MA! MA!"

He led me through the entrance of the building and into barely ordered chaos. We stood in a long, narrow foyer where Cha Ma's people were hawking her wares. Long tables flanked the length of the foyer and were crammed with various articles: prayer shawls, asanas (meditational sit mats), murtis (little statues and figurines), books, incense, sandalwood, clothing, cassette tapes, CDs, DVDs, and a bunch of other stuff that I did not recognize. *This is all just a racket!*

The one thing I did not like when I went to see a guru or spiritual teacher was a huge capitalistic venture. It made me feel that all they wanted to do was make money off us Westerners. Every minute that ticked by I felt more acutely that I was in the wrong place. I longed for the quiet, reserve, and order of my guru's place. "Quiet" and "reserved" were not adjectives known in this place, and "order" seemed to be something that had never been introduced to this group. Here chaos and disorder seemed the norm. People were walking and running about—some with focus, but many with no obvious purpose whatsoever. Many were yelling at each other.

"NO! NO! If you can NOT see that…" I heard a man argue sharply.

"Look, why don't you just…" a woman voiced shrilly.

"In *Tooleetooleemooloolee* [that is what it sounded like] they don't do…" another exclaimed.

And of course my tour guide constantly kept chanting "MA! MA! MA!" loudly in my ear, fiddling—no! *struggling*—with his unwieldy japa mala. Frankly, for all my annoyance, if he had not been with me I would have been intimidated and probably would have left, and that might have been a good thing—I had no idea where my life was about to go. We pressed our way through the crowded foyer-turned-mercantile-obstacle-course and into the main hall. Here, the incense was thick and pungent and had suffused the air with a bluish haze.

The hall was spacious and simple—just a large open room obviously intended to be rented out for meetings, parties, and the like. The walls were made of a cheap, wood paneling. The floor was covered with a thin, industrial carpet of nondescript, greenish-brown color. Centered at the front of the hall was a large, raised platform. On this platform was a short, low-lying bench or couch. Rows of chairs were placed for an audience on either side of the platform and reached almost to the back of the hall. A narrow swatch of space, running from the front of the platform to the back of the room, was free of chairs. At the back were several rows of chairs, which stretched from one end of the room to the other.

My tour guide, MA! Man, led me over to the seats in the back.

"This looks like a great place. MA! MA!" He indicated two chairs that were in the front of the back rows. They were dead-center and would put us directly in front of the platform. We would be comfortably back as the large empty space in the center lay between us and the platform. I would soon discover that the empty space was for people to sit on the floor and approach Cha Ma for darshan. At this point, however, no one was sitting there as everyone was milling around, chatting and watching for Cha Ma.

"We'll be able MA! to see her well. MA! MA!" he screeched into my left ear as he settled back into a plastic chair.

"Okay."

"She'll be coming MA! in a few minutes. MA! MA!"

To while away the time, I looked around at the people. They were very much like the people outside, except inside offered a little more variety: A few Indians—the women dressed in white saris or punjabis (two-piece sets of baggy pants and matching knee-length top), the men dressed also in white. Many Western people—some in suits, many in traditional Indian garb, some in tee shirts, shorts, and Birkenstocks, looking crunchy-granola (you know the type—organic health food store addicts). Only a couple of black people—I was one-half of the couple. The other half of my racial cohort, a man, was walking around talking to people here and there. He looked like a cultural oddity. It never crossed my mind that I probably did too.

As I settled into my chair, my tour guide continued chanting—correction, he kept saying a few words and then hollering "MA!" at me. I could not distinguish between the times he was chanting and the times he was talking to me. To cover my confusion, I kept nodding and smiling, hoping my actions were appropriate.

"MA! MA!"

My gazing was interrupted by his hollering. *Ugh! Would he stop already?*

Suddenly I heard, *"She's here!"* inside of me.

I turned to my tour guide, "Did you hear that?"

"MA! Hear what? MA! MA!" asked he vacuously as he kept wrestling his baby blocks.

"Someone said right in my ear, 'She's here.'"

"There's no one around you MA! but me and MA! I didn't say MA! anything. Hmmm…MA! MA! It seems Ma is calling you. Let's see if she's here. MA! If Ma's here, then, you'll know she MA! was speaking to you MA! through your mind. MA! MA!" He hastily took off his jacket and put it across our seats as we got up to leave. I followed closely behind him.

Freaky! I've heard of mind stuff…could this be? No! Couldn't be! Mind reading's an advanced siddhi! Like astral projection or levitating. That takes years of hard work and great spiritual power. I'm still a baby in all this. Can't be!

As we walked toward the foyer, I felt an energy, an excitement. And I heard a whisper, barely hushed, "She's here. Ma's here!" Over and over. I looked around, but all I saw was just people talking. No one seemed to be preparing for her arrival. *Strange! Am I imagining things? Don't they know she's coming? What is this?* Weaving in and out of all the people, I followed my guide to the front door. *I've got to learn his name.*

Blocking the doorway was a chubby, pasty-faced woman who was kind of short. Her brown hair was long and pulled back negligently, as though it were the last thing to get any consideration. She was wearing a rumpled, light blue punjabi. She stood at the door peering out the window in rapt attention. I looked past her, curious to see what held her attention. *Maybe Cha Ma is coming?* I wondered.

A tall, slim, young guy was running toward the door. He was very pale with a big, Grizzly Adams beard. He was wearing one of those long, ankle-length, male skirts—*What are those things?*—in white, with a white button-up shirt.

"Cha Ma's coming! Cha Ma's coming!" he cried out as he ran—slid—in his flip-flops and that silly, narrow skirt. Because of the flip-flops and skirt, he could not really get his feet moving or his legs pumping. He was holding up one of the corners of the skirt. I could see his hairy, skinny calves.

"Cha Ma's coming! Cha Ma's coming!"

MA! Man turned to me, excitedly, "Ma *is* coming! You did hear her! She spoke to you! And you don't even know her! Wow!" He was so excited he forgot to holler out "MA!"

The chubby woman stood in the doorway. MA! Man and I stood a few paces away. People were rushing to the door—yelling and pushing.

"Make way! Make way!" An Indian man with straight, gray-streaked black hair that flipped up at his collar was ordering everyone about. He was wearing a short-sleeved tunic shirt and one of those narrow skirts (later I was to learn that the narrow skirt was called a dhoti)—both in burnt orange. He strode authoritatively through the foyer to the front door. He was waving his arm, looking extremely irritated. *He's cute. No! I take that back; he's beautiful. What is it about these Indian men? He is fine!*

MA! Man swiftly sank to his knees and pulled me down with him, while he whispered in my ear, "That's MA! Swami Shankarapranatman. MA! MA!" Everyone else had dropped to their knees too. I knew it was protocol: In the presence of a master, a guru, or a teacher, everyone pranams (bows).

"Who's he? What's a swami?"

"Swamis MA! are the ones who wear MA! MA! orange robes. MA! They're the highest MA! ranking after Cha Ma. MA! MA! Not many people MA! become MA! swamis. It's a MA! great honor. MA! MA!" Alternatingly, he whispered and hollered in my ear. I nodded.

I watched the Indian man in orange, Swami Shankarapranatman. He had made it to the door, having cleared a path from the main hall to the door, and was fully engaged in trying ("trying" being the operative word here) to make the woman in the light blue punjabi move from in front of the door. However it was apparent that she was not going anywhere. He was gesticulating furiously while speaking fiercely at her. A smoldering look that bordered on rage dominated his face. She was busily ignoring him, looking out the window, her hands gripping the handles of the double doors, as though intimating, "Try and move me!"

I watched them. I watched everyone. *Ah! This is all so exciting!* I felt myself being swept away.

Right then, I saw a large white van with blackout windows pull up in front of the steps.

"Cha Ma! Cha Ma!" some yelled out.

"Ma! Ma! The Divine Mother!" others were saying.

And still others were murmuring, barely above a whisper, "Ma…Ma…"

The excitement, the tension, in the room quickly intensified. I clasped my hands, prayer fashion, in front of my face and I found myself chanting under my breath, "Ma…Ma…" It all felt so familiar. I stared at the door in heightened anticipation.

First to clamber out of the van was a plump, middle-aged white woman of medium height. She had long, thinning, reddish-blond hair that was pulled back into a ponytail. She was wearing a burnt orange sari. *What's up with that orange? An ugly orange at that!*

MA! Man leaned close to me, "That's Swamini Ma. She's the highest ranking swamini."

"They have female swamis?" I asked in wonder.

"Yes, MA! MA!" he answered the affirmative, "Cha Ma is very progressive."

Behind her another white woman climbed out, this one with more agility than the previous one. She too was wearing an orange sari. She was slim, although slightly hippy. Her face was narrow with clever, sharp eyes and a mouth that turned up at the corners as if she were ready for a good laugh. Her hair was black, shiny, and pulled back into a neat ponytail.

"That's MA! Swamini Atmaprananda, MA! MA!" my tour guide informed me.

Behind her climbed out a tall, well-padded (dare I say—almost fat) Indian man in a dark orange dhoti and long-sleeved tunic shirt. He was exquisitely good-looking, with an aristocratic nose and wide, oval eyes perched beneath perfectly arched eyebrows. He had a big, bushy beard and thick, wavy chestnut hair that extended well past his shoulders. He scanned the building, the crowd, the frenzied activity, surveying the entire situation in one glance.

"And that's MA! Swami. MA! He's the highest swami. MA! MA!"

After he climbed out, I bowed. I do not know why. As I was on my knees, I simply, unthinkingly, pranamed—bowed low—to the ground and did not look up. I could not look up. In my peripheral vision, I saw the entire room pranam. A few of the men executed full pranams by lying down prostrate on their stomachs. Everyone else remained on their knees, touching their foreheads to the floor.

That was when *she* stepped out, rather, when I *felt* her step out. I felt a burst of energy originate from the van and undulate powerfully throughout the building. A couple of seconds thereafter, I knew it was she because I saw her feet pass right by me. As soon as she passed, my tour guide grabbed me roughly by the arm and pulled me up. Simultaneously he whispered hoarsely into my ear, "Get up! MA! MA! Ma just passed by. Did you feel her? MA! MA!"

"What do you mean, 'Did I feel her?'" I asked a bit angrily for being "manhandled."

He went stock-still (which was scary because he had not stopped moving frenetically the entire time I had been with him) and stared into my eyes, "She touched you on the back. You didn't feel it? She didn't touch anyone else! You are so lucky! You are so blessed!" In his excitement, he had forgotten to screech "MA! MA!" after every word or two. I stared at him—his glasses even more askew, arms hanging limply at his sides. Baby-block-japa-mala forgotten. He continued on, words tumbling out one after another, "Don't you know? Cha Ma is a satguru! A guru of gurus! *The* guru of gurus! *She is an avatar*! And she touched you. You will be enlightened in this lifetime! You must go to her ashram in India. Oh, you must! You must! You will! Soon!" With that he seized upon his baby-block-mala again, chanting "MA! MA!" and pressed forward with the crowd. I followed.

We halted after taking a couple of steps because no one was moving. Everyone was chanting something or other in Sanskrit. I heard in front of us horns (or perhaps it was conch shells) being blown and bells ringing, though I could not see what was happening.

I grabbed his arm to get his attention. "What's an ashram?" I asked in a loud whisper.

"Oh! An ashram MA! is a place where all MA! MA! the devotees of MA! the guru live. Cha Ma has one in India." He turned forward again, loudly hollering, "MA! MA!" I stood quietly behind him thinking and listening to the din of horns, bells, and voices. After a couple of minutes, the chanting stopped as did the horns and bells.

MA! Man pushed on into the hall. I hurried behind him as best I could. The crowd was dense. The incense had grown overpowering. My mind reeling around and around went back to what he had said to me. *India?! Me? Go to India? Receive enlightenment? In this lifetime? Cha Ma—a satguru? My satguru?!* I grabbed his red jacket from behind so as not to lose him. Soon enough we found our seats again.

As I settled into my chair for the second time, I perused the crowd. My mind was skipping over a thousand thoughts per second. *I know I've been crying out to the gods to save me, to give me enlightenment, to set me free from this silly, useless, endless cycle of rebirth. I know that I must be at the end of the cycle because of the desire, the burning desire, to be free of this prison-like cycle. I know a satguru has to come, and that to get free, I have to have someone who knows the way. But this? Her?! Cha Ma? No! Not her! Not this! It's too noisy. Too crazy. No! I already have my guru. But, gosh! She's so calm and so ordered and...so...so boring! I don't know how long I can deal with her. What am I saying? But, maybe. Maybe this...Cha Ma...is my satguru? No! I can't take this craziness! This insanity! But, maybe...I know! What I'll do is wait for another sign. If it's meant to be, someone will say something to me tonight about going to India. And if they don't, it's not meant to be.* Having thus resolved myself, I turned my focus to the program. MA! Man had gone partially silent and was now only murmuring, "Ma...Ma...Ma..." under his breath as he stared at the platform and rocked back and forth.

Cha Ma and her crew were climbing up a set of rickety steps that had been placed to the right of the platform. She sat down on the low bench. Someone had covered it with a leopard skin. *I wonder if it's a real leopard skin. No, can't be. It would be almost impossible to get a wild animal skin through customs.* I dismissed the idea.

Later I discovered as I talked with others at the program that the stool was called a peetham and was covered by a real leopard-skin asana. According to Hindu beliefs, the best meditation asanas were made out of leopard skin because such a hide would stop the transmission of all vibrations. Vibrations presented two dangers. One danger was that of vibrations transferring from the ground up into the meditating person if the ground contained "low" energy. The other was the danger of the meditating person's vibrations being absorbed by the ground. No one, particularly a "highly evolved being," would want to lose spiritual power or draw in "low" energy.

Everyone else with Cha Ma sat directly on the platform, cross-legged. No peethams. No asanas. The two women in orange, the swaminis, sat on her left. Three swamis in orange sat on her right. I recognized two of them (although I could not remember their names): the deeply observant, almost fat man and the irritable man with the flipped-up-in-the-back hair. The other I did not recognize. He was tall and bordering on fat, too, although his body was more stocky and solid. He wore wire-rimmed silver glasses and had a kind face that looked prone to breaking out into laughter and smiles at any moment. His hair was black, touched with only a smattering of gray. His appearance put me in the mind of Santa Claus—pursed lips, jolly, rotund face.

"Who's the other swami?" I asked MA! Man.

"MA! MA! That's Swami Shivaramananda. MA! MA!"

Farther to their right was a group of Indian men wearing white. Clearly they were the musicians, as they had instruments sitting in front of them. I recognized the instruments—the two-headed drums called tablas, the harmonium (which looked and sounded like an accordion but sat on the floor), a hand drum, and little hand cymbals called kimini.

Cha Ma began to speak and someone translated. Honestly, I did not process much of her talk. I was too busy examining her, this satguru...this...*avatar*. Her skin was the color of cappuccino. She was plump and, like the other women with her, wore a sari. However, hers was white—vibrantly, unbelievably white, and heavily starched. Immaculate. Her ebony hair was thick and pulled back into a low bun that sat on the nape of her neck. The trailing edge of her sari was pulled up over her shoulders and low hairbun. What was most notable was her face. Simultaneously while she smiled and smiled at us, her visage sailed through a myriad of expressions. Hers was one of the most expressive faces I had ever encountered. Oddly, covering her entire left cheek was what looked like a massive bruise, a dark, dark discoloration.

My mind was everywhere! *She's so cute! Except for that bruise. I wonder what happened. She's so sweet, like a mother! How can she be the center of such chaos and noise? Why are these people in orange sitting with her? Why is she wearing white? How did she get her sari so white? Why is she smiling so much? Is it real or fake? She seems so nice and sweet. Why is her voice so harsh?*

Most disconcerting was her voice. It did not match her appearance. It was rough and gravelly and deep. Guttural. It made me think of a car driving over a gravel road.

After her talk was over (from which I gathered absolutely nothing—I was too busy thinking and analyzing and digesting), everyone on the stage arranged themselves with the microphones and instruments. All the people in the chairs and in the space in front of the platform, which had filled the moment she sat down on the platform, pulled out thick songbooks.

Soon Cha Ma and the people on the stage were singing. The songs were call-and-response with Cha Ma and her crew leading and us in the audience repeating. All the songs (bhajans) they sang were in their native languages—Sanskrit, Hindi, and Malayalam. They sang songs of their gods and goddesses and their consorts. Bhajans of Krishna and Radha. Kali and Durga. Shiva and Devi. Songs of Ram and Sita. The voices of the men and women on the stage mingled with hers leading us, guiding us on a journey. The instruments wove a delicate tapestry that undergirded their delightful melodies and our impassioned responses. I thought to myself—*Ah! This music is otherworldly! These must be, truly, the songs of the gods!* I was hooked!

After many bhajans that seemed to flow one into the other, we sang the last. All I remember is that they were leading us in a song to Kali, and the crowd, MA! Man, and I were energetically clapping and singing the chorus. The voices and the instruments came together, intertwined and pulsed to a crescendo—a sublimely, beautifully orchestrated climax of music. Upon that crest of music, we soared.

All of a sudden, *something happened to me!* It was as though *something* took over my body. I found my body jerking forward and backward, roughly, uncontrollably. I heard myself yelling out, "KALI! KALI!" at the top of my lungs. Everyone else was yelling too, so my behavior was not all that unusual. But for me? It was highly unusual— *I DO NOT lose control in that way!* But…I did. I had. Try as I might, I could not stop myself. Honestly? I did not want to. I allowed myself to be swept away in the current that was racing by and around me. I had no control and I *loved* it!

Suddenly…the song was over, a hush descended upon the hall. I closed my eyes and allowed the quiet to overtake me after the wild high. I basked in the silence as it undulated and vibrated within me. And then, I opened my eyes and saw Cha Ma looking at me. Clearly. Undeniably. She smiled and nodded and I knew, without a doubt— *Yes! She is my satguru, my avatar!* I closed my eyes again and "disappeared," falling headlong into a deep, soundless meditation.

After a long time, I opened my eyes to find that the crowd that had been sitting on the floor had shimmied closer to her. Darshan had commenced a while ago. I sat in my chair, beside my tour guide, who continued to whisper, "Ma…Ma…Ma…Ma…" I watched, enraptured. Cha Ma sat on her peetham, hugging each person who came forward, and whispering in his or her ear. As each person left, she gave them something. I marveled at the care and attention she gave each one. I sat there for a long time observing, oblivious to everyone and everything around me except Cha Ma.

The people who were sitting on the stage with her began to sing more beautiful, melodious songs. *I could sit here all day and listen to them sing.* I sat absorbed in the sights and sounds, allowing myself to be transported to other places, other times.

After an hour or two had passed, MA! Man asked, "Are you going to get in the darshan line?" as he lowered himself onto the floor at the very back of the crowd.

"Uh…yeah…" I murmured distractedly, my eyes still on the stage. I lowered myself onto the floor beside him and sat down crosslegged. *India. Dare I go to India?* I ruminated over this question as we inched forward.

"So, what's your name?" A white woman in a rumpled white sari sat down behind me. She had a bouncy, bubbly voice and an energy to match. Her straight, medium-length hair was strawberry blond, pulled back into a casual ponytail. She was about my height, 5´7˝, and looked a little "big-boned." She had big hazel eyes that looked like they wanted to pop out of her head and a pleasant enough smile. She smiled at me as she spoke.

"Maya," I said, smiling back. *Everyone here is so nice.*

"Well, my name's Sandi. Is this the first time that you've seen Cha Ma?"

"Yes."

"I remember the first time I saw her. I knew when I saw her that she was my satguru, that she'd carry me to enlightenment," she volunteered, her eyes glittering. "As soon as I could get enough money together I moved to India to live in her ashram."

I felt as if I were in a vortex. *Oh no! This is it!* It was one of those decisive, defining moments that occurs in a person's life and forever changes it. I could not put words to it at the time, but I most certainly felt it. My heart sped up. My breath began to come shallowly. The thumping of the tablas grew noticeably farther away. The singing, which was so rich and full, seemed to grow tinny and distant.

"Cha Ma is your guru. You know that, don't you?" Her manner of speaking was demanding, but it did not offend me. I felt an...*inevitability*...looming up behind me.

I barely nodded. I could not speak.

"You have to go to the ashram in India..." That was all I heard. I could see Sandi talking. Her mouth was moving. Her eyes were still sparkling. But I heard nothing. I was caught in my own thoughts. *India! Yes! I must go. This is my date with destiny. What's that question we are to ask ourselves?* "*If you had only six months left to live, what would you do?*" *If I had six months left, what would I do? I would go to India.* I paused in my thoughts, barely able to believe the direction and earnestness they had taken. Before I realized it, I had declared to myself—*I am going to go to India. As soon as I can!* I looked around the crowded hall, hazy with the smoke of incense. *How is it that everyone has a date with destiny at some point or another? Do they live up to it? Will I?* I sat and mused to myself, aware, but just barely, that Sandi and MA! Man were still talking to me.

"Rise up on your knees," a woman on my right whispered into my ear. She put her arm around my waist and "hefted" me up onto my knees. I was in front of Cha Ma! I tried to regain my composure. Cha Ma smiled at me. I smiled back. She hugged me and whispered, "Ma…Ma…" in a gravelly voice. As she pulled away, she took my right hand and thrust a wad of something into it. She smiled at me again, patted my cheek and said, "India."

Pow!

CHAPTER THREE

THE TEST BEGINS

Marie—Maya's Mother

United States

I remember the beginning… What is that cliché? The beginning of the end. Yes, I can remember the beginning of the end of life as I knew it. It was many years ago. One long, arduous, painful year. A prayerful year.

I have come to see that real faith is built on the edge of disbelief, when Satan is gnawing at your heels and you can feel his constant heat. He takes advantage of every single moment: "So, where is your God *now*?" You struggle, wondering whether you're even going to make it without going crazy. This is a head-to-head, toe-to-toe, weapon-to-weapon combat with the powers and principalities of darkness, an intense, passionate warring for every little bit of ground. I had no idea I would know such warfighting so intimately. I remember when war was declared upon my…our…lives.

Emptiness. A gaping, searing gulf. *Are the heavens crying?* I had just heard the worst thing a mother could ever hear next to being told that her child was dead. In effect, my child *was* dead. Perhaps this was even worse than death. At least the absence that death creates is not intentional on the part of the one who dies. My daughter's was.

"I'm moving to India. I have found my real mother and I'm going to live with her," my daughter, Maya, said on the phone, with the oddest, coldest, most distant sound in her voice.

"Real mother"? Did I cause this? I must have! Oh God! I panicked inside. "When are you leaving? Are you coming home before you leave?" I asked, my world crashing down upon me. *Oh God! Oh God!*

"No. I'm not coming home. I have nothing to come home for. I leave tomorrow," replied my life's heart, my baby, sounding like someone altogether different.

What had I done? Why is she running away? "Your real mother?" I asked, amazed that words could come out of my mouth. I wanted to curl up and cry.

"Yes. Cha Ma. She is my guru. My *real* mother. You're just the one who gave birth to me in this life. I've been looking for her for many lifetimes and I've finally found her."

Please help me, Lord. Please help me breathe. Please help me live. Real mother? I asked myself as I thought of all the years with my child, my brilliant and daring (oftentimes too much so) child. *I am her mother!*

"When are you coming back? What about school?" I asked, thinking that she would say she was going in a few months.

"I'm not coming back. I've closed everything here. I've placed myself on a leave of absence at school, but I'm not coming back. I'm giving my life to Cha Ma."

What is she talking about? What is she doing to herself? To leave Harvard? Of all the opportunities... What has come over her? I felt greater and greater panic welling up inside of me. I pleaded, "Baby, before..."

"I am not your baby," she said, her voice hard, flat.

"I just mean, before you do this and overcommit, think about it."

"I knew you wouldn't understand. But then you're not my mother, so of course, you wouldn't understand. *She* understands. I'm going because I can't talk to you. One day maybe you'll understand."

Oh no! I've got to keep her on the line. I could feel the last remnants of her sliding past me. "Well, at least give me your address so that I can know where you are." I paused, hopeful, grasping at the last little straw. "Where will you be?"

"I'm not telling you. I don't want to have anything to do with you again. And if you try to go looking for me, you won't find me, so don't bother. Good-bye."

Dial tone.

She had hung up, just like that. Just like that, my life was over. Completely. My baby was gone. Had been gone for a long time, I could tell from her voice. Such an air of finality. *Oh God! Oh God! What am I to do?* I could not think of a thing so I sank to the floor in my kitchen and wept. I do not know for how long. All night, at least. The sun sank; it rose. Still I cried. Forlorn. Destroyed. Horribly, hopelessly, lost and alone. All from one phone call.

Had Marie only known—she was not alone. Her house was full of supernatural visitors, some of whom were much more comfortable being there than others. The angels of the Lord were everywhere, inside and out. They were her guests and always welcome—through her prayers and intercession, through her music and musings. For many years they had been invited in (sometimes consciously, sometimes unconsciously) to be a part of her family. She had set up an abiding atmosphere of praise and worship to the Lord, and they enjoyed it. From this place, through her continuous prayers and intercession, they were constantly being sent on assignment.

However, this time there were others—spiritual squatters, interlopers—and Marie had no idea that they were present. They had perceived and utilized the opportunity the phone conversation had afforded. In fact, it was not so much that they had perceived the opportunity, but rather that their lord had sent them over. The conversation was bound to happen. The stage had been set months, even years, in advance. Satan had told them to bank on Marie being blindsided and left without a prayer.

They represented two sets of supernatural beings—once upon a time so similar, yet now polar opposites, pitted against each other. They warred in a battle that had been raging from time immemorial. The end had already been decided and settled in a realm beyond and outside of time, yet still the vanquished fought against the victors.

The angels of the Lord, beautiful, awesome, huge, endowed with a fiery iridescence that did not exist within the human spectrum of light, stood at attention. They were waiting…waiting…waiting for a word. A word. A simple word from God would have been all that was needed to permit them to move, to take action. They were waiting for Marie to pray! She *had* to pray in order for them to act.

Instead, she replayed the conversation over and over in her mind. She doubted herself and questioned the past. She muttered fears and worries to herself. She went from bad to worse. She sank into despair. Thus…

Despair entered the house. The Lord's angels had to allow him passage. He had gained legal entry by means of Marie's words of fear and despair. The brilliance of the angels of God was in no way touched by his brownish cast; although their brilliance dimmed his already dull pallor. However the effects were only superficial—for although he was akin to a spiritual black hole and they to spiritual suns, unlike in the natural world, neither had any influence upon the intrinsic state of the other. Having made a binding, eternal choice, out of time, their natures and their fates were forever sealed. Who and what they were was permanent and irreversible.

Oh! Had Marie only been able to see with spiritual eyes, as when Elisha prompted his servant to look upon the hill and see with eyes lit by the supernatural. There were more with her than against her. If she could have seen, she would have taken heart. However she saw nothing. She was to embark upon a "testing of her faith."

Despair slumped past the more beautiful, powerful angels. He was well aware of his diminished, misshapen body, his reprehensible face, his odor, which, though it was not physical, permeated everything about him. His thousands of years of separation from the Presence of God were evident upon him. In fact the dissonance between what he was meant to be and what he had become pervaded his depths and had become his very nature. This essence of what he had become had taken, and would continue to take, its toll upon him. He was Despair, infinitely deep and resolute, with no possibility of respite…ever.

Slinking in behind him, in all their putrid glory, were other hellish angels led fearfully by Fear. Some of these hesitated shiftily at the threshold of the kitchen, overcome by the effects of Fear's fearfulness.

"She'll...never...come...back," Despair slowly hissed, venomously, simultaneously casting a nervous glance at the Lord's angels. Fear and intimidation were evident upon his face. (He did not want to be influenced by his comrades; nevertheless, their presence affected him.) His feverish, foul breath curled its way into Marie's brain, whispering, whispering.... His suggestions wrapped tentacles insidiously around her heart, clutching with their icy-cold lies.

What am I going to do? Marie wondered. She felt despair clutch her heart and weave into its very depths. It felt almost physical. Her heart hurt, ached, burned. "She'll never come back!" Marie whispered to herself.

Worry hissed into her ear, "What are you going to do? There's nothing to do!"

Fear began to pierce at her heart with his barbs, "She's left you forever...forever...and ever."

Marie laid her head on the cold kitchen linoleum and cried bitter, hot tears of despair as Fear stabbed away at her. *I'm so afraid she's left me forever.* With her fearful words, she fed Fear what he wanted, what he needed. His sallow, mustard yellow hue began to deepen into a sickish sulfur color.

"Hehn...hehn...there's no way out..." Despair whispered, sharing with her more of his morose musings. The ripe, brownish cast of his body deepened, growing hideously richer as he warmed to his subject. His eyes cast a furtive glance at the Lord's angels and quickly darted away; their brilliance burned his eyes. "She won't come back," he rasped at her, licking what used to be lips. He, Fear, and Worry commenced a slow, sickening dance around her, scratching at her.

There's no way out. She won't come back. Marie despaired. *I am so afraid. I am so afraid!* In the midst of her agony, an entirely different thought crossed her mind—*I need to tell Paul.* Yes, she needed to tell her husband, share the burden with him. However, he had gone out of town for a few days to visit his sister's family. *I don't want to tell him. Not yet. I don't want to admit it. Honestly, I don't want to deal with what he might have to say. What am I going to do? What am I going to do?*

The angels of the Lord were getting restless. They could not act because a prayer had not been uttered that would release them. Unbidden, they could not make a human do something. *Enough already! Marie, pray! Release us. Pray to the Lord so that He may give us orders to remove these!* they thought. Still, they did not act.

Although Satan's minions' color diminished in the presence of such goodness, the brilliance and beauty of the Lord's angels were in no way affected by them. Even as Marie sank further and further, the angels of the Lord were unperturbed. They maintained themselves perfectly subject to the laws of the Lord in all ways.

One of those laws to which the Lord's angels strictly adhered was that they responded solely, exclusively, to the Lord's commands—the Word of the Lord. They never acted of their own volition. Nor could they be ordered about by a human (contrary to what some humans mistakenly presumed).

Another law was that the Word of the Lord first had to be "activated" in the earthly realm through a human and then commanded by God before it could be acted upon. A human had to pray or speak a Word that was accordance with God's desire—even a simple, "Oh God, help me!" was enough. That prayer—that Word (be it ever so small)—once uttered by a human, would shoot to God in Heaven. He would hear and send it to His angels as an order. They would receive the command and immediately execute the order. However, the movements—a person praying or speaking the Word, God hearing and ordering, His angels receiving the order and executing it—were all simultaneous and instantaneous in a play of time and no-time. In fact, in a profoundly fantastic play between time and no-time, God often would hear a prayer and dispatch His angels with an answer *back into time* for it to be answered before it was ever asked. However, how, when, and why God answered was entirely up to Him.

The Lord's angels ached and burned to battle Satan's angels, to remove them, but no matter the desire, they, unlike their eternal opposites, would not, could not, rebel against the laws of the Lord. Thus, they waited...and waited...and held the promise in their hearts—*Marie, pray!*

More of the enemy came into the house. They surrounded Marie in a macabre dance. She cried and cried, unwittingly inviting even more of them in. The angels of the Lord retreated beyond the outer walls of her home, waiting....

"I can't believe it! She leaves today," Marie stated, "and there's nothing I can do about it. I've gotten no help from the police. They say that as she's an adult and she left of her own free will; it's not their business." Marie paced back and forth in the kitchen, arms folded across her stomach, worry etched in her face. "And I know her, if she says she's going to do something, it's already done." Members of her prayer group sat at the table and watched her. They could see the battle in her body. This woman who was always a support for others, the one who was always the shoulder to cry upon, the one who always knew what to do, had taken a lethal blow. Her face, her body, and even her words evinced the fear, the despair, the anguish.

Marie continued, "I filed a missing person's report. I don't even know if it will be considered, not really. The police said it won't have much effect since she's grown and she called me to let me know her intentions, that she was leaving the country."

Connie, Marie's closest friend, handed her a steaming cup of coffee, "Here…"

"Thank you." Marie's usually laughing eyes showed not a trace of happiness. Her coffee-colored skin looked ashen, as though the life were being sucked out of her. In a sense, it was. She leaned against the sink.

"Did you check for her with any of the airlines?" Connie asked, standing beside her.

Marie nodded. "I tried, but they won't disclose the travelers." Tears began to well up in Marie's eyes. She turned away so that her friends would not see her cry yet again. "I *know* her. If she says she's going to do something, it's as good as done. She's very good at following through on her crazy, erratic plans." She shrugged her shoulders and sighed from the depths of her being—pain, misery, lostness evident in her voice, in her lack of words.

Her shoulders slumped further. Connie and the rest of the members of the prayer group watched Marie in a helplessness bordering upon hopelessness. Their prayerful partner, their intercessory mainstay, the church bulwark was going down.

"What does Paul say?" Mark asked from the table. He wondered if Paul even knew. He could not imagine that he would not hurry home to be with Marie during such a desperate time. Paul loved his wife so much; he would hate to see her hurting like this.

Pause. Marie stared out the window. "I haven't told him yet," she replied in a subdued tone. "I…I don't know why. Except I don't want to worry him."

Mark responded perhaps a little more harshly than was necessary, "But he needs to know. He's her father."

Marie answered, defensiveness in her voice, "He'll be back tonight. I'll tell him then." Her voice waned thin. She stared down at the coffee cup she was holding.

Connie placed her coffee cup in the sink and mumbled to herself, more a thought than an utterance. "Someone has to do something. What should we do? This is awful. Oh God! Tell us what to do!"

An angel of the Lord, the one assigned to Connie, instantaneously received the answer from the Lord. Connie's whispered utterance, made instinctively, was all that was needed. Her angel, whose name in the heavenly language was unpronounceable but in English would have been an approximation of Guardian, immediately moved from without the house to her side the moment she had muttered, "Oh God!" He had received his release from the Lord by her weak prayer. He could help. He could speak. Gently he touched her cheek and whispered into her ear, "Pray!"

Connie turned from the sink and grabbed Marie's hand, "Let's pray!" The others quickly gathered around, each one wondering— *Why didn't I think of that? How did it disappear from my mind?*

How indeed had the idea to pray, to seek God, disappeared from their minds? They had entered Marie's house that morning prepared to pray. However, through the night of pain and anguish, Marie had spoken a universe of fears. She had erected edifices of despair and mountains of anguish. The prayer group had been disarmed immediately when they had walked in—the enemy had been ready for them. As soon as they had stepped over the threshold, Deception,

Intimidation, Fear, and a cluster of others had met them and had blinded them to the knowledge hidden in their hearts. They had whispered ceaselessly, convincingly, overpoweringly into their minds and hearts unspoken fears, horrible imaginations, and vicious lies.

Her friends were unprepared for the warfare, the magnitude of the operation, into which they had stepped. Satan desired, *desperately desired*, to win this war. He believed that many would fall if one went down. If he could ruin Maya for Heaven, he was sure it would bring down Marie and Paul. Such a fall would destabilize their church and create for him an avenue by which to ruin many more lives. Further, he included in his calculation all the souls that were tied to them over the course of their lifetime. People rarely ever took into consideration the soul-count for Heaven or hell that was attached to each human being; but Satan never forgot. Ah! He was counting on garnering for the kingdom of hell thousands of souls at the least.

First he had to ruin Maya, Marie, and Paul. He had planned the operation many years ago—when Maya was still a child. He could see that God had something special in mind for her—*and that just would not do!* So, he had decided to preempt God. Strategically he had dispatched his minion into her life so that over the years she had been assiduously coached, stealthily influenced, and blatantly manipulated to the exact spot. She was now on the brink, on the precipice, of his perfectly constructed plan. He could see it already: The resultant destruction was going to be absolutely massive and deliciously wicked!

This the prayer group did not know. Thus they were horribly ill-prepared for what awaited them in Marie's house. They did not see the deep, ominous shadows that now permeated the house. They could not see the demonic activity within nor the Lord's angels outside, waiting for a prayer-inspired word from God. Outside of the house the air, the very atmosphere, was electric with the Lord's angels' iridescent, supernatural light and their magnificent, perfectly controlled power.

Finally with Connie's intimation, her hint of a prayer, Heaven moved! The angelic troops were mobilized. They had been waiting…poised…and now! Now! All Heaven could begin to move. Immediately, as Connie, Marie, and the rest of the prayer group held hands in agreement and began to pray, relief came. First they prayed in English all those things in their hearts and what the Bible had to say about the situation. Their own words soon became inadequate. So they shifted into another language altogether—the language of the heavenly angels. As the language of the Spirit flowed from their mouths, a light burst forth from the midst of the circle.

The Lord inhabits the praises of His people! As they prayed, not knowing what they were praying but allowing the Holy Spirit to pray for them as He knew the situation they were clueless about, the light grew. It was supernatural light. Living light. Powerful, growing, breathing, flowing light. Exploding. The moment they opened their mouths and prayed in the Spirit, the Holy Spirit, who knew the mind of God, prayed for them. At last, the angels were released to *war!*

Lightning quick, the angels of the Lord were within the house, heavenly weapons brandished, singing celestial songs in an awesome, glorious language. Their voices were magnificent and deeply resonant. They *loved* their work for the Lord. To carry out His Will was their delight and purpose, their *raison d'etre.*

Despair, Fear, Worry, and all the other demonic beings recoiled and shrank in upon themselves. They covered their ear holes and slits, for the songs of the Lord hurt their ears. The Lord's angels beat them back. The evil ones tried to fight. It was impossible. Everything they had or did was greatly surpassed by the Lord's angels. Despair limped out whimpering to himself. Fear and the others were close behind him. The light engulfed them and shot out from the house—riding upon the waves of prayer that rolled up to Heaven and shot back down to the earth.

The prayer group continued to pray in the Holy Spirit. A wondrous, melodic sound swelled and filled the house. The physical effects of their prayers were slight in comparison to the tidal waves being created in the spiritual realm. Yes, the sound of their prayers flowed from their mouths and was heard, but the greater reality was that the atmosphere within and without the house vibrated and undulated due to the sounds.

Had the humans been able to hear it, they would have heard the angels of the Lord joining them, singing, praising, worshiping in the heavenly language, in exultation, in adoration, in bliss. The two sounds melded together, the heavenly and the humanly. Who would have thought that two such vastly different vessels could meld together to create such a sublime orchestration of sound? As the angels sang and the humans prayed in the Holy Spirit, light poured forth from their innermost beings—both human and heavenly— through the house, spreading out in all directions. Into the neighborhood. Into the sky. Even into the ground. It was a living, pulsing, vibrant light—a light of love and of power and of joy.

Suddenly, out of the one-story, red brick house ascended two angels. They paused in the air, hanging high above the house, talking. One was bigger and brighter. His demeanor signified authority and power. The other, also vibrant and massive, exhibited through his attitude a willing submission of his power to the other.

The brighter, larger angel, whose name was Majesty, turned to the other, whose name was Awe. "Yes, prayer works. The fervent prayers of the righteous avail much. Right now their prayer is moving things.

Everything will be set by the time Maya gets to India, to Cha Ma's ashram. No one will know, though.

"First the seed must be planted. This seed will grow and become a full tree. However, for now it is to stay as a glimmer, a mere hint, so that Satan does not find out what's going on. He sees the activity. He knows that Marie is a praying woman and that Paul is a man of God. He is on the lookout for relief to come. He will try to ambush the relief. We will beat him at his game! The Lord has spoken; it will come to pass, no matter what happens. The Lord knows all and He will see to it that His plan is fulfilled and in the best possible manner." Majesty smiled as he spoke. He crossed his massive arms over his chest and chuckled to himself as though he were privy to an inside joke. Awe smiled with him in full understanding of the ways of the Lord.

"I don't understand how Satan can do it…how did he get so lost and how does he continue to be so deluded? You'd think after so many defeats he'd get it." Awe shook his head in puzzlement. At the movement of his head, the air was stirred and glimmers of light—*Oh! If only it were visible to the human eye!*—shot forth like a celestial fireworks display. It was awe-inspiring. Hence, the name, Awe.

Majesty nodded in agreement. "I don't understand, but if I did I still would not be on the wrong side, getting pummeled throughout the ages by the God of the universe. My! The Lord is so awesome!"

He began descending slowly from where he had been in the air. "But right now we must minister to Marie. We must encourage her in the Lord so that she will begin to 'speak those things that are not' in order to create what she wants to see. She needs to speak those things that are not in order to destroy what she does not want. She must speak God's Word so that we can be free to act. And we will need to encourage her to keep speaking them. Come!"

Majesty and Awe moved into the house, right through the roof and into the kitchen, simply by their intent. The other angels turned toward them, smiling, nodding, singing, and praising, eyes glinting with joy as if they knew some marvelous secret. Of course they did—they knew the end from the beginning! The kitchen, the entire house, was packed full of huge, magnificent beings who towered to the ceiling, some whose bodies passed through the ceiling. On the roof were others, sentries standing guard, reaching 12 to 15 feet into the air. Their feet appeared firmly planted upon the rooftop, but in actuality they were standing firm upon the word spoken to them by the Lord.

One of the sentries leaned toward the other, in between singing and praising, and asked, "Where are *they*?"

The other shrugged his immense shoulders, "I don't know. I'd wager that they slunk back to their headquarters to get new orders. They'll be back, though. I'm sure they have a spy or two somewhere, far enough away so as not to get burned by the light of the Lord. They're watching and waiting, waiting for that moment when Marie or one of the others weakens or stops praying or having faith. Then they'll call the others and...you know what'll happen..." He sighed. The other sighed with him. They both looked around watchful for the enemy, but within moments they recommenced singing, as their natures were not given to worry or to thoughts beyond pleasing their God.

Inside, Majesty and Awe stood with the angels surrounding Marie and her friends as they prayed. Their hands were on the shoulders of the humans. Warmth and light poured out of them; their beings could not help exuding their essence.

Majesty spoke, "The Lord says, 'All will be well!'" Immediately the angels cheered. When finally the cheering died down, Majesty continued, "It will be hard for them. We must allow everything to flow and take its course. We are to protect their lives—the enemy may not destroy them—and he knows this. However, they must walk, fully, this path. It is a life-defining test. It will be arduous and difficult, but the Lord our God will see them through."

CHAPTER FOUR

A NIGHT IN BANGKOK

Maya

Enroute to India

HERE I am…*with a layover in Bangkok, Thailand, on my way to India on a 12-month tourist visa. I did it! I can't believe I did it! In three weeks' time, no less!* I replayed the last three weeks in my mind as I peered out the window of a taxicab, lost in thought. I was extremely pleased with myself and with how everything had fallen so neatly into place. The moment I understood that Cha Ma was my guru, my satguru…*my avatar*…and that I was to go to India, I moved to make it happen. *When it comes to enlightenment, nothing is too great or too hard!* I simply had to go. The universe conspired with me to make it happen.

I thought of how easy it was to shut down my life. I had placed myself on a leave of absence at school. Many people do that while working on their dissertation, nothing unusual, just a matter of filling out the necessary forms. Taking a leave of absence gave me room for equivocation—I figured I would deal with my life at Harvard at a later time (regardless of the attractiveness of an invitation to pursue enlightenment with a real satguru in India, I found myself averse—in that arena especially—to closing all doors). I closed my financial accounts, leaving open only the bank account that held my money and one credit card for emergencies. I arranged to leave my apartment.

My apartment…now, that hurt a bit. I loved my apartment and I had felt so lucky to live there. I thought about it with more than a little sadness. For two years now, I had been living in downtown Boston in an old piano factory that had been converted into loft apartments. I had a spacious, two-story, two-bedroom loft on the top floor. The place had such character and beauty. Shiny, oak floors—a vestige of when the building was still a piano factory. One wall was made of exposed red brick inset with large windows that looked out over an interior courtyard. On the first floor were the living room, kitchen, bath, and one bedroom. A steep, iron staircase climbed to the second floor which opened onto the master bedroom. This bedroom comprised the entire second floor and was large and airy. On the interior side of this bedroom was a low, half-wall that ran the width of the apartment and overlooked the living room and exposed brick walling. The other, far side of the bedroom was the exterior wall. It was made entirely of glass with sliding doors that opened onto the roof. This side displayed an amazing prospect of downtown Boston.

At night the lit skyline was breathtaking. Many a night, I had stepped through the patio doors and sat on the roof. There I had thought about the meaning of life, wanting to make sense of it all, wanting to know…the truth…if there was one, if it could be had. Finally, I would go back inside and lie down, still staring out at the night sky, praying for someone…anyone…to come get me and show me the truth. As seekers of enlightenment were wont to say—I desired to know the Highest Truth. As I stared into the night sky, I purposed in my heart—*I will do whatever is necessary to know this Truth!*

Thus, except for leaving my apartment, it was not a difficult thing to shut down my life and run after the satguru. It was easy enough to make a few phone calls, close all my accounts, and leave my friends. *What are friends in this lifetime? A lifetime is so fleeting…a drop in the bucket of eternity…one lifetime out of countless thousands.* No, it was not hard to say good-bye to them. I chuckled to myself at the incongruity—*I don't miss my friends; but I do miss my apartment. Strange!*

My mind went to my parents and quickly abandoned them. *Too much…I can't dwell on them.* I quickly set to thinking about my plans. *No one knows that I plan on staying. Of course, a limited visa is not good. I've got to get a long term one, somehow…. But, I can't do anything about that right now.*

Again I thought about the fevered pitch of the last three weeks and how, when I had finally stepped onto the plane, I had felt vastly unfettered and free—the adventure of all adventures had begun.

And now, here I am on the last leg of my journey to India. Pay attention, Maya! There'll be enough time for reminiscing. But, right now, I'm in Bangkok…Bangkok! Who would have thought! I was riding through the city in a broken-down taxicab. I was afraid it would go, "Eeerrrk kerplump!" at any moment and leave me stranded in the middle of a dangerously packed, chaotic road.

I resolved to devour every sensation and every sight as I stared out the window at the passing scenery. The road was dry and dusty and pocked with gaping potholes. Everywhere I looked there were bodies—walking, running, on bicycles, in rickshaws, driving lorries. Not only human ones. Animals walked about freely—none of them ran. Perhaps it was too hot. Maybe they simply had no need—no one was chasing them or shooing them away. Furthermore, the buildings, which contributed greatly to the sense of chaos and disorder, were crammed together and looked to be leaning on each other. From between the buildings peeked random palm trees and sprigs of vegetation.

Even though it was early evening, the heat of the day had not significantly dissipated with the waning light. The air was still heavy and hot. A humid stickiness clung to everything. As I breathed in, it seemed that the air itself was a viscous liquid with thick, invisible threads sticking to the lining of my lungs. When I exhaled, it felt as if those viscous threads clung resolutely to my lungs making breathing a struggle. Suddenly, free, easy air was a precious commodity.

The taxi drove through the city, almost to its outskirts. Here the air was slightly cooler, lighter. It was still hot and humid, just less so. I breathed more freely. I saw more palm trees and vegetation. The buildings stood farther apart as if they, too, enjoyed having more space. Fewer bodies, human and animal, crowded the road now. *Definitely more pleasant than the city.*

"Excuse me, Miss…hotel?" The skinny cab driver interrupted my thoughts as he swerved around several objects in the road—a couple of them being human. The driver halted the cab in front of a large, manorish-looking building.

"Thank you! How much?" I asked, reaching into my little shoulder bag.

"No charge! Included in hotel!" He grinned at me and hopped out.

I grabbed the duffel bag sitting in the back seat with me and climbed out of the car. *Wow! Pretty lavish hotel.* It was a stately, white building, tastefully situated between palms. A lush, well-manicured lawn encircled the building. White spotlights artfully lit up the façade. *Well done! The lights are striking, especially in the growing darkness,* I thought. Low, marble steps fanned up to the entrance.

Two men in perfectly tailored, heavily starched white uniforms with golden buttons stood on either side of the ornately carved wooden doors. Upon my arrival, they hurried down the steps. One grabbed my huge Samsonite suitcase out of the trunk. (I had not learned the art of traveling light.) The other politely took the duffel bag from me and gently guided me by the arm to the door.

"This way, Miss," said he, as another identically dressed man opened the door from inside and led me into the swanky hotel.

"Thank you!" *Is everyone in Thailand so little? Cute, though! And polite! It's hard to believe that one person, that person being me, needs three men to help her get out of a cab and to the front desk.*

I scanned the lobby as I walked to the front desk. *Oh! This place is gorgeous! I love it!* I had such a predilection for rich-looking wood furnishings and ornate carvings, in which the hotel abounded. The furnishings contrasted delicately with the smooth, white marble floors. Here and there hung or sat pieces of artwork, statues, and paintings that depicted aspects of Thai culture. The lobby was exquisite.

I stopped at the front desk and was checked in efficiently. The airline had arranged everything, as this was a necessary layover. My information had been sent over and my room arranged the moment I had checked in at the ticket counter. The young man, still at my elbow, smilingly took my room key from me and led me away, the epitome of obsequiousness. He guided me past a wide flight of white marble stairs to a set of elevators. Quickly we were transported to the fourth floor.

"Here is your room," he said after leading me down a lushly carpeted corridor. He opened my door and gestured inside. "You like?"

I like? I like?! I love! A hasty scan of the room told me that; but I was not going to tell him. I feigned boredom, "It's fine, thank you." I took one of the smaller bills out of my purse and gave it to him.

"Oh! Thank you!" he responded, his eyes shining as he bowed. The other man who was handling my luggage appeared. He walked in and placed my suitcase on the luggage holder. I gave him a similar bill.

"Thank you!" he responded with unconcealed delight, bowing. They both bowed again as they backed out of the door.

"Ugh!" *I think I may've overtipped them. Oh well!* I closed and locked the door. I walked into the room, sat on the king-sized bed, and surveyed the room. *Beautiful!* It was elegantly lavish. Dark, hardwood furniture. Stunning, heavy tapestries. I checked out the sheets and the cover on the bed. *I hate dirty sheets or seeing even one hair. Nothing. Immaculate. Although a little damp. Probably has to do with the climate.*

I walked into the bathroom. *A hole in the floor.* Literally. There was a small hole in the floor for going to the bathroom. On either side of the hole was a rectangular porcelain platform, just large enough for a foot, ostensibly for the "user" to stand on. *Oh joy!* I had already seen the Eastern-style, squat toilets in my travels. I had not expected to see one in an upscale hotel bathroom. To the right of the hole on the wall was a shiny silver spigot with a silver *(stainless steel?)* bucket underneath and a silver cup hooked onto it. (So far in my travels, every time I encountered a squat toilet, I also found a spigot, bucket, and cup. Every time I asked myself—*What're they for?* I had not been able to get up the nerve to ask anyone so I remained ignorant. Above the bucket was a roll of toilet paper. *Good! Toilet paper!* To the left of the hole a couple of feet away was an almost regular-seeming Western toilet, *almost regular-seeming.* Yet something did not look quite right about it. Something was amiss, but whether it was its shape or height, I could not tell.

On the wall behind the hole, situated high, was a showerhead. I turned it on. A strong shower fell down. *Very nice!* I could see myself taking a shower. I noticed the entire tile floor gently sloped into the hole so that the water drained away quickly. All in all, the bathroom was very nice. *Very Asian, but very nice.* I turned and headed back into the room.

Ahh! Sleep! My next flight was not for 14 hours. *I need to call the front desk. Have them give me a wake-up call.* I did that. Then I took a shower, changed into some comfy clothes, and lay down. I had been traveling nonstop for over a day already and I felt the effects. I fell asleep swiftly.

Brrrng! Brrrng!

"Hello?" I asked groggily, into the phone.

"Hello, hello, Miss. This is front desk. Wake-up call. You asked us to call you," an accent-heavy, masculine voice told me.

"Thank you. Thank you," I mumbled. My tired, travel-weary body screamed for sleep. *I'll just close my eyes for a minute. I still have six hours. I'll get ready to go in a minute. I have…enough…time.*

Help me! Help me! Someone was grabbing my arms and legs, pulling me down, down, farther and farther into the bed. The mattress was engulfing me. Swallowing me up. I felt I was being pulled farther and farther into a dark, murky pit. I could not see who…*What?!*…it was that was grabbing me. Everything was sepia-toned. I could not see clearly *at all.* An odd, high-pitched whine was noising in my ears; but I could not perceive its source. Hands and claws clutched at me. Putrid, corrosive odors offended my senses and ate away at my flesh. The odors were stifling me. I could not breathe. *I can't breathe! I can't breathe! I'm going to die!*

"Heelllppp!" I screamed and screamed but no one heard me. No one came. *I can't see! Just to turn on the light! I've got to get to the light!* I reached out, frantically, and pulled the chain on the lamp. Light flooded the room. *Where am I?! Where am I?!* I looked around unable to get my bearings, acutely disoriented, still feeling fingers and claws clutching at me.

Was I sleeping? Was I awake? Where am I? Slowly, I recalled...*Bangkok, Thailand. On my way to India. Layover.* Understanding came to me in short bursts of thought. My mind felt numb, wasted. Fear continued to clutch at me. *It feels almost real.* I saw something move in the corner of my eye. *What is that shadow? Whew! It's nothing, just my towel hanging on the back of the door. But I could've sworn I saw it move, slink away...me and my crazy imagination!*

I sat up on the edge of the bed, not without great effort, and squinted at the clock: 4:56 A.M. The light of the lamp seemed woefully meager. *These hotel rooms need more lights...better lights.* I shoved myself up. I had plenty of time but I did not want to lie back down. I did not even want to touch the bed. In fact, I wanted to get away from the room altogether.

I know...breakfast! My mind was starting to function again. The front desk had informed me that breakfast would start at six. *I'll take another shower and then meditate. By the time I'm finished, they should be serving breakfast. Hopefully...maybe...I'll be able to shake the dream, or whatever it was, off.*

CHAPTER FIVE

THE NAME

Marie and Paul
United States

"JESUS! Help her!" Marie cried out from the depths of her heart. Her own sleep-shrouded cry startled her awake. *What was that? Was I dreaming?* She peered at the luminous features of the clock on the nightstand—5:56 P.M. *I must've fallen asleep.* Marie was dismayed—napping during the day meant a longer, more restless night. She had stretched out on the bed with the intention of reading her Bible and praying—anything to gain strength and peace of mind. Instead, she had fallen asleep.

Her mind touched upon her dream. Quickly, she whispered, "Oh Lord! If this dream is of You, please help me to remember and understand it. But," her voice quavered as the sensation of the dream washed over her, "if it's not, please help me to forget it. In the name of Jesus Christ," her chest was still heaving in distress, "Amen."

The room was dim, as she had drawn the shades, and quiet. She turned toward Paul for the comfort and safety of his arms. However, he was not there. *Oh yes, that's right. It's the middle of the day, not night.* She was disoriented. *Where is he?* Her thoughts did not stay on him for long. They were drawn back to her dream. She rolled onto her back, thinking—*What was that about, Lord? Was it a dream? A warning? Or just craziness in my mind?*

Marie stayed there for some time, wondering what she had just seen, dreamed. It was all dark and uneasy. Gradually, thoughts of her dream ebbed away as her attention turned to her husband. *I wonder where he is? Probably somewhere praying. Or just sitting by himself. He's been doing more and more of that lately.* Ever since Maya had left, Paul had been spending more time sitting alone in his own brooding world, day or night. Marie did not know if he was praying or what. *I've got to get up.* She roused herself and rolled out of the bed.

She padded silently through the house, praying quietly, only slightly aware of her surroundings. Her disturbed thoughts slipped into whispered praise, "Oh God! I thank You for what You are saying. I praise You. I worship You. I thank You for all Your bountiful gifts, for Your lovingkindness. And most of all, I love You, I worship You, I exalt You for who You are. For simply being You." She used to pray like this so often. Most of the time she had not even been aware of it—it just rose from the wellspring within her. But that was before Maya left. Now her prayers were not so carefree and light and full of praise. Now she had to work hard, dreadfully hard, to stir herself into a place of true praise and worship. This evening was different. The words welled up inside of her.

When she reached the living room, she saw her husband, sitting on the couch in the waning light. *Is he praying?* When she reached him, she observed that his eyes were open. A tear glinted on his cheek.

"How are you?" she asked, as she settled down beside him.

He reached out and put his arm around her, drawing her close to his strong, six-foot frame, "I'm fine. Just praying." He kissed the top of her head. Her hair smelled faintly of his favorite perfume. Unconsciously, he inhaled. "God is working with my heart."

Marie nodded. She understood. She laid her head in the crook of his neck.

"I wish I could do more than pray, Mare," he shrugged. "They say praying is much, but I want to take action. I'm a man of action. I want to go find her, go get her, take her out of India." He sighed, heavy and deep. "What about you? How are you doing?"

"Okay, I guess…" Marie paused. "I must've fallen asleep, because I had a dream. I asked the Lord to help me remember it if it was of Him. I can't remember it all but I do remember seeing a girl…a woman. I couldn't see her face but I knew it had to be Maya. She was in bed and she was being attacked. By what, I don't know. I couldn't see *them* clearly. But they were dark *masses* and they were evil." Paul squeezed her shoulder and rubbed her arm in encouragement.

"I hate to see her being attacked so…so…oh Paul! It was awful…" Her voice petered out. She shook her head. "In my sleep, I cried out, 'Jesus!' That's when I woke up. Even though I wasn't in the dream, I sense…I *know*…that I helped her. But I can't figure out whether the dream was a warning from the Lord or a supernatural link with her that shows me that prayer works or…or…simply an attack from Satan."

She looks like a lost, little girl, Paul thought. He felt compelled to protect her but he did not know where to start. How do you fight that which is unseen and intangible? *It's hard to believe that my strong Mare is being undone before my eyes and there's nothing I can do about it. I hate this.* He squeezed her harder. "You know, in Job, the Word says that the Lord seals an instruction in the night. Maybe He sealed your dream? Maybe He plans to keep it from your remembrance until the time is right for it to be revealed? Maybe He's covering its meaning so that it will not be ruined…so that *we will not ruin it*…until it's time. I think you know, deep inside, what the Lord says and what He wants."

"Yes, I do." Marie smiled gently, her heart aching so much it felt almost physical. "Well, all I can do, all I will do, is pray hard for her. And believe."

Again Paul kissed the top of her head, feeling more than thinking, *My God! How I love this woman!*

"What about you? What is the Lord telling you to do?"

"I don't know…keep praying for Maya, of course…"

"For yourself? What is he telling you to do?" Marie pressed. They had not really talked for some time and now, sitting in the dimming light of evening, they were. She did not want to lose the opportunity. She missed talking to her husband—her best friend.

"For myself? I don't know…keep looking for a job…." His voice waned. After 27 years in the Army, he had retired as an officer, only to find no place for himself in the job market. Or so it seemed. Over the course of seven months, he had sent out over 50 applications, all to no avail. And that ate away at him. It was not that they needed the money, although a little extra would have helped—a little extra always helps. No, he had served his time and was now enjoying his retirement income. On top of it, Marie still worked a well-paying job. No, money was not the problem. The problem was that such constant rejection, even over the most menial of positions, challenged who he felt himself to be. He had always defined himself by his hard work and success. Now to have no work and not be able to get any was a crushing blow. He never considered that, perhaps, God wanted him free for a greater purpose. He struggled desperately within himself. Maya's flight only served to add to the feelings of failure, loss, and doubt inside of him.

"Is there anything I can do for you?"

"No." He shook his head. He wondered if he heard pity in her voice. He did not want her pity. Marie remained silent, as did he. Each was lost in his and her own thoughts, praying, but not fully believing.

Bangkok, Thailand

On the "other side" of a door in a hotel room in Bangkok, as Death slunk through, Despair accosted him. "No! Not yet, you fool! Why are you always in such a hurry?" Despair shoved Death, something he would not have done under normal circumstances. Death was by far the larger, the more powerful, but in this situation—the Maya situation—Despair was in charge. He was getting his orders straight from Satan. In fact, Satan had said specifically that he, Despair, was to lead this case. He was to oversee her demise, destruction, and death and that of as many other people as possible. He had been told the entire game plan by Satan—or so he thought. (He had yet to understand that Satan never revealed *all* his plans. He liked to keep his maneuvers shrouded in secrecy, even within his own ranks. Satan worked to keep them guessing, uncomfortable, jockeying for position so that they would not organize against *him*. *He* did not want any insurrections from within his *own* ranks—he understood all too well that a house divided could not stand.)

For now, Despair was in charge, which Death knew but did not like. This made for an unstable, dangerous situation because Death was, by far, superior. Additionally, he was the loose cannon, the unpredictable element, and he could easily ruin everything. He tended to jump the gun: If the opportunity arose to kill someone, to remove them, Death would seize it, even if their continued existence was more propitious for the kingdom of darkness. It could not be helped—it was in Death's nature to ruin, kill, and destroy everything. He had to be kept under control, always, which was something Satan usually did himself. But not in this case. For some strange reason, he had given Despair veto power over Death. Such a tenuous, volatile arrangement!

"Don't you remember that our dark lord said that we are to play this entire thing out? And that..." Despair paused. "I'm in charge? Hehn...hehn..." He was enjoying his newfound power. Obviously, it was going to his head. "We are only to torment her. What are you doing here anyway? She's not supposed to die, not yet." Despair stepped close to Death, trying to push his face up near Death's. However, his little misshapen, brown body just ended up looking "littler"—ridiculously littler—next to Death's dark bulk. At Despair's words and actions Fear, who was watching from the corner, shrank back, his nature overruling, as always. His doing so showed great wisdom—Death was not to be commanded, shoved, or challenged. No, Death was not to be anything but avoided.

Death. Shiny, jet black. His skin was something similar to the exoskeleton of a rhinoceros beetle. Also similar to that beetle were two jutting "growths" that sprouted out of his head. In fact, his shape and head was reminiscent of the large beetle, but only vaguely. He could and did morph his body into other shapes. When he chose it, his shape more closely resembled that of humans. This ability was a vestigial quality from once having been a heavenly angel. Only a few of the fallen retained it, of whom, of course, Satan was one; Death was quite close to him in skill.

Death was large, much larger than the other evil angels. The others surmised that it was because he fed off his constant "kills," unlike the rest of them, whose occupations were up and down. Suicide and Murder were akin to him and were his favored companions. They, like him, were larger than most of the others, but not as large as he— probably because he often commandeered their "kill" and consumed it.

"What was that anyway? What was it that forced us away from her? What pushed us off?" Despair questioned, unwittingly allowing his inexperience to show. Fear whimpered at Despair's ignorance and stepped back farther into the shadows.

Death pulled himself up so that he towered over Despair, to remind Despair of his superiority, "What? You mean you've never encountered such a thing as this? In the middle of an attack to be repelled? Or in beginning an attack, to be pushed to your knees and forced away?" Death's eyes glimmered evilly, but with hidden elements of fearful intimidation.

"You mean you didn't notice…that after we made it out, we had to pause? Regroup? Reenergize, even if just a little?" Death swallowed hard, trying not to show Despair his very real fear. Despair appeared ignorant of an important element concerning warfare involving humans—warfare with a weapon that never failed—never. Not once. *You would think he would know this after two thousand years of engaging humans…ever since….*

Despair shook his head. "No."

"You mean," Death swallowed hard again and felt himself begin to shake, "you mean, you've never encountered the…*Name*…before?" He whispered the last bit. He hated that his weakness was evident, even if only to himself.

Fear whimpered and muttered to himself, "The Name…nooo…"

Despair shrugged his misshapen shoulders. "What name?" he asked impatiently.

How stupid is this…? Really! How can he be leading? What was Satan thinking, putting him in charge? How does he not know? He must know! Maybe he forgot. Death vacillated between incredulity and seething scorn at Despair's inconceivable ignorance and his own very real fear of the reality of…

"The Name. You know, *The Name…*" Death hissed, feeling aggravation with Despair rise within him, fighting for ground against the fear of the Name. Fear shrank into himself, whether out of fear of Death or of…the Name…only he knew.

Even as Death stared at Despair in a wild mixture of emotion, he observed Despair casting a glance around to see which of the evil ones were watching him with Death. He could almost read Despair's thoughts: *I, Despair, am the superior of Death—if even once.*

Death swore to himself, *Argh! He is such an idiot! He doesn't even know what he's up against!* Despair should have been paying better attention to an angel far superior than him, one with far more knowledgeable and cunning. He should have been listening and observing. But he was not.

Despair asked, distractedly, "The name…what name?"

"The Name…of…" Death paused neither for effect nor for drama. No, he paused out of pure fear. He paused out of a reluctance to have to reiterate it, yet again, as so many times in the past, the supremacy of One. He paused out of an unwillingness to experience what he knew would happen next. "The name," he rasped, "…of…*Jesus.*"

There! He had said it! The effects of the Name…that Name…were instantaneously and horrendously felt. Death's shoulders slumped down and his knees buckled uncontrollably, as did Despair's and Fear's. All the evil ones with them went down. They all fell, as one, to their knees.

"See! See! What happens with just the Name? That Name? Jesus." They fell again, even as they were struggling to their feet. "God has spoken, 'Every knee shall bow and every tongue confess….' We can fight it. We can rebel; but it is inherent within us that at that Name, we will bow. We fear and tremble when we hear it. *It is indelibly imprinted into the fabric of what we are!* Don't you know this?" Death was verging on despair himself. His voice came out as a whine, and he did not care.

Despair despaired, "Oh, help! Help! How are we ever going to win?"

Fear whimpered and moaned, "Oh! Don't say it!"

"When we encounter *His* Name spoken by a saint," Death was unwillingly warming to the subject, "it doesn't matter the distance. All that matters is the intent—the effective, fervent prayers of the righteous avails much—it doesn't matter how great the distance between the praying person and the one being prayed for. Do you know what that means? Let one person pray for another in trouble and really mean it. Let that person call out *His* Name…and we're shut down. Just like that!" Death shrilled, "You saw what just happened when we tried to attack the girl in her sleep!"

"Oh! Oh! What am I doing? I'm on the wrong side. We're done for! We'll never win!" Despair whimpered and all but gave up (alas! such was his nature).

Death asked, "Didn't you *know* this? Haven't you ever encountered this, in the two thousand years since…?"

Despair whined, "Yes, of course…but, I must've forgotten or something…"

Death rolled his eyes. *What am I doing here with this despairing, stupid thing in charge?*

Yet two more supernatural visitors were with Maya. Unlike the evil ones, these two—their brief skirmish won, at least for the moment—stood on opposite sides of the room, glinting swords brandished, their bodies glowing from the exertion of the brief battle. They were angels of the Lord, and clearly they were her guards. One, Brilliant, had been assigned to her from before her birth, so long ago that it would seem to have been before Maya had existed, even in thought; but she had. She had always existed in the infinitely vast Heart and Mind of God. Brilliant was her constant, ethereal companion. Her guardian. She had another more recently assigned, His Strength, who was to help Brilliant. Their orders were to keep her, watch over her, bless her, protect her.

Their huge frames soared unhampered through the ceiling. They were awesome to behold. Brilliant wore an iridescent tunic and pants, which in no way compared to the iridescence and brilliance of his skin, eyes, and even his hair. His body shimmered with a gossamer sheen. He was absolutely lovely to behold. And His Strength was the epitome of his name. His muscles rippled under his white tunic and pants. He looked like power on hold, waiting for an opportunity to be unleashed. At a micro-moment's notice, that held power could, and would, shift into raw, glorious energy and strength made manifest.

A wondrous fragrance, barely perceptible to the human nostril, emanated from them. When she had been younger and less encumbered by the world, Maya, on very rare occasions, had caught faint whiffs of their delightful fragrance. However, it was so quick and fleeting that by the time her senses registered it, it was already gone.

As Maya stood up to start her day, still reeling from the "nightmare," they sheathed their weapons. Brilliant spoke, "I love the name of Jesus!" His Strength laughed aloud and nodded in complete agreement.

CHAPTER SIX

VEGAS CASINO
IN THE MIDDLE
OF NOWHERE

Maya

Trivandrum, India

"LADIES and Gentlemen, we will be landing at the Trivandrum airport in approximately an hour," the captain squawked over the intercom in a thick Indian accent. The flight attendants, lovely Indian women in magenta and gold saris that matched the décor of the plane, walked by opening the hatches to the overhead bins.

That's strange, I thought.

The captain offered an explanation, "Before we deplane, Indian law demands that all people and luggage be fumigated. Do know that the fumicide has been tested by Indian laboratories and does not constitute a health threat."

By the end of his message, the compartment was already filling up with "fumicide"—*Whatever that means!*—I had never heard the word before in my entire life. People began coughing.

I wonder if this is an insidious plot to kill us, I mused between fits of coughing and choking. *Hasn't anyone ever reported this to...to...someone! It should be against international law to "fumigate" people.* I looked around and saw others who looked even more disturbed—physically and mentally—than me. Coughing. Hacking. Tearing up. Some looked like they were ready to pass out. The flight attendants were nowhere to be found. They had abetted in poisoning us and then had disappeared.

Slowly, the fog began to dissipate. I felt the plane descending. After a while, the captain's voice came over the P.A. system again, "Ladies and Gentlemen, thank you for your cooperation with our fumigation." *Cooperation?!* "We are presently beginning our descent..." *Beginning? I thought we were in the middle of it.* "...into Trivandrum airport. Make sure your seatbelts are fastened, your tray tables are locked, and your seats are in their upright position. Please turn off all cell phones and electronic equipment. We will be in Trivandrum airport shortly. Thank you for flying Fly India! I hope that when you have to fly to India again you will choose Fly India." *Not a chance. No way I'm going to be tortured by "fumigation" again!*

Soon the plane landed. Before I could pull my duffel bag out of the overhead bin and check around me for my belongings, the door of the plane opened. The passengers wearily cheered. Many had traveled over 24 hours just to get to the other side of the world. In fact, I was sure that a few, myself included, had been traveling for more than two days.

Upon the opening of the door, I felt the Indian air billow in upon me as though it were a living, breathing entity. Rich, fecund, alive. I could almost feel thousands of years of history and culture within it. I gathered my stuff and waited in line to deplane. When I arrived at the door, I hesitated—the heat and humidity halted me. The air felt denser and "wilder" than what I had felt in other parts of Asia. While I had remained within the plane, the heat and humidity had rolled in softly; now at the doorway, they assailed my body, assaulting my face, my nostrils, my lungs. The heat and humidity felt peculiarly alive—two distinct, pulsating entities, each with its own will. I breathed in deeply. The hot, pungent air filled my lungs. *Ah! I am home! I can feel it. I know I'll never return to America. I have found my home, the place my soul has been seeking for so many lifetimes.* These thoughts passed through my mind faster than I could consciously grasp them. *Something about it…the air, the atmosphere…it's charged, tinged, with a "something" that is so familiar.*

Another reason I hesitated was because we had to walk down a set of rickety, portable stairs that looked as if they would break under the weight of a small child. They shuddered and protested creakingly against the man in front of me. I dared not step onto them as long as other bodies were still on them. Finally I could wait no longer. Carefully, I walked down the wobbly steps. (Visions of falling and breaking my neck before I ever commenced my "Avatar Adventure" paraded through my mind.) I breathed out an audible sigh of relief when my feet touched the ground. Along with the other passengers, I walked across the sticky, tarry tarmac and into the little airport.

It was unbearably hot and crowded within. I followed the line of passengers through customs, which was unexpectedly uneventful. I waited for my suitcase at the luggage carousel, which was not a carousel at all but rather a long counter. Taking it from a hand dolly, two little, wizened men carried my bag between them, struggling beneath its weight. Straining, they hefted it onto the counter. I slung my duffel over my shoulder, grabbed the suitcase, and walked out.

"Taxi?"

"Taxi, Miss?"

"Rickshaw?"

"Miss! Miss!" Drivers pressed all about me. Dark-skinned, dark-haired, very Indian. They were all wearing button-up shirts, although some were wearing dark slacks and others were wearing dhotis. Their dhotis were folded at the knees with the tips tucked in at the waist, exposing bare legs.

"I need a taxi. I'm going to Alleppey."

"I can do it! I can do it!" they shouted at me. A couple tried to grab my arm and pull me with them.

"How much?" I asked, looking for them to barter, though hoping that they would not see that I, myself, did not like to haggle. If they did, they would be able to take me for some exorbitant amount.

"One hundred seventy rupees!" I heard.

"No! No!"

"One hundred sixty rupees! One hundred sixty rupees!"

I let them argue among themselves.

"One hundred fifty rupees!" They were jostling and pushing each other out of the way. "Me! Me!"

"I'll take the one for one hundred and fifty rupees," I said, with some frustration, shoving the hand of one driver off my arm.

Hundred-fifty-rupee driver grabbed my suitcase. "Here with me, Miss!"

He gestured toward a disorganized grouping of taxis—all small, white, and beat-up—and slowly led me to one in particular. The weight of my suitcase slowed him considerably. I had chosen well, though, as I had picked the driver of the least beat-up of the taxis.

Whew! I'm glad I chose him. I think his taxi will make the two-hour drive to the peninsula. I'm not so sure about the others. I slid into the back seat and waited while he struggled to put my suitcase into the trunk. The upholstery was worn, brick-red pleather, cracked, with white threads peeking through. In places, it had been patched up with silver duct tape. *Nice!*

Finally done with stowing the suitcase, my driver climbed in behind the wheel. He turned, smiled at me, and said, "Alleppey."

I nodded, "Alleppey," and then said the name of village where the ashram was located in Alleppey. "Ramancheri Tura."

"Ramancheri Tura," he repeated, although what he said sounded vastly different from what I said.

I nodded and added, "Shri Chamundamayi Ma's ashram."

He smiled. "Oh yes! Shri Chamundamayi Ma!" Again what he said sounded infinitely different than what I had just garbled. *I am butchering the language.* I sighed.

He bobbled his head in a weird movement and started up the car. He gunned the engine a couple of times and maneuvered around and out of the clump of taxis. Once free, he sped out of the crowded parking lot. In his mad dash, he managed to avoid hitting several people and two cows. He kept turning around to grin at me as he wheeled the car through the crowded streets of Trivandrum. *Oh! This is going to be a scary two hours!*

A few minutes short of three hours later, we crossed onto the little peninsula where the ashram was located. The peninsula was a narrow, finger-like piece of land that lay to the north of Trivandrum in the district of Alleppey. It was the longest of many jutting pieces of land intersected by innumerable canals and waterways.

The main road loosely followed the Indian Ocean to its left as it cut through the peninsula. It was paved, but in terrible shape. As we drove deeper into Alleppey, I stared, fascinated by the sights. The houses, if they could be called that (huts would have been a better word), captivated me. They were small, dirty, whitewashed dwellings with thatched roofs. Everywhere were tall palm trees towering over hard-packed sandy dirt, although none stood upright. All were leaning over precariously or were bowed painfully at their midsections. To my left, peeking through the palms, lay the ocean twinkling in the bright sunshine.

People were everywhere. No one looked as though he or she were working or doing anything industrious. Children were running and playing, shouting and laughing. Women and men, young and old, were squatting in various places and talking. Or they were standing and talking. Even in what I construed to be stores, owners and sales-people were squatting, leaning against the doorframe or lounging on long, low cots that sat in front of the store. Everyone stopped whatever he or she "wasn't" doing to watch the taxi pass, transporting someone interesting and different—another foreigner going to Cha Ma's ashram—although at the time, I did not know that she was so well-known and that we foreigners were so infamous.

As we neared the ashram, the road turned from broken blacktop (*graytop?*) to rutted, hard-packed dirt and sand. The driver slowed the car in order to negotiate the sand, dirt, and ruts. People rose from their rest and play to follow behind us. Finally, we halted at a chained and locked entrance. Here, two heavy, weatherworn gates made out of solid iron met each other haphazardly. I noted that a dilapidated, wooden fence spanned out on each side. I could not see how far they went. *Why the need for heavy iron gates when the fences can be overrun by any determined five-year-old?* The fencing appeared to stretch around some large, hulking buildings, many long, thatched dwellings and sandy, dry ground.

The driver honked the horn. We waited. No one came from within the fenced-in area, although the crowd around us continued to grow. The driver honked again after a minute or so. I heard yelling that sounded like, *"Oodoogoodishrunti!"* With the yell, the chain was removed and the gates creaked ponderously inward.

The driver slowly drove the car into the compound. The crowd that had followed us stopped short at the gates. Four young men in white pushed the gates closed with much effort and grunting. The first thing I noticed was a huge, open space—it was larger than it appeared from the other side of the gates. The ground was hard-packed dirt and sand. Grass, crabgrass, weeds, even, were nowhere to be found. Beyond the open space were the large buildings and long huts. *This must be the ashram.* I paused to gaze at the main building with a real shock—*It looks like a huge Vegas casino sprouting up in the middle of "Nowhere," India! Well, I never!*

The sprawling structure appeared to be four or five stories high. It was painted a myriad of pastel colors. *Color coordination is definitely not at issue here!* I was awestruck by the building. Overwhelmed! Enthralled! Repulsed! I could not turn my gaze away from the hulking, Las Vegasy monolith set incongruously in the midst of a severely impoverished south Indian village.

The driver continued to pull forward, cruising leisurely on a diagonal across the empty grounds, talking to a few young men from the ashram. They too were in white. They strolled languidly alongside the car, peering in at me unabashedly. Finally we rolled to a stop several yards away from the casino-monolith. The guys in white stopped with us and stood, holding the hems of their narrow dhotis by the bottom.

None of them offered to help. For that matter, the driver did not either…not this time. He merely opened the trunk of the car and stood with his hand on the trunk door, resting and talking, waiting for me to haul my suitcase out of the hatch. I stood there for a good minute waiting. *So when is he going to take my bag out?* And he stood there waiting for me to take it out. Finally, he won.

I pressed the driver's pay into his hand, minus the good tip that he might have had for helping me. I stood there, lopsidedly, from the weight of the suitcase. People were pressing into me, peering at me, curious. A white woman pushed through the crowd. She was wearing a white sari that was crumpled (to be expected given the heat and humidity). As the crowd did not give, she had to push hard to get through.

"Namah shivaya! Namah shivaya!" she said as most people would say, "Excuse me! Excuse me!"

The men closest to the car would not part, but that did not faze her. She elbowed them out of her way. She was as tall as most of them, if not taller, and she was definitely heavier.

"Namah shivaya!" she exclaimed to me, this time as a greeting. "You must be Maya."

"Hi!" I responded, thrilled to see her—my rescuer. Her blue eyes sparkled as the corners of her mouth tweaked up evidencing some hidden mirth. *She looks so friendly.* I immediately relaxed in her presence.

She continued, "We received your itinerary a couple of days ago."

"You *just* received my itinerary? I sent it out almost three weeks ago!" I exclaimed.

She smiled wryly, "Welcome to the ashram! Welcome to India, for that matter! Everything runs much more slowly and inefficiently here. You might as well get used to it if you're planning to stay." She took my suitcase from me and headed toward the Vegas casino. I scrambled to catch up with her. She talked and walked, veering to the right of the building.

"Oh! By the way, my name's Radha."

"Radha?" I repeated, more as a question than a statement.

"Yes! Radha is the name Cha Ma gave me. She'll give you a name if you ask her. Many of us here have been given names by her. It's a great honor."

"Hold up for a second," I entreated. "I want to check everything out."

"Oh yeah! That's right!" She stopped in her tracks and gestured at the Vegasy looking building in front of us. "This is the temple. The back of it. The first floor...or basement, depending upon how you look at it...has rooms for people to stay. The second is the actual temple. The third and fourth floors are rooms. A portion of the fourth floor is for meditation, as is the roof."

"Wow!" I was overwhelmed. I was excited! We kept walking, and shortly, we rounded the corner of the temple. After a few more paces, she stopped in front of a large rectangular, building-like structure. I halted beside her and examined the area. Its floor was made of smooth concrete and was not too well swept. A low wall, reaching to my hips, bordered its perimeter. To my far right was a small opening in the wall to enter and exit and on the other side was a similar opening. Through the center ran a long, low wall that divided the structure in half—it had an opening in its center. The left side was completely empty, whereas the right had tables and chairs—like a small café. Thick metal posts supported the tin roof. *It's so open and airy,* I thought. *What happens when it rains? Heaven help during the monsoon!* I looked at the edges of the roof for some sort of tarpaulin or covering that could be lowered in case of rain. I saw none.

"What happens when it rains?"

Radha turned and smiled at me, "Oh! We still eat out here. You'll see. Most of the buildings in the ashram don't have any windows, no glass, no covering, no anything. Just open space. When it rains we just continue doing what we're doing. It gets harder when the monsoon comes, much harder."

On the right side were a few Westerners. A slim, severe-looking white woman in a deep yellow sari was puttering around in a tall storage cabinet in the back. A small group of three—a tall white man, balding and skinny, and two women in white saris—were sitting at a table, talking and laughing. As we approached, the-talking-laughing-table-group stopped talking to say hi, laughter in their eyes. *Is everyone here happy?*

"Hey, guys!" Radha called. "We've got a new one!"

"Hey!"

"Hiya!"

"Namah shivaya!"

"Hi!" I responded.

"We'll be back," Radha told them. "I'm going to show her around a bit."

They nodded and resumed talking.

We walked toward the empty side. "That side over there where we just left," she waved her hand back toward the group, "is the Western canteen. That's where we, the Westerners, eat our meals. And here," she halted in front of the empty side and set my suitcase down, "is where the Indians eat their meals."

"Why two different canteens?" I questioned.

"Cha Ma tries to make sure that the Westerners have good food so that we don't suffer from malnutrition."

"Malnutrition?"

"Oh yeah! And if not malnutrition, then definitely protein deficiency. That's something most Western women suffer from here. Men, too, but not so much. One of the first things it affects is our—the women's—hair. We start to lose it. See mine…" She leaned over so that I could peer into her brown hair. *Yep! It's thinning all right.* She wore it back in a long, meager ponytail.

She smiled again. She appeared to have a great sense of humor. Everything seemed funny or enjoyable to her—even such depressing topics as malnutrition, protein deficiency, and thinning hair. Her eyes sparkled with humor. They were big, blue eyes fringed with long, dark lashes. They seemed to shimmer, as if they had a diaphanous layer of water on the surface. *They look so reflective and "glowy."*

"So," she continued, pulling my thoughts back, "Cha Ma tries to make sure that we, the foreigners, have food different from the Indian's curry, rice, and kanya." I gave her a questioning look. She added, "Kanya's a rice and water gruel…soupy and usually salty…it's served with the curry. The Indians have it for breakfast and dinner. They have rice for lunch."

She resumed her explanation. "The Indian food isn't the best quality. As we're working toward enlightenment, Cha Ma believes we shouldn't be so fixated upon our bodies and our stomachs. Part of our tapas…our spiritual practices…is to not eat enjoyable food so that we let go of our egos and our attachment to things of this world, thus, poor food. Often it's too spicy, too yucky, too boring, no nutrition."

I nodded.

"The Indian food doesn't seem to bother the Indians very much. They're skinny anyhow, especially the brahmacharis—the Indian guys who have given their lives to Cha Ma—they're really skinny. Most look like they aren't capable of continuing for much longer on the food they're receiving, but they do. They don't do much work though." She leaned against the low wall of the Indian canteen. I did the same.

"Now," she continued, "the brahmacharinis…the Indian girls who have given their lives to Cha Ma…they're beautiful. Everyone says so. The men are, too, for that matter. But it's the girls that are amazing. And their bodies…they aren't too skinny. They're just right. So the food doesn't seem to affect them much, one way or the other. You'll see."

I shot her another questioning look, "Brahmacharis? Brahmacharinis?"

"Brahmacharis and –charinis are kind of like lower level Hindu monks and nuns. Our equivalent would be Catholic monks and nuns. They've committed their lives to Cha Ma. Completely and totally. They forego all relationships with the opposite sex. They'll never have intimate relationships. They'll never get married. All of their focus is on Cha Ma."

"Oh…" I said, listening hard. I looked, with great interest, at the people milling about, many of whom were looking at us just as interestedly.

"There are different levels, or stages, and it's a little tricky. Let's see if I can explain it clearly…you'll understand more as time goes by. When a young, unmarried Indian comes to an ashram like this one, in order to give his life to the guru or satguru…in our case, Cha Ma…he'll follow all of the guru's orders. He'll wear white and be called a brahmachari. Or brahmacharini, if it's a girl.

"You have to be careful, though," she gestured to the Indians walking around, many of whom were in white. "Householders and regular devotees also wear white. Over time, you'll be able to tell the difference, mainly because householders and devotees come and go and have families; but the brahmacharis and –charinis live here and are alone."

"Okay. I'm with you. Go on…"

"Well, if…and it's a big if…a brahmachari is dedicated enough and progresses far enough…he'll take a solemn vow of sannyasa and give his life, formally, to Cha Ma. He'll vow celibacy and abstain from all intimate relationships and serve the guru his entire life. Once he takes up sannyasa, he'll wear yellow robes. The same goes for the brahmacharinis. As sannyasis, they're addressed as Brahmachari So-and-So or Brahmacharini So-and-So. Brahmachari is not added onto the name until the vow of sannyasa is taken. However, it's a rare thing to take the vow of sannyasa. It takes a lot of dedication and focus and it has to be offered by the guru. Only a few are ever offered."

"That's intense," I said.

"And, if he keeps progressing beyond sannyasa, he *might* be given orange robes. The ones in orange are the highest. It is an extremely difficult position to attain—sort of like the very, very tippy top of the cream of the spiritual crop. The men are called swamis. The women are called swaminis."

"Are there Western sannyasis?" I wondered.

"Oh yes, but only a couple. The woman in yellow in the Western canteen is one." She indicated toward the Western canteen with her head. "And there are a couple of Western swamis and swaminis, too."

I nodded, remembering the two women in orange whom I had seen in Boston, "You mean like, Swamini Ma and…" I could not remember the other Western swamini's name.

"Swamini Atmapranananda," she finished for me. I nodded.

She continued, "The Westerners in white who have given their lives to Cha Ma are called *renunciates*. I'm one of them. We're the equivalent of the brahmacharis and –charinis who wear white. We've given our lives to Cha Ma and live here, but we haven't progressed to the place of yellow. Most of us, Indian or Westerner, never will. It takes way too much self-control, dedication, and determination."

We started walking back toward the Western canteen. "Okay, so back to why the two different canteens…" I prompted her.

"Well, in a nutshell the Indian food is too spicy, tastes bad, and has no variety. Most Westerners are just not going to eat the Indian food for too long. So we make food that's a little more palatable for the Westerners."

"Like what?"

"Soup and salad."

Soup and salad?! That's all?

We stopped before the group.

"Hey guys! We're back. This is Maya," Radha proffered. I gave a little, shy half-wave.

"Hey!"

"Hi!"

"How's it going?" They answered on top of each other.

The tall, balding man gestured toward himself and said, "I'm Dirk." He came over and leaned on the wall with his elbows. Unconcealed curiosity in his eyes. His face was gaunt, but not too severe. He evinced an air of too many years with not enough food.

"Dirk is the cook, baker, and cheese maker for the Western canteen," Radha volunteered.

Dirk nodded slowly, with a half-smile on his lips, "Someone's gotta' do it. And I enjoy it."

"He's from Germany and has been here eleven years."

"What about a visa?" I knew that India was reluctant to give long-term visas.

"Ah! One day I'll have to tell you about it," he said with a knowing smile.

"Oh! Dirk and his stories—don't believe anything he says!" One of the women in white stood up and walked to where we were standing. She was a white woman but had curly, kinky hair—honestly, just like a black woman's. It was dark brown with streaks of blond running through it. It was pulled back into a big poofy ball on the back of her head. It had to be long or she would not have been able to pull it back and it would not have been so poofy. *Wow! That's a really, big ball on the back of her head—a lot of hair's back there. I'd hate to have to comb it. I bet it would take forever!*

She was not slim, but she was not fat either. She just seemed like a normal weight—maybe a size 12 or 14. Her face was extremely pleasant. The corners of her mouth curled up like Radha's, as though she were prone to smiling and laughing a little too much. Her sari looked like Radha's too—wrapped around her well enough but crumpled, with a few spots (which I was to find out were rust) here and there. She hugged Dirk and rubbed his bald head fondly. "He always has some tall tale or other to give. I'm Devi."

"Hey, Devi! I'm Maya."

"Yeah! I know..." She smiled again.

Gosh! They're all such happy people. I like them already. They seem so cool!

Devi pushed against Dirk, playfully. "You're just going to love it here! A bunch of crazy people in a huge insane asylum..."

Dirk feigned losing his balance, adding, "...throw in the heat, the humidity, and Cha Ma..." Dirk, Devi, and Radha laughed heartily.

Maybe they are all a little insane...hmmm, I just might fit in. I think I'm going to like this place!

While they were joking and jostling each other, the other woman who had been sitting at the table came over. "Namah shivaya! I'm Sandi."

"Hi!" I responded.

"Hey...!" she and I exclaimed simultaneously.

She continued, her hazel eyes looking like they would bug out of her head, "I know you! I saw you in America! In Boston, right?"

"Yeah! How crazy!" I replied, beside myself with surprise. *Talk about coincidence!* She looked just like she did in Boston, except "rem-plier." Her sari was as wrinkled and messy as Devi's and Radha's.

"So, you heeded Mother and came?" She was so excited.

"Yeah!" I was growing more pleased by the second.

At that moment, the other woman who was in yellow, came over. The laughter died away. I think it was because of her, although she was smiling too. However, her smile was tight and hard. Her sari fit much too neatly, unlike the others.'

Okay! I don't know if I'm going to like her just because of her sari. Her sari looked to be starch-pressed. *How in the world...?* The folds in the front were neatly pleated like a mini-accordion. Her little "under" top—choli—was pressed, too. Its short sleeves even had a crease pressed in. She looked so neat and so...*crisp*...for it to be so hot and humid and hours into the day (I was to discover, later, just how hard it was to keep one's clothes neat and pressed and white in India—a feat I was never to master.).

She gave a big, toothy smile. "Hi!" she said, with her hand extended.

Strange! She's the only one who's being all formal and shaking hands, out here on a peninsula in the middle of the Indian Ocean.

"I'm Brahmacharini Sita!"

She looks pleasant enough, I assessed. *Why do I feel wary?*

"Hi!" I responded, shaking her hand. "I'm…."

"Oh! I know…Maya! I overheard your conversation. So, how long are you here? Are you staying? How did you meet Cha Ma?" She fired questions at me, machine-gun quick.

Radha held up her hand, "Hold on…I've still got to get her registered at the Foreigners' Office."

"Oh yes! That's right!" Brahmacharini Sita said, nodding her head, still wearing a smile that did not quite touch her eyes.

"But let me finish the canteen tour first…that building there…" Radha paused in speaking, "…is the kitchen." She pointed through and behind the Western canteen to a low, whitewashed building that no longer looked whitewashed. Its exterior was covered with mold and mildew spots and gray splotches. The doorway gaped with no door. It was dark and gloomy inside.

"The kitchen?" *Now that worries me!! Eeew! The kitchen? It's dark and dingy looking!* My face must have revealed my thoughts.

Radha laughed aloud. "I know what you're thinking. Let me be honest with you—it's even worse in there than it looks. Don't go in there if you don't have to! One day I'll have to tell you what the Western doctor and nurse said about the kitchen. They absolutely refuse to go in there."

I shot a quick glance at her. Once again, Radha, Devi, Sandi, and Dirk laughed as if it were the greatest joke in the world. *A kitchen with a health rating of "Double Z"! Yuck! How disgusting!*

Radha changed the subject. "Let's get you registered and settled in." She picked up my suitcase and began to walk to our left, back toward the Indian canteen. "We have to go to the Foreigners' Office.

All foreigners have to get their passport and visa registered and pay for their room and board. We'll assign you some seva after a week or two."

"Seva?" I trotted to keep up with her. She was walking quickly again. I was to find that this was her usual gait.

"Oh yes! Seva is work. Everyone in the ashram does work, some more than others. The Indian men, most of them, don't do much of anything but meditate and tell the women what to do." She cast a glance at me, eyes twinkling.

"What do you mean?"

"According to Hinduism, everyone is creating or burning off karma—by what we say and do, and even by what we think. Our thoughts, words, and actions either create or burn off karma, be it good or bad. Because we're in this ashram, it's clear that most of us are at the end of our karmic cycle—samsara—and so, we're burning off karma. When all of our karma is burned off, be it good or bad, we'll be set free from the cycle. This freedom is called enlightenment or moksha. One of the best and fastest ways to burn off karma is to do service work that's good—seva—in the presence of a satguru. Also, on the practical side, this is a big ashram and in order for it to run properly, everyone has to do seva."

I listened while I looked around. The ashram itself, the building, had me entranced. It was so...so...*hoochie*! It was so...multicolored! Melon-orange and lavender. Lime-green and fuchsia. Sky blue and tart yellow. It simply did not matter whether or not the colors clashed. *I love it! It's hideous!* I vacillated tremendously.

As we headed around the left corner of the Indian canteen, the temple followed the angle, thus creating a wide, sandy path between the two. Behind us, now, was a portion of the temple building that was four stories high and looked like dormitory-style rooms. Here the predominant color was salmon pink, but with dashes of lemon yellow and cobalt blue. The walls were marked by huge mold and mildew spots. The mold and mildew made the colors look slightly dingy, but not too much—the garish colors dominated.

A few Indian men and women in white dhotis and saris walked by, some briskly, others meanderingly. Even more, in the traditional south Indian garb of colorful, patterned saris and dhotis, were standing around, elbows on the walls of the Indian canteen, just…standing…and looking around at nothing in particular.

As we walked, the Indians turned, obviously and uninhibitedly, and watched us…me…go by. *I guess I'm the latest attraction.* Radha noticed, too, "They sure do find you interesting! Not that that's very unusual. The Indians love to watch us foreigners. They stop staring soon enough when they get used to us. There's so many of us." She cast a glance at me and flashed a big grin. "I bet it'll be different for you."

"How do you mean?" My curiosity was piqued.

"Because you're black. In the years I've been here, I've never seen a black person here, let alone a *black American woman*. On two counts you're different," she said by way of explication. "Oh wait! There's Jnani…but she's different…and she's usually not here…"

"Who's Jnani?"

"A British woman. She's black, too. But she doesn't count." Radha paused, her brow wrinkled, as though asking herself why. "She doesn't look Indian. She doesn't look like the brahmacharinis at all. Not to be mean or anything—she's not pretty. Not like you…"

"I don't understand." I could not hide my puzzlement.

"Let me see if I can explain this in a way that you'll understand. I've got to remember that you're new here so you don't understand everything. Okay!" She paused. I figured so that she could think of what to say. "You look like you're south Indian—like a brahmacharini.

But, they're off limits. However, you're an African-American woman, which means you're accessible...you're like an *accessible* brahmacharini." She emphasized the word "accessible." She examined me. "You still don't get it, huh?"

I shook my head. "No."

"See, with the brahmacharinis, the men aren't supposed to interact with them. They're not even supposed to talk to them...but you? Being that you're a Western woman? They *can* talk to you. They *can* interact with you. It's not taboo and you're free to do as you like." She nudged me with her elbow as I gave her a look of consternation. "And then, you're pretty...really pretty. The men are going to flip! Oh! This is going to be fun!"

By now we had passed the Indian canteen on our right. The Vegasy monolithic temple building was still on our left. It appeared as though there were many rooms in the building. Radha walked me around to the front. I halted and stared. It was rather overpowering.

We stood directly in front of a wide set of concrete stairs that led up to two large, intricately carved, wooden doors. The doors were wide open, allowing free access to the interior of the temple. On both sides of the gaping entrance were huge columns. To the outside of these columns stood larger-than-life-sized statues that portrayed scenes from Hindu lore.

We climbed the steps to go inside the temple. Before entering, I cast a quick glance behind me and saw a large, sandy space and a couple of little huts. Farther beyond stretched the dilapidated fence that really appeared incapable of keeping anything out. Not that it needed to—the fence had an entranceway big enough to drive a truck through. People, Indians mostly, were meandering about.

CHAPTER SEVEN

"COME!"

Maya

Alleppey, India

RADHA and I stepped through the entranceway directly into the temple.

Wow! I thought. *Wow!*

"This," Radha declared dramatically while making a wide, sweeping arc with her arm, "is the temple."

Incredulously, I surveyed the scene. We were standing in a wide-open, rectangular space that was about 100 feet long and 75 feet wide.

"Go ahead, check it out!" Radha urged as she set my suitcase down by the entrance.

I did not need her permission to look around. I was too entranced not to. *This is amazing!* Indians, some in white, some in various colors and patterns, sat or lounged on the floor facing the front of the temple. The women sat on my right; the men on the left. A large space ran between them.

Around the perimeter were thick columns, approximately two feet in diameter, with about 20 feet of space between each of them. The columns were painted with colorful frescos and, like the statues outside the building, depicted scenes from Hindu lore. Ten feet behind the columns was the wall of the temple. Set within the walls were huge, glassless "windows" with widely-spaced horizontal bars on them. A balcony sat upon the columns and ringed the perimeter of the temple, except for the front.

I peered at the balcony, which was rimmed by a low, wrought-iron "fence." I noticed that the balcony-floor, the second floor, held rooms.

"Are those rooms?" I asked, indicating with my head toward the balcony.

"Yes. Up there are rooms where people live. There's also the Foreigners' Office and the Westerners' store. Directly above the inner temple is the women's dormitory."

Although I heard her, I did not really comprehend what she was saying. I was engrossed in something else—directly in front of us, at the front of the temple, was a stage—of sorts. It was set back from the main part of the temple. People were crossing in front of it, bending over...over...what?

"Is that Cha Ma?!" I pointed unabashedly. I was so dumbfounded I had forgotten all social convention.

Radha, as was her nature, chuckled good-humoredly, "Oh, yes! You'll have to get darshan with her today before she's done."

I looked at Radha quickly...*I hadn't thought...*

"You hadn't thought…that you'd be able to see her, be with her, so easily?" Radha questioned, smiling almost teasingly at me as if she were hiding a little secret.

How did she know? It's like she…

"…read your mind?" Radha laughed out loud. "Maya! It doesn't take a mind reader to guess what a person would think upon coming to the ashram and seeing Cha Ma."

"True! True!" I nodded in agreement. I stared at Cha Ma, examining the scene that was happening around her. As in Boston when I met her, people were being pushed up to her for a hug. Unlike in America, though, the Indians working with her were handling everyone roughly. Also, unlike in America where she just smiled and murmured, "Ma, Ma!" here she talked to the person she was hugging and to the people around her as the lines on both sides snaked their way toward her.

What is that behind her?

"What is that behind her?" Radha asked for me. "It's a murti of…"

"Kali!" I finished. Kali snatched all of my attention. I began to walk forward through the middle of the temple. Captivated. Gripped. Unaware of my surroundings aside from what was happening on the stage. I stopped halfway through the temple, oblivious to the fact that I had left Radha at the entrance. The people who were on either side were staring at me. I did not notice. All I noticed was…Kali.

Kali!

It was a human-sized murti, a life-like statue of Kali, as tall as a person. I knew Kali to be one of the female deities of Hinduism and not an awfully kind one either. She was considered the most pernicious and destructive of all the deities—male or female. It, she—the murti—was jet black, which was Kali's usual color (unless someone wanted to "sweeten" her up). Around her neck hung a huge, grotesque japa mala made of human heads (plastic, ostensibly)—108 to be exact. A "human-limb" skirt hung about her hips. She had six arms (usually the more malevolent the deity, the greater the number of arms), each of which held a different weapon. One arm held a bloodstained machete. One held a sickle. Another arm gripped a knife. Still another brandished a sword. One arm, uplifted in triumph, clutched a skull by its long black hair, dripping fake blood. Underneath that arm, the bottom-most arm held a shallow bowl that caught the blood that dripped from the severed head.

I stood and stared. No thoughts. Almost as though I were in deep meditation—a deep walking meditation. A trance. Noticing, but not noticing, I saw Cha Ma stop talking to the person who was kneeling before her. Then slowly, deliberately, she raised her head and looked directly at me. Her eyes pierced me. I felt a shudder of pure, white-hot fear tear right through the center of my being.

"Come!" I felt the command rise from the place where the white-hot fear had seared through my bowels. I vaguely "sensed" a hand on my right elbow. I looked to my right, barely registering anything. It was Radha. It was as if I were looking at her through a telescope. She seemed so far away and so distant.

"Cha Ma says, 'Come!' So c'mon! Let's go get your darshan." Radha pulled me to the right side of the temple. "Because she's called you, we'll cut to the front of the line."

That was when I noticed that on either side of the stage—the inner temple—was a door that led within. Radha guided me through the large crowd of Indian women, who appeared completely enthralled with us—the Westerner show—not Cha Ma. Cha Ma would always be there. But! The spectacle of a black Westerner? One who looked like them? They were entranced. As we passed by, they followed us, not only with their eyes, but with their bodies. They turned and stared—their entire bodies actively engaged in staring. *I wish they'd stop staring! What's so different? I look like them? Well, okay…my hair is different and so are my clothes, but come on!* I felt a couple of hands touching me. When I looked back to see who was touching me, all the women bobbled their heads and smiled. Nothing more.

"Are they touching me?" I needed Radha to confirm that I was not going crazy.

"Oh yes. They definitely are! You're so interesting to them."

We could not make it to the side door quickly enough for me. "Do they have to stare so hard…and touch me?"

"You'll get used to it…at least the staring part. They enjoy staring at foreigners. We're entertainment for them. As for you, as I said, you'll really catch their attention because you look just like one of the brahmacharinis, but you're actually a Westerner…an African-American, and you're pretty." She giggled mischievously. "Really pretty…I said that already, didn't I?" She giggled again. She seemed to be having great fun with it all.

Radha and I stepped through the side door and into the inner temple. It was cool from several fans blowing—all pointed toward Cha Ma. I noticed that between the main temple area and the inner temple was a thick wall, a ceiling-to-floor partition, made of wood. Beautiful, elaborate designs were carved into it. The walls on both sides stopped short to allow someone in the inner temple a view of the outer temple, or if one were standing in the outer temple a view of the inner. Heavy curtains hung on either side and were drawn back to allow a full view into the inner temple.

In the center of the inner temple was Cha Ma sitting on a low peetham like the one I had seen in Boston. This one was covered with a leopard skin, too. *I wonder if it's the same leopard skin? How does she get it through customs? Or is it faux?* She was hugging an Indian man and looking at all the people in the outer temple over his head.

Directly behind her on a raised dais was the murti of Kali. *Wow! Kali's even scarier up close!* On both sides, people snaked toward her—on their knees in partial pranam. The women were on our side; the men were on the other.

Our side, the "women's side," was teeming with women's bodies, disorderly and tightly packed. All were sitting; however, some were meditating or doing japa, while others were watching Cha Ma. Some were simply vegging out. Still others were busy looking around at everyone else. There was no room anywhere…not even a little space to put a foot down. Arms and legs and saris and asanas were everywhere. But…it was the faces of the women that was most astounding—not a one looked happy. The women looked angry, upset, irritable.

I dared a glance over toward the men's side. *Hey! What's the meaning of that!?* The men's side was orderly and spacious, the complete antithesis of the women's side. The men were seated in rows. Space was between each of them. Unlike the women, the men were happy. They smiled and whispered to each other, nodding in agreement.

I was willing just to stand in the back and watch Cha Ma. I tried to force my way into a space between two women who were standing against the wall. They were none too enthused to share their space—they refused to budge.

"Come on, Maya! Cha Ma said to come! You don't want to miss darshan with her!" Radha exclaimed.

"Oh, okay. Sure." I know I sounded nonchalant, but I certainly did not feel it. I felt terribly nervous and excited.

Radha grabbed my hand and pulled me through the throng of unsmiling women. They looked resentful to see me passing them. Most had waited for hours and hours for their moment with Cha Ma, so of course, they were not thrilled to have a woman walk right past them upon arriving and get darshan.

Radha placed me in the line very near to Cha Ma—two people away from her. Just enough time to steal a perusal. I examined her slyly. She was busily whispering into a man's ear. As she whispered to him and rubbed his back, she reached her hand out to a small group of women sitting at her elbow. They were putting something together and passing it forward to the woman closest to her, who would place it into her hand. Cha Ma, in turn, would stick it into the person's hand to whom she was giving darshan. In this case, she stuck it into the man's hand. I was to discover that that something was a piece of candy and a packet of vibhuti—sacred ash that came from the religious ceremonies, pujas, that were conducted at the ashram.

Smilingly, she looked at me...scrutinized me, actually...with unveiled curiosity. It seemed as if she were looking right through me...as if she were reading my every thought. I smiled back feeling nervous. She continued to rub the man's back and smile...and study me. Then she lifted his head, stared into his eyes and said a few things to him. He bobbled his head from side to side, a decidedly Indian gesture that meant "yes"—although it appeared to be a "no."

The young Indian man who was helping her with the men pulled him up by his arm. *I wonder if he's brahmachari.* He was wearing a white dhoti with a white, short-sleeved tunic top over it. He was about 5′ 9″, very slim. He had brown wavy hair and a big, soft beard. However, it was his eyes—he had striking eyes. I stood there waiting for my turn, surreptitiously examining him. *He is cute!* I thought. *No! He's fine! Really fine!*

"Pssst!" Radha said behind me, pushing me down. "It's almost your turn."

I got on my knees and put my hands in front of me "prayer style" and waited. Simultaneously, I watched Cha Ma and observed the brahmachari out of the corner of my eye. He was not paying any attention to me. All of his attention was for Cha Ma.

Cha Ma reached for me and pulled me close. She smelled good. My head was in her lap as she rubbed and rubbed my back. Then, she lifted me up and said, "Ma…Ma…" into my ear. When I looked up, she smiled at me and said, "You…stay…India." Her voice was a deep, gravelly whisper. I felt a chill of excitement fly down my back. And that was it. I was pulled up by the Indian woman who was helping her.

I stood up in a daze. I saw, but I did not see, all the people looking inquisitively at me. I was lost. In a stupor. I followed Radha back out the side door that led into the temple. I trailed her along the wall back to the entrance of the temple where we had left my suitcase and duffel bag. She slung my duffel over her shoulder and picked up the suitcase. I stopped and turned to stare at Cha Ma still giving darshan. I felt something in my hand—a packet of vibhuti and candy. *When did she give me this?*

Gently Radha grabbed my arm and urged, "Come on! We need to get you registered." Just inside the entrance was a wide set of concrete stairs on either side. We went up the stairs to our left. At the top I turned and walked, automatically…unconsciously…straight ahead toward the balcony. I gripped the rails and stared down at Cha Ma.

"Come on," Radha said again, tugging at me. "If you think that's something, just imagine when she does Kali Leela."

"Kali Leela?" I asked vacantly, overwhelmed by my darshan.

"You don't know what Kali Leela is?"

I shook my head numbly, distractedly, "Huh uh…"

"Kali Leela is when Cha Ma allows a layer of her humanity to drop so that we may see a glimpse of the goddess…of who she really is. But more about that later. Come on!" She tugged at me again, this time more emphatically.

I turned to my right and followed her into an office with a sign hanging above it: "Foreigners' Office." Inside was an Indian man sitting at a desk. His head was down, all of his focus upon reading a newspaper that lay on the desk. He was wearing a white dhoti and tunic like the guy helping Cha Ma in the temple. *He must be a brahmachari too.*

Loudly, Radha cleared her throat, "Namah shivaya, Narayana!"

"Namah shivaya, Radha Devi," he answered, without looking up. His voice was thick and rich with a deep Indian accent.

He has pretty hair. It was about six inches long and hung gently about his neck. It was a rich chocolate brown with a loose wavy curl to it. It looked so soft. I wanted to touch it. I clasped my hands behind my back.

"Namah shivaya!" Radha responded to his lack of attention rather emphatically.

"Namah shivaya!" He looked up and smiled at Radha.

Oh my gosh! He is absolutely bee-you-tee-full! His eyes…his eyes… I found myself staring at him, enthralled. His eyes were big and almond-shaped. Clear and expressive. They sat above an aristocratic nose, full lips, and a close-shaven beard that followed a strong jaw. His skin made me think of melted caramel that blended perfectly into his neat beard.

"So, who is this?" With that question, he looked at me and the open, happy face he had for Radha shifted…shifted into something else, an altogether "different" expression. I did not understand it. I could not. This was my first encounter with the passionately contradictory nature of the brahmachari, the sannyasi, the celibate Hindu monk—the repressed, never-to-be-expressed-or-discussed sexuality and the fiery, yet unacknowledged, desire hidden behind a stoic wall riddled with minute cracks and fissures. I simply did not understand ashram brahmacharis and sannyasis, yet. In many ways, I never would.

Radha smiled, oblivious (so it seemed) to the decided shift in his countenance, "Oh! This is Maya. She just got here from America."

"Has she received darshan with Cha Ma?" asked he, inexplicable disdain for me upon his face. His voice sounded harsh and condescending.

"Yes, that's what we just finished doing. Cha Ma called for her. Cha Ma told her to stay here." Radha sat upon the desk, swinging her feet, which were crossed at the ankles, under her. *Can she not see his "attitude"? Maybe it's me? Maybe I'm just imagining it..."*

"Really? Cha Ma told *her* to stay here?" he asked incredulously as he looked at me as though I were a cockroach he wanted to squash. *Man! Talk about animosity! What's wrong with him? He acts like he hates me already and he doesn't even know me!*

"Oh, yes!" Radha nodded her head. They were talking about me as though I were not there. Or as though I were some little puppy with no brain. "Anyhow," Radha continued as she pointedly, but good-humoredly, turned away from him to me, "this is Narayana. He's in charge of the Foreigners' Office."

"Namah shivaya," he said in a flat voice, not even looking at me. "Do you have your passport and visa? It costs one hundred dollars per month to stay, which will cover your room and board. All Indian meals are included. If you want anything from the Western canteen, you'll have to pay extra."

As he spoke, I began to root around in my bag for my passport, visa, and money. My documents had shifted somehow to the bottom. I kept digging and digging. Finally, I found them. When I looked up quickly with a smile of triumph upon my face, I caught him staring at me…lost…in looking at me with a strange, beautiful, captivated expression upon his face. I felt a jolt within me—a pull. Desire. Quickly he looked away and I looked back down at my documents and money.

"Here you go!" I proffered, completely flustered, wondering whether Radha had noticed. I dared not look at her. I dared not look at him. I simply could not. Would not.

It seemed to be the same for him. He looked at neither Radha nor me—all of his attention upon my documents and money. He examined them intensely. After what seemed a long time of staring, he began to write my information into a notebook, still not looking at either of us.

I ventured a sidelong glance at Radha. She seemed unaware, as she was picking lint off her sari. *Maybe there was nothing there. Maybe it was my imagination. I'm sure it was.* He finished writing down my information and counting the money.

"Here you go." He handed my papers to me, his face closed and hard.

"Thank you," I responded as I took the papers. He did not answer me. I kept my eyes averted; I could not risk looking into his eyes. Not that it mattered. He did not look at me. He gazed at Radha as he flicked his hand toward me condescendingly, "Put her into the women's dormitory above the inner temple."

With that, he picked up his newspaper, snapped it open with disdain and began to read—we were dismissed. I turned on my heel and walked out the door behind Radha. When I had passed the threshold, she leaned toward me with a twinkle in her eyes and a smirk on her face, and said, "Methinks the man likes you! Poor thing…you!" She picked up my suitcase and duffel bag where she had left them sitting by the door and walked off laughing.

I ran to catch up with her, "What do you mean?"

Radha did not answer me, at least, not about that. Instead she said, "This is the store," as she gestured toward an open door.

"I want to see!" I exclaimed like a little child.

"Okay!" She let me lead the way and, after setting my bags down again, followed me in. "Shruti, this is Maya. She's come to visit for a while."

"Namah shivaya," Shruti said pleasantly. She was an older British lady who looked nice enough. She had massive, black and gray (at the roots) hair pulled back into a gargantuan ponytail that reached almost to her waist.

"Namah shivaya…" I tried the phrase out myself. "Uh, what does 'namah shivaya' mean?" I asked.

"Basically: hello, good-bye, excuse me, what did you say? Literally translated it means, 'Salutations to the Shiva in you,'" Radha informed me.

I walked around the little shop looking at the wares. I saw a section of clothing. Most seemed to be white. "What is this?"

"Oh, saris and punjabi sets, for ashramites."

"I want a sari!" I had noted the white saris and I wanted to wear one like the other women.

"Okay. Let me help you pick out your size." Radha started rifling through the stacks of clothes. "Now, you can get cotton—which is cooler, but wrinkles. I'm wearing cotton." *It does wrinkle!* "Or, you can get a polyester blend—which is not so cool, but it doesn't wrinkle."

"I think I want the poly-blend."

"Okay!" She pulled out a couple of folded pieces. "Here you go! Sari and petticoat." She held up a little shirt that looked like a front-button, half-shirt. "This is the choli that goes under the sari."

I went to Shruti and paid for the clothes. As we were walking to the dorm, I asked Radha, "Will you help me put my sari on?"

"Sure, but first let's put your bags in the dorm and then we can go to my room." We set my bags inside the door of the dorm before continuing on around the balcony and to a room on the other side. The room was very small. No cot or anything. Inside a fan was ineffectually stirring the air.

"Where do you sleep?" I asked, puzzled.

"Oh, on the floor. I unroll a mat to sleep on. So does my roommate. Here, let me help you with the sari."

Right then a knock sounded on the door. Radha poked her head out. After a moment, she informed me, "I have to step out for a minute. Attend to a problem with a Western resident. Hang on, though. I'll help you with your sari in a minute, okay?"

"Okay," I responded.

She stepped out. I unfolded the sari material. It was long—easily a few yards. *I can do this...* I put on the petticoat and choli. The choli fit me a little snugly. *Is it too perfect a fit?* I tucked one corner of the sari material into the waist of the petticoat and began wrapping it. I thought of the women I had seen wearing saris and attempted to imitate them. After wrapping it twice, I folded the fabric four times, back and forth, over my hand in order to form the front pleat. Then I wrapped it around my body again and placed the remainder over my shoulder so that it hung down behind me. *There!* I could not tell what it looked like. *I'm sure I messed up. But, that's okay. I'm just getting a feel for it.*

Soon, Radha returned. As she stepped in, she exclaimed, "Oh, Maya! You found someone to help you with your sari?"

"No, I just tried to do it myself."

"Uh uh! That couldn't be! It's perfect! Really! How did you ever get your sari so perfect? It took me months to learn how to put one on. How did you do it?" she asked, smoothing the fabric and pulling at the train that hung behind me.

"I don't know. I just saw a picture in my mind and did it..."

"Wow! You know what?"

"What?"

"You must've been an Indian woman before...in another lifetime. How else would you know how to put on a sari?" She fastened the front pleats of my sari with a safety pin.

"Really?" I asked, holding in my stomach so that she would not poke me.

"Oh yes, most definitely! Hey...do you have chappels?" she asked.

"What are chappels?" I looked at her quizzically.

"Chappels are cheap Indian sandals. Made out of plastic. Like those." She pointed to a pair of tan, plastic sandals that sat by the door. "You'll need them. You don't want to wear those nice sandals." I looked down at my leather thongs. "Somebody will steal them for sure." She walked over to a duffel bag sitting in the corner and began searching through it. "Here!" She held up a pair of brown plastic sandals very similar to the ones at the door. "You can have these. I think they'll fit and they'll work much better around here—no one will steal them."

I can see why! I thought to myself but I answered, "Thank you!" I slid my feet into them. They fit almost perfectly.

She looked me up and down with a look of immense satisfaction on her face. "You know what?" she asked, big grin beginning to spread across her face. I shook my head. "You're *definitely* going to have a time with the Indian men, especially the brahmacharis! You *look* so Indian. Just like a brahmacharini. They're going to fall in love with you!" She laughed heartily. "C'mon! I'll take you to the women's dorm. Hopefully we won't run into any of the brahmacharis on the way!" She snickered as she walked out of the room with me in tow.

We had walked halfway to the dorm when I realized—*I've got to go to the bathroom.* Not really anything that would cause a crisis except for the fact that I had just mummified myself in miles and miles of fabric. *How am I going to do this?* But, I could not put it off. I *had* to go.

"Uh, Radha…I've got to go to the bathroom," I said.

"Oh, okay." She turned around and headed in the opposite direction. Quickly she trotted up one of the staircases, the one on the right that I had seen upon entering the temple. She made a sharp right. There were the bathrooms!

Well, I never…! I was disgusted. Shocked. Before I could stop my mouth, I blurted out, "This *can't* be the bathrooms!" Six connecting stalls stood side-by-side and looked to be about three feet wide and five feet deep. *Definitely not enough space for a full-sized adult.* They offered some privacy, but not much. The dividing wall between the stalls was approximately six feet high—any tall person could look over into the next stall.

I cringed—privacy was not something to be had here. Several Indians and a couple of Westerners walked back and forth. Men and women. Children. Namah shivaya-ing. Talking to and yelling at each other. Singing songs. Clothes slung their shoulders. Some of them carrying plastic buckets over their arms. They walked in and out of the stalls. A couple of them were showering—I could tell because the showerheads were mounted above the walls of the stalls. All the doors were closed.

I waited with several people who were standing just outside the doors. Finally an Indian woman carrying a bucket stepped out with a threadbare towel wrapped around her head. She had just finished showering and washing her hair. It was my turn.

I opened the door to go in and stepped back out. I threw a quizzical, repulsed look at Radha, to which she just laughed. Inside, the stall was a nightmare. Although the walls were whitewashed, there was a foot-high swatch of brown stains, which ringed the walls of the stall. It looked like the juice from betel leaves and perhaps it was, but given the location of the ring (in the toilet) and its color (chocolate brown) I could not help but wonder if it was something else. The floor was a rusty-brown color and looked as if it had never seen cleanser. A wide hole was positioned toward the back—I knew what that was for. Disgusting or no, I had to go and I knew what to do. I would have to squat.

"Uh, Radha...where's the toilet paper?" I asked.

"There is none." She giggled. "You see the bucket?" There was a spigot with a faded orange plastic bucket underneath. It was half full. "Scoop some water out of it with the little cup." I noted the small measuring cup that was hanging off the side of the bucket.

"Okay..."

"...and pour it on yourself." *So, that's the reason for the spigot, bucket, and cup in the toilets.* "But, remember...use your left hand, not your right. You use your right hand for eating and shaking hands. Your left is for washing. And when you're done, your petticoat is great for drying." I did not say anything. I was beyond disgusted! *How in the world am I going to do this? I can't squat!* I had never been a squatter. I always fell backward when I did.

The moment I began to squat down in the stall, I did what I most feared...*I fell backward!* Onto the nasty, gross, yucky brown wall and floor! *Gross! Yeechhh!* I did not want to even look at my new, beautiful, white sari!

"Oh! Let me guess," Radha called from outside the stall, "you fell!" She erupted into uncontrollable laughter.

I'm glad she finds it funny!

CHAPTER EIGHT

KALI LEELA

"TONIGHT is Kali Leela night," Radha informed me as I stopped by her room on the way to lunch. It was my fourth day in the ashram and she was still acclimating me to the schedule.

"Kali Leela night?" I queried as we walked around the balcony to the stairs.

"Oh yes! Notice the crowd?"

"That it's growing?" I had noticed that the crowd of a few hundred had been steadily growing over the course of the morning. I had seen people trickling in through the front and back entrances.

She nodded. "Yes, the crowd will grow to several thousand. During special Hindu holidays the crowd can grow to over twenty...thirty...thousand people."

I shot her a look that was a mixture of incredulity and skepticism.

"Seriously! And when Cha Ma travels around India, the crowds are easily that large, if not larger, every night."

"Really! Why? What's Kali Leela?" I could not understand what could be so different about Cha Ma as to draw so many people.

"Kali Leela is a special night," Radha said as she and I joined the line in the Indian canteen. The Western canteen did not serve lunch, only breakfast and dinner, which was fine. I figured, as I was in India, I would eat Indian food; although, I did find it extremely spicy and bitter. "As Hindus would say...an auspicious night. One night out of the week, Wednesday night, Cha Ma gives a special darshan. It is the one time when she allows who she really is...Kali...to show for the world to see...if only for a few hours." The line inched closer to the servers. Radha continued, "Cha Ma says that Kali Leela is the only time that she'll peel away a layer...just one layer...of her 'humanness' so that more Kali can be revealed. She also says that if she removed any more layers, we'd all leave her."

"Why?" I asked.

"Because she's an incarnation of Kali," she paused and flashed a smile, "if she were to show any more of *who*...and *what*...she really is, it would be too much for us to handle. We would all run."

"That's wild!" I found the thought strangely titillating—*We'd all run away...unreal! How many people get to live with such a terrible goddess?*

"You'll get to see it all tonight. After lunch I'm going to put our asanas down so that we'll have a good spot for the whole Leela."

"Really?" I questioned. "We have to save a spot?"

"Oh! You have no idea how large the crowd is going to be. If we want good seats, we've got to claim them!"

A few minutes shy of four o'clock, Radha and I made our way through the masses of women sitting on the women's side.

"Namah shivaya! Namah shivaya!" I exclaimed as I tried not to step on anyone. I followed Radha as she wove her way toward the front of the temple. I noticed that the brahmacharis and –charinis sat in the front, closest to Cha Ma. *I didn't know there were so many of them!* They took up almost half of the temple floor. They were obvious because of their white clothing. Interspersed throughout the brahmacharis and –charinis were Westerners, also in white, and a few, very few, yellow-garbed sannyasis. Indians in brightly colored, traditional garb sat behind the ashramites. I could not even guess at the number of people, easily several thousand.

Radha stopped toward the front of the sea of brahmacharinis. I could not see our asanas or even an inch of space on the floor. I thought with dismay, *There's no room. They took our spot.* Next thing I knew, Radha sat down in the midst of the densely, packed brahmacharinis. They shifted enough for her body to squeeze in. She turned to me and beckoned. I clambered over a bunch of women's bodies to stand beside her. The brahmacharinis parted to allow me a space as I sat down. We were in a very tight spot. It was like sitting on a dime.

I peered around. *This is amazing!* I was overawed by the sheer number of people squished into the temple. The brahmacharinis to my right and left looked at me and smiled, heads bobbling. I smiled back. I looked over toward the men's side. All I saw were more bodies, albeit more orderly.

Behind us, sitting in the middle aisle, were the musicians and singers. The swamis were sitting in this group, chatting and laughing. A couple of brahmacharis and -charinis sat with them, tuning their instruments and adjusting their microphones. They all sat on the men's or women's side, respectively.

I could feel in the air the anticipation of the crowd as we waited for Kali Leela to begin. With every second that passed, the excitement and sense of expectation grew, as did the noise level. The air was heavy and hot, in great part, I was sure, from all the bodies packed together.

At precisely four o'clock, conch shells began to sound and bells began to ring. The crowd began chanting and singing. The songs were simple, repetitive chants, so I joined in with the thousands of voices. As we sang, Cha Ma came out and started performing a ritual in the inner temple. Billows of incense rolled out upon us from where she was.

Radha leaned toward me and whispered under the din, "This is where Cha Ma begins her transformation into Kali."

I nodded, enthralled. I watched while a couple of sannyasis in yellow and one brahmachari in white assisted her. After staring for long moments at the scene on the stage, recognition hit me—*Is that brahmachari in white Narayana?* I was surprised to see Narayana up there passing plates, bells, and flowers to her as he chanted along with the crowd. Finally the curtains to the inner temple were drawn closed, to our deep anticipation.

After many minutes, as we continued singing and chanting above the sound of the bells and conch shells, Cha Ma emerged as "more" Kali—one layer of her humanness removed! I was spellbound! She was dressed in a vibrant, red sari with a thick border of golden embroidery. Her hair was hanging loose, down to her waist, and was blowing in the heavy breeze of the fans. (I was to learn that she demanded the fans because in the mood of Kali, she was always hot.) I blinked. I blinked again—*It can't be true!*—her skin appeared to be a darker hue. Instead of its normal cappuccino coloring, it was like dark chocolate. She looked over the temple of people, her face set in a fierce glare. A thought shot through my head—*She IS Kali!*

That was when I noticed she was trembling. Visibly trembling. I leaned over to Radha, whose eyes were glued to the inner temple and who was singing passionately with the crowd, and asked, "Is Cha Ma trembling?"

Radha nodded her head, yes, and stage-whispered under the ferocious din of the bells, horns, chanting, and singing, "Yes, she always trembles in Kali Leela. I think it's just who she is manifesting. It's like…she—Cha Ma the human—struggles to keep who she really is—Kali the goddess—under control."

I nodded, fascinated, still staring at the stage.

Cha Ma sat down and began giving Kali darshan. I sat mesmerized. After a couple of hours the swamis stopped singing and disappeared. (Radha informed me that they would be back at the end of the night.) The brahmacharis and –charinis continued singing non-stop the entire night while I stayed in my tight, on-a-dime spot. Observing. Soaking it all in. Hour after hour. At one point Radha left, saying that she was going to get dinner and that she would be back. I nodded, not taking my eyes off of Cha Ma.

After many, many hours, the crowd swelled as people came back and sat down. Radha was one of them. The darshan lines had thinned. The swamis returned and took up singing. The atmosphere revived as all of us in the over-packed temple sang passionately to Kali. Song built upon song. I wondered if the exuberant, festive excitement in the atmosphere could grow any more impassioned.

Finally, Cha Ma finished with the last person. Once again the conch shells and bells began sounding as we sang a final song to Kali. Slowly, deliberately, Cha Ma…*Kali*…stood up and walked to the edge of the inner temple and peered down on us. Once or twice, it seemed her eyes flashed gray as she looked down at us with an odd, frowning smile—I had never seen such a look in my life. It seemed she looked over each and every one of us. Meticulously examined us. Masses of incense rolled out from behind her into the temple—thick and overpowering. For long minutes, Kali, thinly veiled as Cha Ma, gave us a pure, unadulterated Kali darshan.

Then she stepped back and the curtains closed. All sounds—bells, horns, chanting, and singing—ceased. Kali Leela was over. I did not move. I felt thrilled. I was exhausted. In shock.

"Come on, Maya," Radha urged me. I looked toward her. She was standing with her asana draped over her arm. *When had she stood up?*

"Come on," she said again. "They've got to sweep the temple so that archana can begin."

I nodded. "What time is it?" I asked as I looked around, noticing for the first time that it was light outside.

"7:38 in the morning..."

CHAPTER NINE

PRAYER AND ETERNAL TIME

Marie

United States

I *wonder where she's at…what she's doing….* Marie's mind turned to her daughter, again. *I've got to keep my spirits up. I'm not going to allow myself to get down.* Marie washed her face in preparation for sleep. It had been a long day. Every day, ever since Maya had left, had been tediously long. She could not keep her mind from circling around and around—stuck between worry, doubt, guilt, and fear. When she was done with her nightly ritual, she kneeled before her bed, happy for the time alone—just her and the Lord.

"Dear Lord, I pray, be with Maya. May no weapon formed against her prosper. May nothing of the enemy come upon or against her. I bind and declare void every single plan of the enemy. Lord, protect her! Your Word says that the angels hearken to Your Word. Oh God, please release Your angels, legions of angels, to war in the heavenlies on Your behalf in her life. Bring her back to us.

"And Father, I pray, protect my husband. Give him strength. Oh! God…" Marie looked up from where she was praying and stared at the wall. In her mind's eye, she could see her Lord smiling upon her.

Quietly, gently, inside she felt a whisper waft up to her consciousness: *"Pray Psalm 91 over her. Every single day. It will protect her."* That was it.

"Pray Psalm 91 over her? Was that You, Lord?" Marie asked, still seeing Him. *I'll look it up in my Bible.* She looked down at her Bible, which was lying open between her elbows upon the bed. She flipped to Psalm 91.

"He who dwells in the Secret Place of the Most High God shall say of the Almighty, You are my strength and my refuge, my God in whom I trust." Marie read the entire Scripture. It was a Scripture detailing God's supernatural protection from catastrophe, danger, illness, and every plan of the enemy. "Oh yes, Lord, clearly this is of You. Thank You." Marie smiled to Him.

"Insert Maya's name into the Scripture. Apply it to this situation." She felt another whisper from within her from the One she loved so much.

"Okay…" Marie peered down and began to pray the words. Little did she know that one day, she would be able to pray Psalm 91, the entire Scripture, from heart. Little did she know that she would have prayed it so much, it would become a part of her—eternally living, breathing, powerful.

"One day, Maya will dwell in the Secret Place of You, the Most High God. She will say..."

"No! Do not pray in the future tense!" Divine instruction welled up from deep inside of her and touched her understanding. *"I AM the eternal God. All is the present to Me. You must speak those things that be, not as though they are. You must speak what you want as though it is already here in order to destroy what you do not want in your life. That is how you create what you want. The mystery of time is within Me as time is nothing before Me, except a construct. My construct. Pray in the present! Regardless of what you see in the natural."*

Marie exhaled, this time in wonderment. "Okay, Lord. Maya...is...she who dwells in the Secret Place, of You, the most High, most Wonderful, most Magnificent God. She *says* of You...Yes! She...she... says of You, You are her strength and her refuge, her God, in whom she trusts. You, and You only, my dear Lord, deliver her from the snare of the fowler."

Marie began warming to the prayer...it felt so wonderful and freeing, "You deliver her from every snare, every trap, every trick of the enemy, regardless of whether it is a person or a thing or demonic spirit. You deliver her from *every single thing*. You deliver her from all perilous pestilences. Every sickness, illness, and disease that she comes across wherever she is, You protect her and deliver her whole and complete from it."

Marie prayed in the present tense—feeling awkward in praying this way while simultaneously feeling so comfortable, so *right*, in her spirit. She had no idea the magnitude of the power she released when she prayed God's Word over the situation. If only she had known...if only she could have seen the flurry of activity the moment she began praying the Scripture—the literal Words of God.

When she had finished praying Psalm 91, she began to pray in the Holy Spirit…in tongues. Quickly, smoothly, she shifted into singing in the Spirit…lost in the Lord. Tears began to stream down her face. She sang…glorifying…exalting…magnifying God.

Marie could not see into the heavenlies—*Oh, if she had been able!* Every one of her utterances rose to Heaven, and as they were in accord with the Word of God, Jesus interceded for her. Her prayers—every single prayer and her heart behind her prayers, "heart-prayers"—and those of the Holy Spirit praying through her were heard. Her prayers had fallen upon willing ears. They were pleasing to God. A prayer asking for help? A prayer asking for angels to war in her daughter's life on His behalf? It was definitely in His Will. He was thrilled to respond!

Thus, in the Throne Room, in a transcendent realm in which time was non-existent, the Lord of all Glory commanded. Immediately, riding upon His Word, legions of majestic, warring angels began to move forth into the earth realm. They were brilliant in color, flashing with an ethereal luminosity that could not be perceived by the human eye. Heavenly trumpets sounded. Undergirding the trumpets pierced another sound, slicing from Heaven down to the earth—the celestial shofar. Angelic weapons of warfare glinted in the Light of the Lord. The warring angels moved in unison, in order, in power, and in might! They saluted the Lord, in worship, in exultation. They were primed to do His bidding, to bring glory to His Name.

Instantaneously these thousands of majestic, powerful angels began to descend upon a dark place in southern India, a place ensconced in great darkness and from which proceeded this darkness. It was a darkness that spread and pulsed across the Indian continent— its tendrils reaching even into other continents. However, *now* was the time for change. It was time to overthrow one of Satan's major principalities. War was on!

From before the foundations of the earth, God knew He would desire to deliver a crushing blow to this principality, at this very time, and so He had conceived in His vast Heart and Mind, before the earth had any form, a young, questioning girl. He had given her parents who were strong Christian intercessors. He had allowed her to grow disenchanted and disillusioned with Him and to run far away. How it hurt Him to see her so distant from Him. But…He had *made* her. He *knew* her. She was His handiwork, His workmanship. He knew and had fashioned every single aspect of her person and her life from before the beginning of the world. He knew it would come to this. He had planned for it to come to this…at exactly this time.

Ah! To think, Satan felt *he* had *her*. He felt *he* was leading *her* along by a corrupt, tarnished ring in her nose. He felt he had her family and the hundreds of others he planned to destroy with her and through her, right where he wanted them. And yet this time, like every other time, *every single time*, he was walking in the plan of God. *Knowingly, wittingly, Satan was walking in—and helping to unfold—the plan of God!* Whatever—*anything* and *everything*—Satan meant for evil was merely a tool in the mighty hands of God to bring His Righteousness, His Glory, His Goodness, His Light into the earth. Oh! This was going to be good!

Yet God's sense of time and timing was vastly different from that of humans. It was time—yes! However, embedded in the timelessness of eternity was the necessity of a linear progression of time upon the earth that the unfolding of a destiny demanded—humans were bound by time within a spiritual realm that was beyond time and in no-time. Maya would have to walk out the journey God knew to be before her. A journey that would end, that had already ended, in victory.

CHAPTER TEN

CRAZY FOLK

Maya

Alleppey, India

"C'MON, Maya! Get up!"

I could hear the voices; I just could not see the people. Not that I needed to. I knew who they were. I recognized them by their voices.

"C'mon! Hurry up! Cha Ma is giving darshan to the residents and we don't want to miss it!" One of the voices wheedled me from outside the dorm.

The women's dormitory housed 40 women and was located directly above the inner temple. Only Western women slept in the dorm. The Indian brahmacharinis slept in a set of huts a distance from the temple, away from everyone else. The best thing about the dormitory was its proximity to everything that happened concerning Cha Ma. We could go out the dorm's front entrance (entrance, not door—

there were no *doors* to the doorways of the women's dorm. Nor were there any real windows—just large, square openings with horizontal bars. Anyone, male or female, could look in at any time—and they did. We had virtually no privacy.). This entrance opened onto the second floor balcony that spanned the interior perimeter of the temple. We could walk in either direction around the balcony until we came to the staircases at the entrance of the temple. From there we could go down the wide concrete steps, on the right or left, and into the main temple area or out the front door of the temple.

The dormitory also had two back entrances that opened onto an outdoor balcony. These faced the back field (the one I had traversed in the taxi upon my arrival) and the brahmachari huts. One of the back doorways was directly across from the front entrance. And the other entrance, if one were facing the brahmachari huts and field in the back, opened at the right corner of the building onto a spiral staircase. The staircase spiraled from the ground floor up to the top floor. Down one flight of steps from the women's dorm, the staircase opened onto the outdoor balcony behind the inner temple. Up one flight, it opened onto a hallway that led to the rooms on the floor above us. We, the women in the dorm, often sat upon this staircase and watched Cha Ma's (and everyone else's) comings and goings.

At this moment, though, I was lying down on my bunk. All the bunks in the women's dorm were made of thick iron piping with a twin-sized board upon which to lie. I had been fortunate to get a lower bunk—fortunate because I did not like the idea of falling off a top bunk. Unlike children's bunks, these were high and had no rails or even ladders upon which to climb. One side of my bed was against the outer wall and underneath one of the windows, a rather large window. I could look out upon the big open field and the brahmachari huts.

The bunk was positioned so that my head was pointing toward the door, which was right beside the window.

My feelings about my bunk's location was a love/hate sort of thing. Sometimes being placed by a window and door was great because of the ventilation, especially at night. The women's dorm grew extremely hot during the day, and although during the course of the night some of the heat would dissipate, it tended to remain stuffy and overly warm all night long. The only stirring breeze came in through the windows and doors. Night or day it was better to be near a source of ventilation. However, due to my location, I often found myself being spied upon by someone, usually male, standing in the field. Or when visitors to the ashram cut through the dorm to get to the temple, I was stared at as though I were an animal on display.

So, there I was, late afternoon, in my bunk. I was trying to be as still as possible. I did not want to be noticed. I hoped that the owners of the voices would think I was asleep and would leave me alone. I was not in a bad mood, just tired. And I was thinking. I had been there for some time, contemplating a conversation I had had with Radha the night before about things spiritual. It was a conversation very similar to the ones I used to have with Manjula—eons ago, it seemed.

Radha and I had been in the women's dormitory relaxing. I had been lying in my bunk. She had been lying prone on the floor because the painted concrete was cool. The night was hot and muggy, as usual.

In the few weeks that I had been at the ashram, I had grown to respect her opinion immensely. She was unusually insightful and analytic, but unlike many with a penchant for critical thinking, she was not prone to negativity or pessimism. Her head was grounded and well-placed on her shoulders. Her sensibility had not made her boring and staid; instead it had made her rational and able to accurately assess a situation within minutes of observing it. If ever I wanted a balanced, honest opinion, Radha would have it.

"So, what do you think about Cha Ma?" I had asked her, following a lengthy discussion about Hinduism, reincarnation, enlightenment, and the like. "Where does she fit into all this?"

"Cha Ma?" she had responded with that characteristic mirth in her eyes. She paused for a moment and then exhaled audibly. I had not noticed that she had been holding her breath until she exhaled so. "I don't know...I know what Hinduism says and what a lot of people say..."

She stared up at the ceiling, hands behind her head. She had unwound her sari from around her torso and had drawn up the skirt so that her midriff and calves were resting bare upon the concrete—much cooler. "They say that toward the end of samsara—the cycle of reincarnation—when we are about to be released from the cycle, we will begin to encounter gurus and divine beings meant to help us get free from this cycle of rebirth. In fact, many...most...believe that if you come into contact with a divine being, it's an indication that you're at the end of your karmic cycle, that enlightenment is near."

I nodded in agreement, "That's what I've learned, too. Okay, keep going."

"That's where darshan fits in. They believe that to see a guru or a divine being—darshan—is the result of great karma and is a great blessing. To actually talk to one? Even better. To live with one and be touched by him...or her, as in our case? Well, that would be a clear indication that the person is at the end of the cycle. At least, that's what people say...." She paused here and rolled over onto her side facing me. She propped herself up on her elbow, her head resting on her hand. "What do I think? I try not to think about it." She gave a wry smile. "And honestly...I don't know how much I believe all of this…stuff…about being at the end of the cycle and the guru coming. I do believe that Cha Ma is something unusual and that I'm drawn to her." She sighed. "And that once here, I can't seem to get away from her, *not* that I'd want to," she quickly added. "But, as to *who* she is and what she does and will we get enlightened? I just don't know…"

Undeniably, our conversation had provided "fodder" for much musing on my part. "What do *you* think?" she had then asked me. Good question!

What do I think? I had asked myself that question many times since our conversation. Something about it compelled me. *I believe I'm at the end. No doubt. Honestly, I don't want to believe otherwise. Why else would I run all the way to the other side of the world, unless it's to be set free? And then, why else would I have this burning desire to be free, unless it's because I'm at the end?*

In fact, I believe that we all, who live in the ashram, are at the end of the cycle. We live with Cha Ma. We talk with Cha Ma. We work with Cha Ma. We hug Cha Ma. We do everything with Cha Ma. She is a sat-guru. No! She's more than a satguru…she's an incarnation of the goddess Kali. I let this thought roll around in my head. *An incarnation! An avatar! A real goddess! And I live with her. We all do. We're all going to be free from this crazy system of birth, life, and death. Someday…*

"Maya! C'mon!" A voice, now much closer to me, urged.

At the moment I just wanted to be free of the women behind the voices—Anneshwari, Rukmini, and Alice.

"Leave me alone!" I said with my eyes squeezed shut.

"Maya!" I heard Alice's voice through the window.

"Okay! I'm getting up! I'm getting up!" I would have covered my head with my pillow if I had had one. But I did not. I slept with no pillow. All I slept on was a narrow bamboo mat—that when folded was no more than one foot wide. When I rolled it up it was no thicker than a coffee cup in diameter. Nor had I a blanket. When I needed covering against the morning chill, I used my woolen prayer shawl. For mild nights, I simply used the extra fabric of my sari (the part that draped around the body a couple of times) and laid it over my body lengthwise. It was suitable for a sheet. For the extremely hot, stuffy nights, I took off my sari and slept in my petticoat and choli. Being that I had lain down fully dressed in my sari for a few moments of afternoon "quiet time," I had nothing with which to shut myself away from the trio.

"Get up! Get up!" exclaimed the big one (well, they were all big in different ways—if not in body, then, in personality)—but this one, Anneshwari, was big in terms of width. She was of average height and chubby bordering on fat. She was the one I had seen at the program in Boston, the one who had stood in the door, who had so angered the swami.

She had a pale face that was riddled with acne, probably due to the poor food. Her hair was thinning and mousy brown. (She claimed, as did all the Western women, that it was not only the poor food but also the black sand that made her—their—hair thin. They argued that the black sand harbored a radioactive isotope that wreaked havoc on their bodies.) She loved her punjabi sets, and in her huge pants and baggy, knee-length shirts, it was easier to see her as a young girl than a grown woman. She had an agreeable face, always smiling (if she was not crying because of something Cha Ma said or did). Something about her demeanor made me want to smile with her, talk to her. She was likeable enough. As long as you were ever mindful of one thing…she loved Cha Ma. No! She ate, slept, and breathed Cha Ma! Whatever you did, you did not cross her or even get in her way when it came to Cha Ma or she would leave you out to dry. For all of her "likeableness," when it came to Cha Ma, it completely disappeared if you got in her way.

I suppose it was in this way that she and Rukmini were so well suited: They both displayed a single-minded—bordering on pathological—focus upon Cha Ma. Even so, Rukmini was much scarier than Anneshwari. Considering her looks and her behavior, she was distant, unreadable, downright intimidating.

For where Anneshwari was rotund and looked pleasant and smiling; Rukmini was tall and thin, exceedingly gaunt, and she never smiled. At 6′3″, she towered over the Indian women and men. She looked the quintessential "Aryan" through and through. Pale skin, wholly unaffected by the equatorial sun. Wheat blond, coarse hair pulled back into a bedraggled ponytail. Blue, steely, never-to-see-you eyes. High, hollowed-out cheekbones. Dark circles under her eyes from staying up, night after night, prowling—stalking—after Cha Ma, looking out for Cha Ma, ever on the hunt for Cha Ma. The perfect sportswoman, it seemed she never slept; instead, she was always watching for her prey, Cha Ma.

Like Anneshwari, she wore punjabi pants although hers were too short for her (of course). Or she wore men's pants, which were too short for her too. Either way she paired her ill-fitting pants with a grungy tee shirt that was dirty and smelly from working with the cows. Her toenails and fingernails were perpetually caked with dirt and cow manure. The heels of her feet were cracked and packed with dirt and dung too. Everything about her was coarse and harsh and severe.

Every once in a blue moon, she would wear a bright, colorful sari, which would be perfectly arranged upon her body. This was unnervingly strange, because of the nature of the wearer. Rukmini in a sari was akin to putting a shotgun in a piece of black velvet or a machete in a fur stole. What would be the purpose? To disguise her intent? But that was Rukmini—to wear a sari in order to hide, to be stealthy, and to sidle closer to Cha Ma without being obvious—although a gorgeous, colorful sari upon her frame was louder than any bellow.

As far as Rukmini was concerned, Cha Ma was all that mattered; anything and everything that came between her and the object of her obsessive focus was to be ignored, removed, trod upon, or beat up. Anneshwari was talkative as long as it was about Cha Ma. Rukmini was not. She did not talk to anyone about anything. No, but you could always find her hiding...*lurking*...somewhere, waiting, watching for a glimpse of Cha Ma.

And then, somewhere between the two, or perhaps on the far side of the personality triangle...lay Alice. Good ole' plain Alice. Nothing special about her. It was a wonder that she ended up in India at all, let alone that she had lived in this place for six years. Alice with brown hair and brown eyes. Average weight and size. There was nothing unusual in her looks.

She wore a sari every day. The same one? I could not figure it out. Regardless, every sari she wore was off-white and riddled with rust spots. The fabric had lost all sense of stiffness—it sagged and waved and sailed and lay as it chose. She kinda, sorta wrapped and tucked it the way it was supposed to be.

Alice. So ordinary, so friendly, so talkative, so gossipy! If I wanted to know anything about anyone at anytime all I needed to do was go to Alice, offer her some peanuts (or cookies if peanuts were not to be had), and she would tell all. She was the information hub of the ashram.

She did not seem to hold any special regard for Cha Ma. In the weeks that I had been at the ashram, she had not taken darshan even once (from what I could observe). Nor did she seem to care. She did not show any particular devotion to Cha Ma. She did not meditate. She did not do japa. She would sing bhajans, if others were around. More often than not, however, when I looked at her during bhajans or meditation, she was consumed with watching everyone else. The only thing she seemed interested in and good at was obtaining and disseminating tasty tidbits of salacious gossip—and eating peanuts. She loved peanuts. All sorts of knowledge could be exchanged for a handful of peanuts.

I could not figure out why she hung out with Anneshwari and Rukmini, and even got in trouble with them, as she did not seem to care one lick about Cha Ma. But she did. If you saw Anneshwari, you would see Rukmini nearby and Alice pulling up the rear. They were constantly together. Perhaps she hung out with them for the excitement, because if anything interesting was going to happen, it would probably be around Anneshwari and Rukmini.

So, there they were...the ragtag team standing on the balcony yelling through the window by my bunk, "Wake up! Wake up, Maya! It's almost time for darshan!"

"For us?"

"Yeah, c'mon! Cha Ma has called all of the residents. It's still a little early and she's called us for darshan!" Anneshwari took off for the spiral stairs. Rukmini was right behind her.

Only Alice lagged, "Do you have any peanuts?"

"Yeah," I replied, as I swung my legs over the edge and stood up. "Look on the far side of my bunk. Don't eat all of them and make sure to screw the cap on tight so that the ants won't get into them."

"Okay," Alice said, already reaching into my bunk area. She grabbed the plastic jar that sat at the back of my bunk and unscrewed the top. She thrust her hand in and grabbed a handful of peanuts. Quickly, she put her hand to her mouth and began to eat.

I hustled out of the women's dormitory behind Anneshwari and Rukmini and down the spiral staircase to the next floor, which was the balcony of the inner temple. Alice walked at a leisurely pace behind us, munching on her highly coveted peanuts. This time as in all the others, her interest seemed more upon the peanuts and what everyone else was doing, than upon getting darshan with her satguru, Cha Ma.

I stopped in the balcony entrance and scanned the inner temple. There was Cha Ma hugging a Western woman. Of course the men were on the men's side, the women on the women's—that was a rule, never to be broken. The women's side was the usual crowded and chaotic mass of bodies—arms, legs, torsos, and feet. The men's side was calm and orderly. Ashramites, Indian and Western, were standing along the back walls. Everyone seemed to be either anxiously waiting, if they had not yet received darshan…or happily enjoying, if they had. Many were standing in the traditional stance: palms pressed together in front of the face as if praying. Some were doing japa on their japa malas. Others were meditating. Almost all, with the exception of the meditators, were staring at Cha Ma, observing the goings-on around her.

Anneshwari and Rukmini pressed through the women's side, oblivious of the crowd's density and the disturbance they created. Clearly they were women on a mission—to get as close to Cha Ma as was humanly possible. I was not certain who was scarier— Anneshwari or Rukmini. Both had a terrifyingly single-minded focus upon Cha Ma. Rukmini led the way, shoving standing women out of the way, stepping over sitting women's bodies, not once letting her eyes leave Cha Ma. Close behind her followed Anneshwari, generally friendly and laughing, but not right now. Both were like moths drawn to a flame.

Rukmini pressed her way to the very front, much to the chagrin of all the women she stepped on or pushed out of the way. She stood in the spot closest to Cha Ma although an Indian woman was already sitting there, still not allowing her eyes to leave Cha Ma. The Indian woman faced a decision: move over or be sat upon. She chose to move over. Wise decision. Rukmini was not an easy "opponent"—considering her height, strength, and ferocity—she was frighteningly Amazonian. The woman glared at her with a mixture of hatred and fear. Rukmini did not even notice. No, she sat down in the woman's hastily vacated spot, still staring at Cha Ma, unmindful of everyone else.

Anneshwari pressed in behind Rukmini and moved in even closer. She put her knees upon the marble steps right beside Cha Ma's peetham and leaned toward Cha Ma, as Cha Ma looked at her with a pleasant gaze. Cha Ma gave her a smile and said something into her ear. Anneshwari beamed at whatever Cha Ma had told her. She plopped down right where she was on the marble steps, impervious to the rule that no one was to sit on the steps beside the peetham. Anneshwari would have sat on Rukmini's legs had Rukmini not shifted; but Rukmini, still staring at Cha Ma, adjusted her legs a bit to allow Anneshwari space on the steps.

I stood in the back against the wall and observed. I really did not want darshan. Sometimes Cha Ma scared me—repelled me—I was not too sure why and I would not allow myself much time to speculate. Whenever the wisp of a thought like that drifted by, I brushed it aside. Unconsciously, I chose to stand as far back as I could without leaving the inner temple.

After a while, I heard, "Psst! Hey, Maya!" It was Devi whispering to me as she peeked her head around the corner into the entrance of the inner temple. "You wanna go to the village with me?" Several of the women turned and cast nasty glances at her for being too noisy. A couple put their index finger before their lips indicating, "Silence!"

I walked to where she was standing on the balcony. "To where?"

"To the village across the backwaters."

"The backwaters?"

We stood looking out over the empty brahmachari area—all were inside with Cha Ma. "You don't know the backwaters? How did you come, by bus or by taxi?" she asked.

"By taxi..."

"Oh! I understand! Well, come on! You're coming with me," she declared emphatically, taking me by the wrist. "You've got to experience the backwaters and the village."

I hesitated.

"Come on! You need to see this," she said, pulling me along. "We'll be back before evening bhajans."

"Wait! Let me get my money and passport!" I pulled her up the spiral staircase to the women's dorm. Once in the dorm, I went to the lockers, opened mine, and took out my little black and pink embroidered shoulder bag. I checked inside for my money, and more importantly, my passport and visa documents—already a deeply ingrained habit of carefulness. If I were to lose my passport and visa, I would be sent from the country lickety-split as India only gave a 15-day grace period to remain in the country in the case of lost documents. I double-checked—*money, passport, visa...documents... sealed in a Ziploc baggie* (the baggie was to keep the moisture in the environment away from my documents). When I was certain that all the important documents were secure in the Ziploc baggie, I zipped up the shoulder bag. "Okay! I'm ready!"

We headed out of the ashram by way of the front entrance. It was all novel to me because I had never been this way before. *To have been here a few weeks already, and not to have stepped out of the front entrance...not to even know what the surrounding neighborhood or the nearby village looks like. How strange!* It did strike me as unusual that I had stepped into the ashram over a month ago and had not stepped out since, and further, had no desire to. We turned right at the large gate—it was always open to allow devotees of Cha Ma to come and go freely. We walked down a dirt path that was bordered variously by fences, sparse grass, and dilapidated houses. We walked only a couple of minutes before we came to "the backwaters."

As we approached the water, Devi spoke, "We're going to have to wait for the ferry." We stood with the crowd of people who were waiting for the sole ferrying boat for our stretch of backwaters (there were other ferries farther down on either side of us) to come back from the other side laden with passengers. As we waited, I looked around, absorbing it all.

First I examined the people who were typical for Kerala. They were all very thin and weathered-looking, as if life had beaten them down a long time ago. Their clothes were colorful and bright, although worn. Children were running around everywhere, boisterous and free. Everyone was talking animatedly, some yelling. As I examined them, they gave me the same consideration—staring unabashedly and smiling. I smiled back.

Next my attention shifted to the backwaters. The backwaters was a canal or a thin section of river that stretched between us and the mainland. It was as if we were on an island but I knew from my first-day taxi ride that we were on a narrow peninsula. I recalled that when I had ridden in the taxi we had traversed a narrow land bridge, which I surmised was the place that connected the peninsula to the mainland. The backwaters was the channel that ran between the peninsula and the mainland. It ran as far as my eyes could see to my left and right—the length of the peninsula. Its width was about 400 feet. I could not tell how deep it was, although it could not have been too deep, because men propelled and "steered" their boats using long bamboo poles that they pushed against the canal bottom.

The water was a brackish, murky, greenish brown. Clumps of scum hung about the slippery, muddy edge. Boats were all over— mainly two types—flat boats that were used as water taxis, overloaded with too many people carrying too many parcels, and spindly fishing boats with spindly men hanging off like spiders on a leaf. On the edge of the backwaters were little narrow houses on stilts, much smaller than any house I had ever seen. They sat half on the bank and half over the water. No person could possibly live in them. They were only large enough to be—*outhouses! Yuck!* The implication struck me: The backwaters was the place that all "wastage" was sent! *Double Yuck!*

"Are those…outhouses?" I asked, my common sense outraged.

Grinning widely, Devi nodded, watching me as I examined the backwaters.

That is when I noticed the smell—a weird, unusual mixture of overripe pond scum, waste, and fish—surprisingly, the fishy smell overpowered the other smells. Strange, indeed! *How had I not noticed the smell before?* I wrinkled my nose and continued observing the scene.

The fishing boats fascinated me. They looked like spiny lobsters— very, very spindly, with many legs. The men were lithe and graceful on the long, narrow contraptions. The boats were delicately fashioned with long tendrils of bamboo masts jutting out everywhere. The men looked like acrobats standing and moving smoothly, deftly, over the bamboo poles suspended above the net of murky water. *Okay! I can understand having to cross the backwaters, but to fish in it? Ewwww!*

I said as much to Devi, "I can't believe they fish here!"

She smiled and winked at me, "I know…but before you criticize, you should consider…where do you think we get our water from in the ashram?"

Immediately, the gist of her question struck me. "The backwaters?!" I exclaimed.

She nodded.

"That's nasty!"

"Uh huh! That's why some of the Westerners, those who know, get so upset when the water's not boiled long enough or when the filter breaks and the Indians are so slow in fixing it."

I stared at the sick-green canal. "I can see why…"

We continued to wait. She chatting, I silent, nodding, observing. I was fascinated by the backwaters.

Soon (a little too soon for my taste) it was our turn to climb onto the boat, which rocked dangerously from side to side every time someone stepped on or off or even shifted bit. Devi skipped on as if she were a Keralan boatman and gracefully sat down. *How in the world did she do that?* I looked at her, waveringly. *I hate the thought of falling into this water. If I do…I will freak out!* Disgust rose within me.

Reluctantly I followed. As I stepped on, the boat swayed violently. There was nothing to hold onto to steady myself. Fear clutched my chest—*Oh no, oh no!* I quickly threw myself down onto one of the plank benches. An Indian woman lunged out of the way of my body. I turned and smiled sheepishly at her. Devi chortled at my discomfort. I looked down and noticed that the hem of my skirt was hanging in the water that had collected in the bottom of the boat. I felt the water slosh between my toes in my cheap plastic chappels. *Ugh! This is so yucky!*

Our trip over was without mishap. I scrambled out behind Devi, thrilled to leave the swaying, scary boat for solid ground. The little village was dry, dusty, and poor. It looked to be only a couple of streets, very busy, crowded. Just like any other Indian village. Our errands were not too demanding; however, we lingered so that we did not have to hurry back to the ashram. I was in no hurry to traverse the backwaters again—never was too soon for me.

CHAPTER ELEVEN

A HOUSE
SWEPT CLEAN

"MAYA, have you seen her?" Alice asked me in a melo-dramatic, hushed tone. Alice, Anneshwari, and I were sitting in the women's dormitory on Anneshwari's bunk. Alice and I were talking, as Alice scarfed up my peanuts and I plied her for gossip. Not that it took much—Alice loved gossip. Further, I had given her freedom with my peanuts and peanuts were the bribery tool of choice for Alice.

Anneshwari was ignoring us; her focus was on Cha Ma, of course. She was busy peeking out the window at the head of her bunk. She had a highly coveted resting spot—a bunk with a direct view of Cha Ma's quarters. She could observe Cha Ma's comings and goings at all times.

For over a year (so I had been told), Anneshwari had bided her time, patiently waiting until the previous occupant of the bunk had grown too sick to stay in India and was forced to return to the United Kingdom. The moment the bunk had opened, Anneshwari had "seized" the opportunity and taken the bunk. For the prize, she had to beat a couple of women down and bribe a few others.

The only real competition, though, had been Alice. I could not help but wonder at Alice's motivation: Had she joined in the race for the bunk merely to create competitive tension or for amusement?…Or just because she could? Not that she actually cared about Cha Ma's goings-on. Apparently, as the story went, when Anneshwari and Alice had squared off for the bunk, Alice would not capitulate. Bribing had not worked with her. Nor had hitting her. Finally, Anneshwari had dissolved into a mass of inconsolable tears. After four straight hours of Anneshwari's profuse weeping, Alice had given up the bunk, showing no emotion one way or the other.

So, there we were—Alice, Anneshwari, and I—an odd grouping (I was not sure I liked being grouped with them.). Alice and I were enjoying a moment of rest and gossip between the weekly residential darshan and evening bhajans. Anneshwari was at the window, watching, waiting like a predatory animal. She probably would have waited at the door of Cha Ma's apartment had Cha Ma allowed her. In fact, she had tried that route; but after three days of her camping out on Cha Ma's doorstep, Cha Ma had said no, firmly and unambiguously. So, instead, Anneshwari posted reconnaissance at the window.

If one had looked down, one would have seen Rukmini below, watching from the garden. Hiding her gaunt, yet hulking frame behind a palm tree. She, too, was watching…waiting…*Does she think she's invisible hiding behind that palm tree?*

I shook my head no. "Her…who?"

"You know—the crazy lady. You must've seen her," Alice whispered even more melodramatically through peanuts, if that was at all possible.

I shook my head no again. I studied Alice: the narrow brown eyes, darting hither and thither, the mouth with a pronounced overbite, munching away at the peanuts. The mousy brown hair caught up in a loose ponytail—limp and greasy from infrequent washing. Alice did not seem to notice the scrutiny.

"You know…the lady who walks around and around and mumbles to herself," Alice shoved another handful of peanuts into her mouth.

Anneshwari interjected, not losing focus from her vigil one bit, "Oh, you mean, crazy Kartika!"

"Yeah!" *Munch.* "Her!"

"I've seen her, I think," I answered, my forehead wrinkled in thought. "She's the lady who walks around like a zombie, her clothes half hanging off of her." My mind, along with Anneshwari's and Alice's, went to the woman.

The woman, Kartika, was memorable. Once you saw her, you would never forget her. She was average height. Average weight. However, it was her looks that burned her into memory—she had the appearance of pure, unmitigated insanity. Her madness was neither outwardly nor inwardly directed. It was not directed at anyone; because no one was home to direct it. At all. Kartika was *120 percent* out to lunch.

What had happened to make her this way? Her eyes failed to tell the story. They were frighteningly vacant. Always. Staring at something or someone no one else saw. Rarely did she blink. Never did she focus. She walked with a lopsided gait, favoring the left side—shuffle, lean…shuffle, lean…shuffle, lean…. Wherever she was, she paced back and forth, back and forth. She never ran into anyone. Probably because everyone walked a wide arc around her. No one wanted to come into contact with her body or even be near her. Her once-upon-a-time white sari was now an indefinable grayish color with large, faded splotches of reddish-brown rust spots. It was crumpled, old, and threadbare. She draped it around her body as if she did not care whether it was there or not. Some days it made it halfway over one shoulder. Other days, it hung limply about her waist, almost suggestive and obscene had she not been so scarily disconnected and vacant, so decidedly insane.

"I saw her yesterday," I recalled, "walking back and forth in the bathroom wing."

"I know," Anneshwari confirmed. "She often walks there or up on the balcony of the temple."

"I know what," Alice said excitedly, "let's go and see if we can find her. Let's go watch her!"

"Okay!" I responded quickly and jumped off the bed.

"I don't know…" Anneshwari was more reluctant, instead wanting to stay and watch for Cha Ma. She was not one to neglect her favorite pastime.

"Oh! C'mon! Let's you and I go, Maya," Alice said, grabbing a handful of peanuts from the jar on the bunk before she headed off.

"Where are we going?" I asked, trotting double time to keep up with her.

"To the bathrooms on the third floor. That's where I saw her earlier today. She doesn't change where she is once she gets there. I've seen her walking at four in the morning and then hours later still be walking back and forth in the same spot, not stopping, not doing anything but walking. Hmm, I wonder…" I could almost hear Alice's mind churning along with her mouth chewing peanuts, "I wonder, you saw her by the bathrooms yesterday?"

"Uh huh," I affirmed.

"And I saw her there today…I wonder if she ever left. Maybe she's been there since yesterday?"

"I don't know…" My voice trailed off, weakly. The idea of being that crazy scared me. I did not like the thought so I pushed it away.

We walked to the bathrooms by passing through the balcony above the temple. As we walked by the Foreigners' Office, I tried to glance inconspicuously toward the office. *Is Narayana there?* I hoped that Alice would not see me looking. I could see her with *that* piece of knowledge.

Right then, Alice turned to me, stuck a couple of peanuts into her mouth and said, "I wonder if Narayana's there. He's always there or with Cha Ma. He's really close to her and spends a lot of time with her."

I did not say anything. I did not want Alice to figure out how I felt. Alice peeked into the office, I behind her. I did not want to seem like I was trying to talk to him. I did not want anyone, particularly Alice the ashram gossip, to think I was interested in him; although truth be told, I was forming one huge, gargantuan crush. For some inexplicable reason, he took my breath away.

"Namah shivaya, Alice." I heard his voice. He sounded bored. Not that it mattered to Alice.

"Namah shivaya, Narayana!" Alice responded.

I peeked in to see him flashing a big, beautiful smile, in direct contradiction to his bored-sounding voice…that was until he saw me. Upon seeing me, his smile died, faded, disappeared from ever having been on his face. In its place arose that look of disdain and barely-concealed disgust. *He acts like he hates me! Why? Why?*

"Namah shivaya, Narayana!" I tried to say it as cheerily as I could, although he had deflated all my joy with one acidic look. He did not deign to answer me. Instead, he announced to the air as he pushed past us, "I'm going to the balcony to watch Cha Ma."

Unperturbed, Alice walked out, still munching on peanuts. I trailed behind her, stealing a glance at Narayana. His back was toward us as he faced Cha Ma. *Why does he hate me so?* He had completely disconcerted me. *I can't believe this. I barely know him and he upsets me!* I chided myself as I followed Alice. She began to climb the stairs to the third floor.

I paused at the stairs and looked behind me one last time, wishing I would not, but I could not stop myself. That was when I saw him…Narayana, staring at me. Unmistakably at *me*. An unguarded, inexpressibly tender look upon his face and in his eyes. Lost in staring at me. He continued to stare until he seemed to come to himself. His eyes "refocused" and went blank. He turned his back to me to face Cha Ma.

I followed Alice up the stairs and around the corner to the bathrooms. *Ugh! I hate these stalls! It's so nasty here!* The third floor toilet stalls were so much dirtier than the ones on the top floor. I tried to avoid them and just use the nicer, cleaner ones at the top; but sometimes it could not be avoided.

We crept up to the row of toilet stalls and peered around the corner. I avoided touching the nasty, filthy walls. I wished my feet did not have to touch the floor, even though they were in chappels.

"There she is," Alice whispered with excitement, her eyes glittering ever so slightly.

"Uh huh," was all I ventured to say. There she was, indeed. Pacing…slowly, ever so slowly, lopsidedly…one measured step, lean…another measured step, lean…. Her feet were broad and flat, the toes splayed out, as though she had walked too many nights. The soles were cracked all around, painfully cracked, with deep, dirt-encrusted fissures. Her sari was threadbare and dirty, which was to be expected. It was wrapped loosely, carelessly, about her body. The portion that normally would have been draped around one or both of a woman's shoulders was sloppily tucked in around her waist. Her choli was too big and looked too bare without the sari draped over it. It did not matter because what would have been alluring with a sane woman, with Kartika was frightening and ominous. Everything about her hinted at an internal torture, a never-ending nightmare, that dared anyone to come close and risk contracting whatever it was she had.

She did not mind that no one ever went near her. She was not aware of anyone anyway. If you stood in her way, she would slowly walk around you as if you were a fire hydrant sitting in the middle of a path. She held conversations with herself. Her eyes blank and unfocused. Sometimes she drooled while she mumbled. She never bothered to wipe the drool, as she was not aware enough to perceive the fact that she was drooling. She was horribly frightening. Revoltingly mesmerizing.

"What happened to her?" I asked partially awed, partially revolted.

Alice looked back at me, incredulously. "You mean, you've never heard what happened to her?"

(Unfortunately, Alice and Maya could not see into the spirit realm. If they could have, they would have seen the demons that swirled around and through and in Kartika. She was a place of residence for them. The leader of them, Insanity, whispered random suggestions to her all day long. If they could have seen into the spirit realm and into the past, they would have seen the events that precipitated her madness. They would have observed the willful and willing letting down of subconscious walls that protect most people from outside spirits. They would have seen the opportunistic invasion of evil spirits into her body. Years ago, she had laid herself wide open.)

"No, I've never heard what happened to her," I replied.

Alice looked at me wide-eyed. "Well, I'll have to tell you. But, not here! I don't feel right telling you here." Alice paused for a second and looked around, "It has to be because of these bathrooms; they're so dirty and smelly. Just not the place to tell a good story."

Vigorously I nodded my head in agreement, not so much because of the filthiness of the bathrooms but because of the "feeling" I got whenever Kartika shuffled near us, because of the uneasiness that seemed to slide along my neck and up and down my spine. *Creepy!*

"Let's go to the Western canteen," Alice suggested, already moving off toward the back stairs near the bathroom.

I hurried behind her, casting a glance at Kartika as I went. No change. She continued to pace, mumbling to herself, oblivious to the fact that two women had been staring at her and talking about her, let alone that they had left.

We circled down the back stairs. Alice looked around furtively, as if she had done something wrong or was planning to. I knew her a little better…I knew she was scanning the near and far horizon for any glimpse of Cha Ma. One sighting of her and our little talk in the Western canteen would be shot. But fortunately…no Cha Ma.

As we entered the Western canteen, we encountered Dirk, Devi, and Radha sitting and chatting. The high ceiling fans twirled themselves languidly, not quite stirring the unbearably hot, moist air. I felt sweat trickle down my back. Their faces were flushed various shades of pink and red due, I was sure, to the heat and humidity.

"Hey guys!" Devi called out, lazily gesturing us in. "Come join us."

"What are you guys doing?" Alice asked as she moved toward a seat.

"Nothing much…just chatting. Don't feel like meditating," Radha volunteered, "so decided to come to the Western canteen. Keep Dirk company."

I sat down in a seat, quiet. This crew, although they were extremely friendly, had me a little in awe of them. They were so "knowledgeable" of things of the ashram, of Hinduism, of Cha Ma. *Best to remain quiet and absorb.*

"What are you two doing out here?" Devi asked, a little smile playing around her mouth.

Alice's eyes grew big, "I was going to tell her about Kartika…"

"Oooo! That's a good story," Radha said, her eyes growing wide too.

"You mean…she doesn't *know* about *Kartika*?" Devi asked incredulously.

"Maybe you shouldn't say anything. Let sleeping dogs lie," Dirk suggested. He waved his hand dismissively.

"Oh, Dirk!" Alice exclaimed.

"Dirk!" Devi and Radha responded together.

"You know you're lying. You like a good story more than anybody. In fact, since you've been here so long, you probably know the whole tale," Devi said.

"Oh! I could tell you some things…" Dirk teased.

Radha leaned over and pinched Dirk's arm playfully. "Yeah, but it looks like we're going to have to beat you up just to get it out of you!"

"Look, I'll begin! Just give me a minute," Alice said, looking around furtively, like a little rat.

"What are you looking for?" Dirk asked.

Devi broke out laughing, "Need you ask? Peanuts! What else! Am I right?"

Alice nodded quickly. "Do you have any peanuts, Dirk, here in the Western canteen?"

"Even if I did, I wouldn't give them to you," Dirk responded quickly with a wit that teetered between too sarcastic and just plain mean. *Where'd that come from?* I wondered. His remark was out of nowhere and much too harsh given the light, bantering conversation.

Alice did not seem to notice, "Oh, okay! Well, I've got my own." She grabbed a corner of her sari. It was knotted up in a teeny bundle. "You guys want some," she asked as she undid the knot. Out fell a small handful of peanuts, grubby and dirty. Probably old.

"Uh...no thank you!" Dirk said, throwing his head back with a laugh.

Radha and Devi just shook their heads, laughing and holding their bellies.

"No thanks," I responded, still not quite knowing what to think of Alice and the crew.

"Okay! More for me!" Alice said with utter aplomb as she picked up a peanut and stuck it into her mouth. "Ummm yumm!" she smirked for emphasis.

"Okay, already!" Devi said, laughing. "Go ahead and tell her about Kartika."

"Oh yeah! Kartika..." mumbled Alice between chews.

Dirk interrupted, "I remember her...when she first came to the ashram. She was absolutely beautiful. She was one of the 'beautiful ones,'" Dirk reminisced, staring off with a glazed look in his eyes.

"What's a 'beautiful one'?" I asked, intrigued.

Devi leaned back and placed her legs on the table, crossing them at the ankles—very un-Indian-lady-like. Grinning, she replied, "Ah! The beautiful ones are those brahmacharis and -charinis who far surpass all the others in beauty. They're all beautiful..." Everyone, including myself, nodded earnestly in agreement. "...but the beautiful ones are even more beautiful, more exquisite..." She paused, looking for the right words, "...more innocent and untouchable in their beauty."

"It's as if their devotion to Cha Ma, their focus upon Cha Ma, makes them unusually beautiful," Radha added.

"So," I interjected, "who would be considered a beautiful one, of the ones in the ashram now, that I would know of?"

"Narayana!" Radha, Devi, and Alice said in unison. Dirk rolled his eyes and snorted.

I tried to feign as if I did not know that. "Him?"

Radha and Devi eyed me slyly and smiled knowingly. Alice just focused on grabbing another peanut and, after popping it into her mouth, proceeded to chew like a chipmunk.

"Oh c'mon! YOU know...Naaraaayaanaaa..." Devi said, dragging out his name for emphasis, "is one of the beautiful ones! He's absolutely gorgeous!"

"But, he's so obnoxious!" I interjected, hoping I sounded appropriately whimsical, hoping they would not notice my crush on him.

"That too!" Devi agreed.

"Oh, I don't know...he's really cool if you get to know him," Radha noted.

"Okay! Okay!" exclaimed Dirk waving his hand impatiently in front of his face as though he were fanning smoke from his face. "Anyway, *Kartika* was one of the beautiful ones!" he said, drawing us back to the story. "Remember, this conversation's not about Narayana."

"Dog, dude!" Devi exclaimed, smiling. "You don't have to get all upset 'n' stuff!"

Dirk smiled wryly at her and chucked her chin, "Kartika was so beautiful. Kali! She was breathtaking to look at." His eyes glazed over again as he stared out of the canteen toward the ashram itself. "She came in her late teens…I don't know why. No one does, I don't think. Except maybe Cha Ma. She loved to meditate. It started slowly. At first she'd meditate thirty minutes here or there. But over time, the amount of time she spent in meditation increased from thirty minutes to an hour, from an hour to two hours. By the end of it, she would meditate hours and hours on end…all night long…sometimes all day long. But, that was at the very end."

"Hey! How do you know all this?" Devi asked with fake suspicion.

"Ah! Because I used to follow her and watch her goings about," Dirk replied coolly. "She was so beautiful. So quiet and mysterious. Intriguing, actually." He looked down at his hands. A hint of a smile played about his mouth. "I found myself following her around, curious about what she was doing. She was so beautiful to watch…especially when she was meditating. I could watch her for hours…"

I thought to myself, *He's a stalker!*

Alice added, "That's weird!"

"Okaaay…" Radha and Devi responded in unison. *Do these two always speak and think the same?* I asked myself in wonder.

Dirk ignored the comments. "From the very beginning, Cha Ma would tell her to mix work with meditation, that she needed to make sure she worked."

"Why is that? Why would Cha Ma push so for her to work? Did she need people to build her ashram? Does she use the money for herself?" I asked, engrossed in the story. I could see Kartika when she was younger, outrageously beautiful, captivatingly mysterious—my mind was weaving a story, an image of her, as we sat there. I was enthralled.

"Oh, no! Nothing like that!" Radha corrected. "It's not that Cha Ma needs people, particularly women, to work for her. No, it's that women are urged to work a lot in order to keep grounded."

"Huh?" I asked bewildered.

Radha continued, not missing a beat, "Cha Ma says that because of the way women are built…wired…we are more 'open' to things spiritual. When we meditate we open ourselves to a bunch of 'influences.'" She made quote-unquote marks with her fingers. "We can easily get swept away. So, we have to ground ourselves…"

"Ground ourselves?" I repeated quizzically.

Devi nodded, "Oh, yes! We have to ground ourselves or we may get burnt."

"Burnt how? What do you mean?" *This isn't sounding too good!*

Radha continued, "Because women are so much more open to spiritual things…too much can come to us too quickly when we meditate or do other sorts of tapas, which are spiritual disciplines, too much. So, Cha Ma tells us that we have to ground ourselves."

Devi added, "We have to do work in order to stay spiritually grounded so that we don't go 'spinning away' or 'flying off to La-La Land.'" She whirled her arm over her head like a helicopter.

"Wow! That's different!" I'd never heard of anything like it. I began to muse upon the everyday happenings of the ashram. *Now it all makes sense! I see the brahmacharinis and Western women working so hard from before the sun rises until the wee hours of the morning; whereas, the brahmacharis and Western men just sit around meditating.* Still, although it made sense, I could not help being a little critical. *I know the theory has its reasons but it sure does sound extremely chauvinistic. How fortuitous for the men! I can't believe Cha Ma would push this stuff!*

"Um hmmm, that's what happened to Kartika," Dirk interrupted my thoughts. "So beautiful…so innocent…so, so lovely…" His voice faded away as he remembered. "All to disappear. It started happening over time. Slowly, though. When she first got here she would meditate only a little…just like most people."

"Yeah!" Devi laughed, snatching one of Alice's peanuts and depositing it in her mouth before Alice could protest. My stomach turned at the thought of all the germs, bacteria, parasites, and amoebas that could be attached to that one grungy little peanut. *Ugh! Not worth the risk—amoebic dysentery in exchange for a germ infested, stale peanut! Oh no!* "It *is* really hard to meditate for any length of time." Alice smiled at Devi completely oblivious to the import of the theft. Although she saw it, it did not register with her.

"I know!" Alice agreed. "I can't meditate at all so I just stopped trying. Cha Ma will have to see me through and get me to enlighten—"

"Yeah. Well," Dirk interrupted Alice, "as I was saying—Kartika started like most everyone else—meditating just a little. Soon it became enjoyable to her to the exclusion of most of her other activities. It became an obsession. It began to rule her. Cha Ma told her to stop meditating so much. I can still remember. She'd come to darshan and kneel before Cha Ma or she'd be on Cha Ma's lap looking dazed and a little out of it from her meditations, all the more beautiful because of the 'lostness' in her face.

"Cha Ma would pat her cheek and tell her, at first gently, but over time more and more emphatically, that she had to stop meditating so much, that she needed to work. See, Kartika would avoid work in order to spend more time meditating. She started not eating so much. In fact, we'd not see her at mealtime at all. It got to where she wouldn't sleep at night. At any given time, during the day or night, she could be found on the top meditation roof, 'out' in deep meditation.

"Cha Ma warned her, though." Dirk sighed heavily. "Over and over. And then one day, she just snapped and became who she is now. I don't know the particulars of what happened. No one does, except maybe Cha Ma who, when she saw the 'new' Kartika, began to cry. She was probably busy meditating one of her mega-meditations and her mind snapped. But no one knows for sure."

"Why not? Hasn't anyone ever asked her?" I queried.

"Yes, but after that day, her mind has never been back to normal…in any way. No one has been able to have a conversation with her since then. She doesn't see anyone. She doesn't talk to anyone. She doesn't respond when she's spoken to. She doesn't even show when she's been hurt. Absolutely nothing."

He continued, "It's strange. In the beginning she was so beautiful, even though her mind had 'snapped,' was gone, never to come back…still she was so beautiful to look at. Such beauty but also such innocence and purity and devotion to Cha Ma. Quickly, though, she started to change. With her mind gone, her looks left too."

I sat back in my chair. We all did. During Dirk's recollection, we had leaned forward in our seats, spellbound by the story of Kartika—an enchantingly beautiful and innocent brahmacharini transformed into an ugly, frightening, mindless "something." The story affected me profoundly. I felt chills rush up and down my spine. *Ugh! To think…that could happen to me? To any of us?* My heart froze at the full implications—the dangers inherent in this "way."

Little did Maya and her newfound friends know the true nature of Kartika's madness. As she meditated, she had grown increasingly more adept at emptying her mind and removing all thoughts, beliefs, feelings, and emotions within her—the goal of meditation. What she did not know was that such an empty mind, such an empty soul, is an invitation. Most people sweep their minds clean only momentarily and their souls even less so. But she, by her constant and habitual striving over longer and longer periods of time, was quite successful at emptying her mind for hours on end. Therein lay the problem: Such emptiness begged for an occupant. The universe demonstrates that nature abhors a vacuum. Always with emptiness, something of substance will opportunistically rush in to occupy the vacuous space. Even Jesus had warned, "When an evil spirit comes out of a man, it goes through arid places seeking rest and does not find it. Then it says, 'I will return to the house I left.' When it arrives, it finds the house swept clean and put in order. Then it goes and takes seven other spirits more wicked than itself, and they go in and live there. And the final condition of that man is worse than the first." Such was the case with Kartika.

One day, one random day, while her mind basked in a place of nothingness, the demon named Insanity rushed in. Finding such empty, inviting space within her, it brought along a few of its cronies: Dementia, Pure Craziness, Depression, Ugly, and a couple of others. In the realm of the demonic, illegal opportunism prevails—they exercised squatters' rights.

By the time Maya and her crew were observing and discussing her, many more had moved in. She had an entire enclave of demons that swirled about, through, and in her. Some had nested for so long, so comfortably, so *uncontestedly* in her, they had lost all semblance of constraint. They no longer felt they needed to hide the fact that they had co-opted her body as their vehicle. They allowed themselves to manifest upon her. What Maya and her friends saw that was so hideous and ugly in Kartika was the countenances of the more "confident" demons superimposed over hers. Her gait was that of a human dominated by the demonic. It was indicative of the evil ones always trying, though never truly being able, to get used to the much heavier, cumbersome, albeit divinely inspired and purposed human body. Never would they be able to adjust to the human body because it was never intended to house rotten, opportunistic, illegal spirits. Never was it intended to accommodate demons. No, the human body was created to house the human spirit—and the Spirit of the One True God, who came only upon invitation.

Oh yes! They were squatters in the ultimate sense. Unfortunately, they had "squatted" for so long, they had ceased to hide themselves. They did not kill Kartika outright because it was more "fun" this way. It was advantageous to keep the vehicle alive. Further, it was not in their nature to kill. Those whose nature it was to kill—Death, Murder, Suicide—had yet to really notice her; however, one day they would. Then it would only be a matter of time before they would motivate Kartika to kill herself, or some other human to extinguish her.

"Have you ever noticed how her face seems to change? Some days it's all swollen? Other days it's darker? And sometimes it just looks crazier?" Radha asked in a rushed whisper as if she had been waiting for so long to get these words out. Everyone nodded rapidly in agreement.

Everyone had seen the manifestation of the demons upon her face; they just did not know what it was they were seeing.

Devi declared, "Some days she doesn't even look human!" Her face wrinkled up in distaste.

"Yeah, well," Dirk added, "you should have seen her in the beginning. Then you would be shocked by how she's changed. There's nothing in her that looks like she used to look." He shook his head sadly.

Alice rolled her eyes. "All I know is that I don't ever want to end up like her."

Devi added, "Yeah! I almost think it would be better to be dead than to be like that."

"Then at least," Alice said, "I'd come back in another lifetime."

"If we come back…" Radha said quietly and slowly, almost too quietly and slowly. "Sometimes I wonder…what if we don't come back? What if we don't reincarnate? What if…this lifetime is our only shot?"

Deadening, uncomfortable silence fell upon the group. I looked down at my hands. My heart clutched in fear, shrinking back from a nameless something. *What if we don't come back? What if all of this is wrong and this is our only chance?* I wanted to run away from where these thoughts led, from what it all could mean.

Alice jumped up. "Well! I've got to go! I'm going to go see what Cha Ma's doing!"

I seized at the opportunity to escape my own hidden doubts and questions. "Me too!"

Our group broke up, each heading his or her own way, needled by the thoughts and questions the conversation had stirred.

CHAPTER TWELVE

OF ANGELS
AND MEN

Marie

United States

IT had been a difficult night for Marie. In fact, the nights were getting harder and harder, as were the days. During the day, she felt hopelessly depressed. All she wanted to do, all she ached to do, was sleep, just to get away from the thoughts, the fears, the worries that constantly barraged her. She prayed against them. Oh! How she prayed and prayed and prayed! It seemed she was getting nowhere. Then at night she felt oppressed and could barely sleep. She tossed and turned most of the night, yearning to go to sleep only to have ominous, harrowing dreams and colorless nightmares once slumber overtook her. Finally tonight, as with all the other nights since Maya had left, Marie fell into a deep, nightmarish state.

"Marie! Marie! Wake up!" Marie heard a voice calling to her in her sleep.

"Hmm?" she responded sleepily.

"Marie!" Again the voice. This time, sharp in her ear.

"Yes!" Marie opened her eyes and saw no one but her husband who was sleeping and thus could not have called her.

"Marie!" That voice again. This time she was awake enough to recognize the voice—the voice of the One she loved. She looked around and answered, her voice hushed, "Yes, Lord! I'm awake. What do You want to tell me or what do You want me to do?"

"Pray right now! In the Holy Spirit!" the Lord commanded her.

Immediately she began to pray in tongues. Still lying in her bed. The room was silent, but she did not feel alone.

And she was not alone, far from it—for all around her stood the Lord's angels. Some guarded her. Some encouraged her. Still others waited for a prayer, particular to a specific need, to fall from her lips so that God could command them to move.

An aerial view of the invisible supernatural realm would have shown three concentric circles of angels. The first circle stood guard 200 feet away from her house facing outward. They were between 12 to 15 feet tall, broad-shouldered and strong, with iridescent skin of different hues. Living light flowed from their bodies—a constant effusion that came from the core of their beings, made stronger from existing in the Presence of God. They were clad in silver battle armor. Gleams of light shot from their armor even when they did not move. The armor itself appeared alive and vibrant. Their faces exhibited rapt attention as they stood facing the darkness, watching for nothing the human eye could see. Their eyes peered into the supernatural realm. They were observing Satan's angels drawing near and then pulling away. Each side was waiting…waiting…

The next circle stood just a few feet outside the house. They were facing outward also, as though they were back-up to the first circle. They were the same height as the first group of angels, tall and powerful and in full battle regalia, which sparkled and gleamed. They too stared intently into the darkness, on guard against Satan's forces.

The final circle was in and around Marie's room. Disregarding walls or solid objects, this circle of angels faced inward and was more intent upon ministering to her. They too were in battle gear—silver and full of light. They were as tall and as large as the others, but there was a "something else" to them. They were more massive and exhibited a greater mastery. They too exuded light; but it was more pristine and radiant as it poured forth from their beings.

As Marie prayed, she felt the load, the pressure within her, lifting. She slid off the bed and onto her knees. She raised her arms to Heaven as gratitude poured into her body. She did not know why she felt so thankful at this time, which was surely the most painful and confusing time of her life; but as she prayed she felt peace and thankfulness suffuse her body. She began to sing in the Spirit songs to God. She did not know what she was singing, except she knew that the sounds and melodies flowing from deep within her were full of joy and peace and adoration for her Lord.

The angels around her began to sing in their heavenly language. Had she been able to hear them, she would have heard a most wondrous, beautiful melody. She would have heard voices that were more pure and rich in tone than any instrument found on earth. Their song poured forth from the room and spread out—a tangible force of light and power and might. As their song flowed forth, it touched the angels outside. They, too, began to sing in the celestial language until every angel within a few hundred feet had joined in—a heavenly wildfire was blazing!

The nature of their voices lifted high in unison, in exultation of the Lord of Hosts, sent the evil ones scrambling away, hands covering ear holes. The pure beauty and majestic power of the angelic song devastated the enemy's forces. They scampered farther and farther away, screaming from the burns inflicted by the heavenly wildfire. They could not get far enough away.

Had Marie known, she would have been astounded by how her song melded with that of the angels. The angels, smiling and saluting the Lord of Hosts, sang with all their being. God's Glory filled the room. His Presence flowed, real and heavy. Somehow the heartfelt, transparent worship of Marie and the angels had supernaturally transported them into the very Throne Room of God; while it had simultaneously drawn His Manifest Presence to the earth.

The angels bowed down before Him, their voices quieting to a deep, undulating hum that was no longer even a vocal utterance but rather a flowing forth of melodic tones from the eternity within them—they were lost in worship to their Lord. Marie did the same. She bowed down before the Lord, although she did not know she was doing the same thing as so many angels all around her. Her song slowly quieted to a whisper, then to nothing. She was overwhelmed by His Presence. She began to cry. Even her tears were silent in His Presence. Every part of her saluted and glorified Him. She lay down, fully prostrate.

She felt that familiar feeling within her chest—the fire. The same fire that the two men on the way to Emmaus felt as they walked in the presence of Jesus but did not know it was He. She burned. The burning increased until it felt as if all her cells were afire. On fire with Light and Truth. White-hot and living. Her God was a consuming fire, a living conflagration. She gasped for breath.

The Lord began to speak to her. *Yes, Lord...* Her entire being assented. He spoke beyond her mind, beyond her soul, into her spirit. Her spirit bore witness with His Spirit. *Yes, come what may...* A hint of a whisper echoed within and without her, "I have sealed the instruction..."

Yes, Lord... Marie looked up from her fully prone position. She peered at the luminous numerals on the clock. Wonderment flashed through her. Somehow she had been lost in the Lord for over five hours...It had felt like five minutes.

She felt much better. She *knew that she knew*, deep inside, everything was going to be all right. She also knew she had a fight on her hands—a fight unlike anything she had ever known, a fight that most humans on the face of this earth would never have to undergo. She knew this in her spirit. However, she, in her soul, did not know the full extent of what she was fighting.

The Lord had informed her spirit that she was to battle and intercede to withdraw her daughter from the grips of a most powerful principality—that of the Queen of Heaven. This principality under the leadership of feminine-appearing spirits was like all others— assiduously and cunningly controlled by Satan and comprised of thousands of evil angels. It was a consortium of spirits hidden under the guise of the feminine goddesses of various religions throughout the world. The assumption of the feminine aspect was solely to lure people in—Satan would appear however a person desired in order to draw that person—a trick he had been using effectively since the beginning of human history. He was willing to manipulate, play, and be any and everything in order to lure people in. In India, the Queen of Heaven was often called Kali. Chamunda Kali and Bhadra Kali were variations on the name.

Few people faced the Queen of Heaven and came out alive. Few people could stand strong enough, long enough, to withstand the warring devices of that particular principality. The Lord had decided that although Marie's spirit was to know, it was best that her soul remain completely uninformed. She could not have conscious knowledge of what she was to fight. For had she known, she would have lost heart. Had she known, she would have given up. No, all she knew *consciously* was that she had a battle and that she was not to give up. She was to pray hard and ceaselessly for her daughter.

As she came back to consciousness, Marie began to pray in the Spirit again. Every angel instantaneously moved upon the orders contained in the prayers uttered by Marie while she prayed in the Spirit, for she was allowing the Holy Spirit to pray the mind of God into the earth. The Lord's angels hearkened to the Holy Spirit's prayed orders. Ah! Such was the mysterious outworking of a person praying in the Holy Spirit and the unfolding of the Lord's will in the earth. As she prayed, the three circles of angels began to move from their positions of watchful and alert waiting.

The outermost circle shot like bullets out of a pistol, brandishing fiery weapons of Heaven and singing in unison. They flew—flashes of brilliant, otherworldly light. Some people thought they saw flashes of lightning on the horizon. Others thought they saw something similar to the northern lights. No, it was simply the Lord's angels warring on His behalf in the earth realm, so caught up in their assignment for Him that they had forgotten to keep their brilliant light concealed. They reveled in the warfare. The demons scampered and limped away—howling, covering their ear slits, begging for mercy.

The circle just outside the house moved into Marie's bedroom to continue to protect her and now to minister to her as the innermost group of angels, who had been standing in her bedroom, shot straight up into the air.

Majesty, the leader, was in this innermost group. These were the ones to whom most of the Lord's thoughts and plans concerning this family had been revealed. They were close to Marie and her family, as they had been assigned to this family three generations ago when her great-grandmother had given her life to Christ, and thus had willingly stepped into the destiny God had for her and her family from before the beginning of time. Majesty and the members of this circle of angels knew each person in Marie's family through and through. They had been present at every birth, every funeral, every heartache and heartbreak, every celebration and party. This was *their* family. It was their duty to enable each person in the family to fulfill the purpose for which God had created him or her. And now, it was Maya, Marie, and Paul's time.

Majesty let out a deafeningly loud war cry to the Lord, *"Yes!"* He turned to Awe as they soared straight up from the room into the air with the others. "We are going to India! It is time!" Awe smiled at him as they found themselves moving through a space/time vortex. Heavenly angels are not constrained by the elements of time and space. They have the ability to "think" themselves somewhere or have an "intent" to be somewhere and that was where they were sooner than the next instant. At will, they could be here or there in no time at all. Or if necessary, they could move within the confines of time to accomplish what God wanted, completely unconstrained by that element. How much time "should" something take? It did not matter. How much distance had to be traversed? It did not matter. An answer or a resolution, which could be expected to take several human days, weeks, or months, could be compacted into a small unit of "no-time," given the nature of the Lord's angels. However, if time did elapse, it was because of any number of factors—constraints placed upon the angels by the humans involved, limitations due to lack of prayer or lack of faith, or the necessity of the humans involved to develop certain characteristics such as faith, patience, righteousness, love, and joy, all of which needed to simmer in the crucible of time and tribulation in order to be perfected.

Satan's angels were woefully deficient in this mastery of time and space. Granted, they must have had it once in Heaven. But no more. Not after the First Rebellion. No, their mastery had greatly diminished over the play of time, although Satan and a couple of the most powerful spirits, Death being one, still had it, in part. Why did they not have it as powerfully and fluidly as God's angels? Perhaps Satan limited their ability to use this aspect of their nature (doubtful, as he was more likely to use every means available in his arsenal). Maybe God limited their ability to use this skill. Or perhaps, simply being away from the Presence of God diminished this ability. Suffice it to say that Satan's angels were nowhere near as proficient as the Lord's angels in manipulating time and space. They were unable to move thousands of miles within a nanosecond. They could not manipulate, fold, or weave time according to the dictates of their lord. They were unable to create and mold circumstances to take place in an hour's time that should take days, weeks, and even months.

Satan's team knew about this deficiency. Thus, what they lacked in true angelic attributes they made up for by illegality. Their forte was illegality. Their power was in illegality. Unlike the heavenly angels who were delightedly bound by the laws set forth by the Lord and thus observed them perfectly; Satan's angels cheated, lied, and calculatedly breached God's laws every opportunity they could get.

Thus, as the play of time unfolded, the evil ones grew heavier, denser, more hideous, more bound by time and space, and more driven to violate as many of God's laws as was possible. However, where great darkness abounds, so does great light—God's angels grew increasingly more brilliant and beautiful and powerful. They grew increasingly more capable of manipulating time and space and of influencing and controlling elements within time and space.

"What about Marie?" Awe asked as they shot to India.

"Mighty, Paul's angel, and Jovial, Mighty's second, are going to oversee the care of Paul and Marie," Majesty answered. "Of course they will be over legions. The legions will be necessary as there is intense warfare in store for the two of them. It will be starting soon. When it does come, we may or may not return to help them. The Lord has yet to reveal that. For now, He wants us in India to protect and minister to Maya."

"What is our legal entrance?" Awe asked.

"Marie has been praying for Maya—in English, but even more powerfully and effectively in tongues. As she prays in the Holy Spirit, as you know, the Holy Spirit has been speaking the Mind and Will of God through her. His Will is for us to help Maya. We are to join Brilliant and His Strength in protecting her, ministering to her…watching over her. She will be fine; but we will have our share of intervention and warfare as she is in the grips of Chamunda Kali…deeply in the grips…we will have much work to do."

"That doesn't sound too bad. I love hard work," Awe responded as they landed on a busy street in Madras. He looked around, "Ah! Madras! Do you remember Thomas?"

"Yes, that he lost his life in a village near here?"

"Yes. Who would have thought that the one who so doubted the Lord, the one who had to have proof, the one who had to place his hands into the Lord's wounds in order to believe, would be so strong in the Lord?"

"Yes, to love the Lord so much as to come here to India and end up being martyred in..."

"...Mylapore," Majesty picked up his thought.

"...which is just outside this very place! Many lives were saved and many more seeds planted."

"Ah! But, you must be meaning when he first arrived in this country and went to Kerala?"

"Yes! Many people came to believe in Christ through him," Majesty said. "Don't you think it interesting that we are again to be in Kerala?"

"It does seem to be almost full circle with the work Thomas did." Awe turned slowly in the middle of the street. Two lorries rumbled through him. "This place never ceases to amaze me! Fascinate me! The evil that permeates it..." Although he said this about the evil, he did not cower or seem perturbed by it. In fact, he appeared to be expecting a momentous occasion. "I cannot wait until we get to battle with the demons and evil spirits entrenched in this principality again!"

"Whoa! Hold on," said Majesty in his wisdom. "Everything must be prepared. God has a major victory set up. Of course in His time it has already been won. However, now it has to be played out in the earthly realm. Every single person must be in place. Every single event must be set up according to God's Will. Every heart must be open and ripe. But," he clapped Awe on the shoulder as he looked about, grinning jubilantly, "I have to agree with you. It will be very exciting and enjoyable to battle this principality again! And then, at the end of times...to trounce it...to trounce *all* of Satan's principalities once and for all! To see them all destroyed forever—*our forever*—now *that* will be heaven…as humans like to say!" Majesty stated wryly.

He and Awe "walked" along the busy streets, looking about. Cars whizzed through them. People walked through them. Dogs looked at them curiously. A cat skittered away, yowling.

"Why are we here?" Awe asked as he followed Majesty through a closed door into a dank, dusty warehouse. It was nondescript in appearance. Obviously it had been abandoned for a long time.

"We are meeting with several of our own who are assigned to this area. We're going to brief them on developments with Maya's family. Also, it is possible one will be coming directly from the Lord to give us further instructions. We will see whether there is anything more the Lord would like to reveal. Or it may be that He will prefer that most information remain perfectly in Him, that way we can more easily take Satan's troops by surprise." As Majesty was explaining this, he and Awe walked a straight line "through" walls and doors toward the largest room in the building. The entire building appeared suitable for an angelic meeting with its huge rooms and soaring ceilings (not that the physical dimensions of the building or the rooms mattered in the least).

"Many of us who are involved in this will be here," Majesty continued, "with the exception of Brilliant and His Strength. They are with Maya and are to remain with her at all times. She is too unstable and the situation is too dangerous to leave her even for a moment. When we are done here, you and I will go and brief them." Awe nodded.

Even before they reached the main room of the warehouse, they encountered several angels—all of whom they saluted and who saluted in return. The main room was teeming with angels…all large and powerful. One, in particular, seemed in charge. It could have been his immensity—even more hulking than the others—that indicated his superiority. Or it may have been his beauty, which had nothing to do with appearance but rather his very nature. Whether he moved or stood at ease, his muscles rippled and pulsated minutely as if, although they were a part of his body, they were also consciously thinking, individually functioning parts of his body. His skin shimmered and glowed with a golden radiance. His burnished golden hair reminded one of butterscotch laced with a delicate filigree of pure bronze and gold. He was awesome to behold, incomprehensibly powerful, a force to be reckoned with.

Awe turned to Majesty with a look of wonder, and although he did not ask, a question was obvious in his countenance: *Is that...Michael? The archangel? The one who is constantly in the Presence of the Lord in rank and in service? The one the Lord implicitly trusts to conduct warfare on His behalf?*

Majesty smiled and nodded. He could recall the first time he had met Michael eons ago, which could have been yesterday as in the Spirit, time was insignificant, a mirage to be seen through. The wonder of it all! He and Michael had warred together against Satan's angels a few times. He smiled privately remembering the last "engagement." *Hmm, it had to have been about fifty years ago—human time, that is....*

Michael flashed a gargantuan grin and "zipped" to within inches of them as they stepped through the wall, clearly knowing that their arrival was imminent. "Sixty-four years, seven months, twenty-four days ago...human time...to be exact!"

"Ah yes! World War II...the Western Front!"

"That was a war that engaged many..."

"...of us," Majesty finished Michael's thought. "The Lord does not like the loss..."

"…of human life," Michael replied. "And how He hates the encroachment of evil!"

They spoke rapidly back and forth, nodding in agreement. Awe's head flitted back and forth at the verbal repartee as though he were watching a tennis match. *This is Michael! The one they say never loses. Of course, how could he?*

"A most magnificent play of the ages…" Majesty continued, philosophically.

"…constrained by time and space!"

"Human time…"

"…who can fathom it!" Michael responded, grinning heartily. He spread his arms wide in a gesture of magnanimous welcome. They appeared to grow until they almost spanned the width of the room. "Majesty! So good to see you! It's been such a short while…it seems only a day!"

Majesty smiled and embraced his angelic comrade. "The pleasure is all mine! We must war together again!"

"It looks as if we may have our opportunity sooner than we could have ever guessed."

"Yes?" Majesty urged. "How do you mean? In what way?"

"Well, you know that intricately linked to the Maya situation is the Lord's intention to deliver a debilitating blow to the Queen of Heaven principality in that region. It has grown virtually undisturbed for several centuries…" Michael paused, deep in thought. "Our Lord has been intimating that this would come to pass very soon, within the lifetime of this generation. We are to help them get themselves into *alignment*… into *agreement*…with His Will. To that end, He has given us permission to do deep intervention."

"Really?" Majesty stepped back in surprise. "We're not given permission for that very often because of the..."

Michael picked up his thought, "...free will of humans. Yes, and they maintain it, always. They must. However, as you know, a deeper mystery sometimes operates."

Majesty nodded. Awe listened intently. By now, every angel within a 500-foot radius was listening closely.

Michael paused again. Finally, he resumed, "I don't understand all the human mysteries. It is our lot to wonder and to ponder *this* between the Lord and humans...and to perform the desires of the Lord in the spirit and human realms. Perhaps they will be revealed when the human play is up, when we are all fully ensconced in eternity again." He shrugged, his voice fading away.

Majesty urged him, "Please continue."

"Yes. What I do know...what the Lord has told me...is that there is an incredible mystery unfolding here. This mystery deals with the dynamic, yet subtle, interplay between His Will and Pleasure, the intercession of the saints, the innermost cry of the heart, and a human's free will.

"Of course, the plans that He established for Maya from before the beginning of time will succeed—not even a question about it. And...her mother and father have immense favor with the Lord. Their prayers are powerful—they have been crying out and He hears them." Michael smiled as Majesty nodded in agreement. "And when we consider the girl's heart, no matter how misguided...we find, then, that free will is other than what it seems—a part of a deeper, grander mystery hidden in the Lord. Given all of this, the Lord has declared that we are to intervene.

"But that is concerning the girl's life. As I mentioned, the Lord also has great plans for the region. Does He ever do anything for one person where it does not affect many? Due to the fervent and continuous intercession of people from around the world, the Holy Spirit will exert His 'pressure' from within and we will work from without to bring about His Will. Everything is on a timetable…God's timetable. And this area, this little place in India, is key. Once the Queen of Heaven…Kali…falls in this area, it will weaken this principality in other regions around the world.

"Earth time is wrapping up." Michael smiled, his eyes flashing sparks of crystalline, golden light. "It is time for the lovers of God to arise and shine. God is beginning to execute His plan; and Satan and his principality, the Queen of Heaven, are going to help Him. Whether he…*they*…want to or not." Michael rubbed his hands together with relish. "I can't wait!"

The angels continued to talk strategy, battle plans, and field preparation for what seemed to be days as the sky darkened and day turned into night and lightened again, as night moved into day. Countless day to night transitions passed as they talked and strategized and consulted the Lord; however, for them, so often in the Presence of God where a thousand days is as one…time flew by as though it were only a minute on the face of a clock. When they were done, they all shot up out of the roof to their different places and times of assignment.

"What is that? Who is that?" shrieked Eritoi, a lesser, a "demigod." For all intents and purposes, he was at the bottom of the demonic hierarchy, an imp. He had felt "them" the moment they had come near the peninsula. In fact, every demonic being had "felt" them in varying degrees depending upon that being's strength and power. "Why am I *burning so?*" he exclaimed in pain, his ruddy, reddish skin flushing to an even muddier hue. The lumps and warts all over his body seemed to shrivel and expand with his frantic breaths.

"That is *them*," answered Chamunda Kali icily, as she…*it*…sat hunched over herself on the upper meditation deck, chin on her fist. She looked like a grotesque and altogether hideous version of Michelangelo's *David*. Her jet-black skin hung from what appeared to be bones…the problem being that demons did not have bones. How could her skin look shiny and dull simultaneously? Her eyes were gaunt from leanness. She never "fed" enough. She could never "kill" enough to satiate her hunger. At this moment, she…*it*…looked searchingly out toward the far end of the peninsula. She was peering into the "air," the "air" that her prince ruled. She could not see them coming…but she certainly could feel them.

They all could.

Wailing—thin, eerie, high-pitched, imperceptible to human ears— had begun. The demons had commenced lamenting. Only dogs and bats could hear them…barely.

Eritoi continued to pace in front of Chamunda Kali, rubbing his warty, mud-reddish hands worrisomely, "Oooo! Oooo! What is this? What is this? I feel awful. So awful…" Back and forth he paced, limping slightly.

"*Move!*" Chamunda Kali hissed at him, anger furrowing her brow. She slammed the back of her bony hand against the side of his face— or what used to be his face. In the mush of what was supposed to be his face, only one eye was left. He had lost the right one in a battle long ago. An angel of God had pierced his right eye with a sword. As he had plunged the blade into Eritoi's eye, he had spoken the Living Word at him. Instantaneously, Eritoi's eye had shriveled up and fallen out. Soon thereafter, the flesh had begun to ooze over the orifice, almost as if he had some sort of satanic leprosy. In fact, his entire face on the left side had begun to slide down.

Eritoi spun around from the blow and landed face down on the ground, four stories below, having fallen through all the floors. He had forgotten to remind his ethereal body to mind the physical laws and thus his body acted as it was…physically nonexistent and unhampered by physical laws. He crawled himself through the air, hurting, face smarting, back to the meditation roof. He warily presented himself to Chamunda Kali.

"Yoooou stuuuupid, insiiiiipid, speck of…" Chamunda Kali looked at him with pure disgust, her skin flushing an even darker hue of black. "Why was I assigned such a being as you? You are worthless. Stupid. You didn't even remember to make your body mind the physical laws!" She looked away from him in disgust, hatred oozing from her body. "I would kill you if I could. I hate you so much I cannot wait to see you thrown into the lake of fire and brimstone at the end of time."

Eritoi hung his head in shame and anger. "And I cannot wait to see you thrown into that same lake!" he muttered to himself.

"*I heard that!!*" Chamunda Kali shrieked as she flew across the meditation platform grabbing his stringy, oily hair with one of her hand-claws and swiftly pulling out her machete with another. She slowly slid it across his neck so that a mustard-yellow ooze that resembled pus appeared. "I cannot kill you. But I can surely maim you so that you will be in even greater pain."

She leaned over and kissed his sliding, warty cheek. As she pulled away from his face, it smoked from the contact with her vile lips. The contact began to eat away at his skin. "I still have power over you. I am still your leader. Satan put me here. I am in charge. Do not forget where that limp came from." She peered into his eye and smiled flatly. She shoved him away from her in disgust.

Then, she cast a slow, hard look about the meditation roof. Whimpering and cowering from her glare were many other demons, one of whom was Despair. "I know what you're thinking," Chamunda Kali spat at Despair. "You thought you were in charge…. *No!* Never! His Darkness would never let you be in charge of something for too long. You'd give up before you even started." Despair hung his head in acknowledgment of the truth. "You'd ruin the whole thing!"

She walked to the center of the meditation roof and spun around slowly, "*I am the Queen of Heaven!*" The air reverberated with her words. Despair, Fear, Eritoi, and the others cringed.

"Now! If we are done, I have a girl I must attend to!" Chamunda Kali sat back down on the roof of the meditation platform. As she settled into her grotesque position, she whispered pensively to herself.

"I could deal with her if she were by herself. But it's the prayers! They must be shut down! Oh! The damage Christians—real, powerful, praying Christians—create. I thought perhaps God had not noticed this place. I thought maybe He was allowing us to keep this place. But now…this?!" Chamunda whimpered to herself. "What am I to do? What is going to happen if they continue praying?

"Their prayers draw *everything* awful! The Lord's angels…the Holy Spirit…" She…it…was whining. It could not help it. "Heaven help us, if their prayers stir the Lord to come…to come…" It gulped in raw fear, "…Himself!"

"What is going on here? The angels are coming…we can feel them…we can feel the parents' prayers…" Chamunda was muttering nonsensically to itself, "…we can feel Him, the Holy Spirit. Oh! There is nothing, absolutely nothing, that that girl's parents cannot do, if they know and believe in the power of the Holy Spirit who is with them…in them….

"I hate that the angels are coming." Her blue-black brow furrowed into deep funnels of worry. "Yes, we have squatters' rights on this place. We have held a total reign over this peninsula since…but even one stupid idiot can mess everything up if they or, in this case, *she* has someone praying for them. Ahh!" Chamunda shrieked aloud an otherworldly screech that startled the dogs again.

"The power of God! Even now, I can hear their prayers in the wind. I can feel their prayers in the atmosphere. Their prayers are proceeding from them and stirring up the atmosphere. Their prayers ride upon the air and cause us to burn! And their prayers cause the angels to come and…*we burn!* And then…and then…His Spirit comes and…*we burn!*" she hissed, then whimpered.

"This is going to be absolutely dreadful! I cannot leave because Satan has given me this place as an assignment. I cannot stay because of the intensity of the burn! This is horrid. And all these underlings under me…they will go crazy, panic, be what they truly are…fearful and despairing and worried. How will I ever control them?

"Well, at least I have Death and Suicide. They, even if they are afraid and suffer and are in pain, will stand strong." Chamunda mumbled to herself, "And that Despair! What was Satan thinking…to put him in charge? If even for a little while…I am glad Despair has been given to me! I can control that simpering wimp! Oh! We can do it! Death and I! We will control the others! We must…"

On and on Chamunda Kali muttered to herself, deep in thought, lost in worry. The other demons shifted around her, uncomfortable, in pain, from the Presence that rolled in with the prayers, that rolled in with the angels.

"Oh yes! Why didn't I think of that earlier?" Chamunda Kali clapped her hands together in delight at having found a solution after many human hours of worrying. "We'll just have to kill them. The girl or her parents. The girl *and* her parents. Yes, I know the Lord has said not to kill them, but…it's not my fault if…one of them messes up even a little—that will be all we need, a loophole, a *gap,* in their *protection.* We'll take advantage of a sin and kill them. Ahhhh! Killing them, even one of them, will solve all our problems." Chamunda Kali smiled to herself. "And that stupid girl! She's so foolish and dumb, it will be easy to kill her! Ha! We can even get her to kill herself—*that* will be even easier. Silly girl!

"Underlings! Come here!" Chamunda jumped up energetically, startling the others. "I have a plan!" She looked around, "Where's Death and Suicide? Go call them!"

CHAPTER THIRTEEN

POT WASHERS, UNITE

Maya

Alleppey, India

I sat on the balcony of the temple, my face pressed against the cool iron bars, watching Cha Ma give darshan. The crowd was scant, only a few hundred people. Last night had seen several thousand people as it had been a Kali Leela night. But now, the day after, the crowd had cleared out. Most would not be back until the next one.

Ahhh! Kali Leela nights…how I loved them! Long nights that poured madly, fervently, into morning. But a heavy price was to be paid. For all of us ashramites, the next day was extremely difficult as we suffered from what I termed a Kali Leela Hangover. We all moved slowly and spoke very little. We would recuperate as the day wore on. Wonderfully excruciating Kali Leela Hangover!

That was my state as I sat on the balcony, still nursing the effects of my night of spiritual inebriation. The cool bars felt wonderful against my hot face and burning, tired eyes. I closed my eyes. *Lovely rest.*

"Maya!" I heard a voice bark at me from the Foreigners' Office. I would know that voice anywhere. Immediately, I felt my emotions swing insanely and land, decidedly, in resentment. *Why doesn't he ever suffer from a Kali Leela Hangover? He spends the whole night either helping her or playing and singing to her and the next day, he's as energetic as ever. How come he's immune?*

It did seem the case. He stayed awake and was busy with her the entire time. While she made her transformation, invariably, he served her—he was by far her favorite. And then during the long evening, he could be found either passing people to her or sitting with the musicians, playing his kimini and singing to her. And yet, the next day....

"Maya!" Narayana's voice was even more demanding this time. "Come here!"

I struggled with whether to just keep watching Cha Ma and act like I did not hear him…but before I knew it my body had taken control and I found myself standing in the doorway.

"Yes?"

"Do you know how to cook?" Narayana asked me with his usual air of condescension. He did not bother to look up.

"Oh yes!" I answered as I nodded my head enthusiastically. "I started cooking when I was…"

"Good," he said without even listening, waving his left hand lazily at me in a dismissive way. He checked off a couple of places on a form he was filling out and put it in the desk drawer. "You can report to kitchen duty tonight after dinner. Be there at eight. You'll be washing dishes."

"*After* dinner? I thought you asked me if I knew how to cook," I questioned him in confusion.

"Oh yes…I did," he replied absentmindedly, still not bothering to look up at me. *How I hate him!*

"Well, why did you ask me if I knew how to cook if you weren't going to assign me to cooking?" I asked, feeling strains of anger rising up within me.

"I don't know." He shrugged, his attention focused on the papers. "We need people to wash dishes." With that, he began to jot down some things into an officious-looking notebook that was sitting in front of him and ceased having another word to say to me.

"But I thought I'd get to cook in the kitchen."

No response. Narayana was done talking to me. I turned on my heel feeling dejected and hurt. I walked back to my spot on the balcony and sat down, desperately swallowing back the tears that threatened. I did not see Narayana look up and watch me after I turned away. I did not see the yearning in his eyes, the desire and passion. He looked like a man who was being desperately torn between two worlds. However I did not turn around, so I did not see how he really felt about me. I saw only the rejection.

"Namah shivaya!" A tall, smiling, white guy greeted me enthusiastically when I walked around to the back of the kitchen that night. He was wearing a dirty, white dhoti in the casual manner that was characteristic of so many men—the bottom was tied loosely around his hips so that the dhoti stopped at the knees—I suppose to allow for a little more ventilation.

"Namah shivaya," I responded not so enthusiastically.

"My name's David. What's yours?"

"Maya."

"So, you're here to wash pots, huh?" he asked. I nodded, barely. "Good! Here, let me give you a little tour of the kitchen and what we do. Then we'll get you all set up." He headed off in the direction of the building.

As I followed him, I looked around. He stopped by a man and a woman, who were washing two *huge,* fire-blackened pots. The pots were easily five feet in diameter and three feet deep. The man and woman were each standing inside of one of the pots, scrubbing away, chappels and all. The woman's skirt was hiked up and the man's thin, white trousers were sloppily cuffed up to the knees. There was something disturbing about seeing a man and a woman with hairy legs and chappels standing inside vast pots—pots that they were supposed to be cleaning. It appeared as though they were scrubbing the inside of the pots with some type of branch or brush or shrub. Nothing was "sudsing" up. *Strange.*

I looked up and saw that we were standing beneath an awning that did not seem to serve any real purpose. It was covered in patchy thatching that looked like it was going to need to be redone...very soon.

"This is where we wash the rice pots." David waved his hand non-chalantly about him, indicating the area.

He continued on, skirting around two more dirty rice pots, and stepped through the doorway of the kitchen. "This is the kitchen." I followed him, looking around. Yes, I had been at the ashram for almost two months, but I had yet to make it into the kitchen. I had taken Radha's advice and steered clear. It was absolutely astounding in its dirtiness (if that was a strong enough word!), dankness, dinginess, darkness, and disorder. We had stepped through the "back" door of the kitchen. On our right was a big rust-encrusted water heater. On our left was a stone oven that was used for frying. It was black from soot and use. Its surface had three holes with the charred remains of branches and twigs sticking out. A single, dim lightbulb hung from the ceiling. There was only one window near the ceiling, which was about one foot by seven inches. It was covered with dirt and let in no light. The floor, wet and sooty, was made of bumpy, lumpy concrete.

"This room is the fry kitchen." He stopped in front of the rusty boiler. "Most of the hot water for the kitchen is made here. This is also where the kitchen ammas fry spices and make small portions. When Cha Ma wants something special, they fry it here."

"What's a kitchen amma?" I queried.

"The older women who work in the kitchen." He stepped through a door to our right that was just beyond the rusty boiler. "C'mon…" He beckoned me to follow him.

"Here is the brahmacharini kitchen." He flicked a switch on the wall. A dim ceiling light flickered on, emitting even less light than the first dull lightbulb in the fry kitchen. "This is where the brahmacharinis eat." It was a big, empty room. Several low, squat stools that had oval metal pieces with jagged edges attached to one side sat in a corner. (Later, I would learn that the stools were used to scrape out the meat from the inside of a coconut—a kind of "de-coconut-ter.") He turned and headed back into the fry kitchen. He stepped through the door on the right. It was a straight shot from the back door to this door.

"And this is the main part of the kitchen. Wild, isn't it?" he asked, certain I would say yes. And for good reason. I had never in my life seen a kitchen like this! Nor could I have imagined one like it. This room was dingy too, but at least it had two ceiling bulbs, instead of one. There was a place for one more lightbulb as wires were sticking out of the ceiling, unused. The floor was like the rest of the kitchen, concrete, lumpy, bumpy, and wet—and dirty. No, "dirty" was an inaccurate description. Filthy was much better. Yes, rank and filthy.

Closest to us, along the left-hand wall was a row of six shiny stainless steel boilers. They ranged from largest, three feet in diameter and three feet deep, to smallest, one foot in diameter and two feet deep. They were used for steaming and boiling. A horizontal pipe at the top was the water source that linked all of them together.

Two Western women were busily scrubbing the insides of two of the boiler pots, alternating between pouring water into the pots from the pipe, scrubbing, and then dumping the water out. They dumped the water out into a shallow gully that ran along the back of the kitchen—basically, an open drain—and out a hole in the wall. All waste water from the kitchen flowed to and through this drain, which, eventually I figured out, drained its way to the backwaters. They looked up when we walked into the room.

"Hey, Anjali and Purna, this is Maya. She's here on pot-washing duty."

"Namah shivaya, Maya!"

"Namah shivaya!"

They stopped scrubbing and smiled at me. "So, you're brave enough to take on the pots, huh?" said one of the women. She had on a dingy red skirt and white top that was covered in soot and ashes. She had a pleasant face. "My name's Anjali."

"And I'm Purna," said the other woman. She was wearing punjabi pants and top. "Have fun! I hope we don't lose you!"

"C'mon! Let me show you where you'll be working tonight." He led me farther into the main kitchen. On the left-hand side, sitting randomly in the middle of the floor, was a bunch of square, stainless steel, contraption-like baker's ovens. Intermingled with these ovens were huge mixing bowls made of stone that looked large enough to hold several gallons of liquid. Each bowl had a stone pestle. These mortars and pestles were sitting atop machines that made them go around and around. It all looked archaic, medieval, and just plain dirty.

"What are these?" I asked, curiosity winning out. I placed my hand gingerly on top of one of the stainless steel ovens.

"Oh, those…?" He looked. "Iddly makers, I think."

"Iddly makers? What's an iddly?"

"An iddly is like a…" He screwed up his face thinking. "Well, we don't have anything like iddlys in the West. They're small, round," he formed a small circle with the thumbs and index fingers of both his hands, "…and disc-shaped. They're a little mushy and a little sour tasting. I think it's made out of fermented rice."

"Yuck!" I wrinkled my nose at the idea.

"Actually they're really, really good. Especially with curd and honey."

"Curd?"

"Yogurt. But it's nothing like what we have in the West. It's real curd. The kitchen ammas make it."

"Really? How?"

"I've been told that they put a special kind of bacteria into a pail of milk and overnight the milk turns into curd."

"Bacteria, huh?"

"Yes, but that's something to ask the kitchen ammas." He kept walking. "Now this here is…" He gestured to a large, flat, square surface. It looked to be eight feet by eight feet. Waist-high. Its top was blackened by years of cooking. Under the top was a six-inch space. "…a chapati stove."

"Chapati stove?" I asked, feeling silly. All I seemed to do was repeat him.

"Oh yes! Chapatis! Have you ever had one?"

I shook my head. "No, I don't think so. I don't recall the word. What is a chapati?"

He stopped by the chapati stove. "Be careful of the top because it's often hot from where the brahmacharinis cook chapatis."

"*What's* a chapati?" I was starting to get aggravated by his little digressions.

"Oh yeah! Chapatis are like fried flat bread. They're really good! I remember the first time I had a chapati—I was in America, not India…" He chuckled to himself as he reminisced. "It was summertime, in California…"

I shot him a castigating look.

"Oh, chapatis!" he said with a grin. "Yeah, so what they do is mix up some dough. I don't know what's in it—wheat, I think. They roll it into little balls and pound the balls flat. Then they cook it on top of this stove."

"I'll have to try a chapati," I said. They sounded tasty.

"This is where…" He took a few more steps and stepped over a six-inch high "wall" that seemed to be a border or boundary for a particular area. "…we wash everything else…all the other pots and the smaller things like plates and cups and, every once in a while, silverware—what little there is."

Here the floor was even dirtier. It was littered with grains of rice, pieces of vegetables, and chunks of curry. Nestled in the corner between the left-hand wall and the far wall was a rickety, wooden shelf upon which sat two pots full of dirty water.

In this area, three Westerners were working—two women and a man. A woman was standing in front of each of the two pots, scrubbing away; although there were no suds. *What do they use for soap?* They were washing small round plates, tins, cups, and silverware—all of which were made out of stainless steel—and dropping them into a large pot, which sat behind them. As the pot was full of water, I figured it was for rinsing.

"As I said, we wash pots here, except for the big rice pots you saw outside and the steamers." He gestured to three "towers" of dirty pots that had been stacked one on top of the other. Two of the stacks reached his chest. The shortest came to his hips. *That has to be at least thirty pots! What an awful job!*

The pots ranged in size and, I figured, in use. The serving pots ranged from two to three feet in diameter and a foot or two in depth, and they were not too dirty. The frying "pans" were various sizes—ranging from two feet in diameter and six inches in depth to little woks that were about a foot in diameter and a few inches in depth. Still others were larger and rounder. They looked like cauldrons in varying sizes. *These pots will take hours to wash!* The outsides of the fry pans and cauldrons were crusted black from the cooking fires and their insides had food and spices seared into them. The man was squatting on the floor furiously scrubbing away at the inside of a large, bottom-blackened cauldron.

"We'll put you with this crew, okay?"

I nodded my head reluctantly.

"Hey, guys! Show Maya what to do, okay?" David squeezed my shoulder, winked at me and walked off back into the bowels of the kitchen.

"Namah shivaya," the guy muttered who was battling the cauldron. He did not say anything else to me. Evidently, he was consumed with his task. I looked at the women. I recognized one—Sandi! I was so happy to see her.

"Namah shivaya!" Sandi sang. She was wearing a not-so-white-anymore sari that had huge spots of black soot on it. "So, you've come to join us?" she queried with a grin.

"Yes."

"Cool!" she responded gaily.

"Namah shivaya! I'm Victoria," said the other woman. She was short, about 5′2″, with dark brown, mid-shoulder length hair that was pulled back out of her face. She was wearing a brick-red, calf-length skirt made out of a heavy, canvas-like material. For a top, she was wearing a simple, light blue shirt that was dirty and covered with soot.

Both of them were busily scrubbing even while turning around and talking to me. "This is great!" exclaimed Sandi. "Okay! Let's see…we've got to show you the ropes. Hmm, well, first things first…we need to get you set up with some ash." Sandi pointed to a round plate that was sitting on the floor. It had a heap of wet, lumpy ashes in it.

"Ash?" I asked. "What about soap?"

"Oh sure! We use soap," Sandi responded as she scrubbed a large, round plate, "but only a pinch. Mostly, though, we use ash from the fires. We take a bit using a coconut husk."

"Wait a minute! Wait a minute! Coconut husk?"

"Oh yeah! Coconut husks make extremely good 'brillo pads.'"

"Brillo pads?" I asked incredulously. *They use ash and coconut husks to clean dishes and pots with not a single thought about how prehistoric it is, not to mention how unsanitary!*

Sandi handed me a piece of coconut husk. "C'mon," she said, as she grabbed the ash plate from off the floor. "I'm going to get some ash. You can come with me."

"Okay," I said, following her, curious as to where and how they got this ash. I followed Sandi back through the dank, dirty kitchen. We stepped out to where I had seen the man and woman washing the rice pots. They were still there; David had joined them. All three were standing inside of a pot—chappels, hairy legs, and all. *Yuck!*

"Hey guys! I need some ash," Sandi announced. "Anyone know which fire pit is the coolest? I don't want to get burned."

"Sure," David said with an almost imperceptible nod of his head in the direction of a certain pit. "I think the middle pit was either unused today or it burned out a long time ago."

Sandi gingerly stepped her way over to the middle pit and scooped up some of the ash with the steel, round plate. "When you get ash, try to make sure that it's as fine as possible. See? Look!" she commanded as she extended the plate so that I could see. I looked but I did not know what I was looking for. "This has big chunks, which isn't so good for scrubbing pots. Finer ash is better. Let's look a little harder for some good ash." We dug around in the ash pit for some time looking for "good" ash until Sandi was satisfied. "Okay! Let's go back; time's a-ticking!"

When Sandi and I got back to our "station," Victoria and the guy were still there, scrubbing. Victoria handed me a wedge of strawy, coconut husk. "Here you go! This is a good piece." I took it. "Okay, first you dip the husk into the water in order to soften it. Then you scoop up a little bit of the ash with your husk and you start scrubbing."

"Okay." I did what I was told and commenced scrubbing.

It was a different sort of work—menial, endless, fun. We chatted and played while we worked, scrubbing away the mountains of pots, pans, plates, containers, cups, and silverware. It took us well over two hours.

The final step was "cleaning" the floor of the entire kitchen (with the exception of the fry kitchen floor—which was never cleaned the entire time I lived in the ashram). When asked about it, Sandi informed me that the floor got half a packet of soap (approximately a quarter of a cup) two days out of the week—Tuesdays and Saturdays. The other days we dumped the tubs of dishwater onto the floor. That is what we did this time. Then, Sandi took a contraption she called a squee-gee (which was like an oversized windshield wiper—except that the rubber edge was held against the ground) and pushed all the water on the floor into the open drain.

By the time Sandi, Victoria, and I were done (the guy had disappeared at some point) the crew that had been washing the huge rice pots and the steamers was gone. We were the only ones left. We headed out by way of the Western canteen. It was dark, but we did not need any light—the full moon made everything bright.

CHAPTER FOURTEEN

"YOU HAVE TO BE CAREFUL WHEN IT COMES TO KALI!"

"I want one!" I said, looking yearningly at the little doll in a white dress. I was sitting in Victoria's room on the fourth floor. Ever since I had started pot-washing duty, I had been hanging out with Victoria and Sandi. Our common duty made for an immediate bond.

We hung out often, usually in Victoria's room, as it was on the top floor. I liked to visit the top floor rooms because of their privacy and their relative coolness. The light breeze from the ocean, which did not reach the lower floors, blew in through the windows. The fan, twirling lazily above, helped reduce the temperature.

However, for all the privacy and coolness of a private room, I preferred the ladies dorm. Its location above Cha Ma's temple was ideal—anything and everything that happened—we, in the dorm, knew about it. Also, with the location we were closer to Kali's fire. We sat right above the epicenter of immense spiritual power. When I wanted a break from the fire and the lack of privacy, I headed to other people's rooms.

"You like my Cha Ma doll?" Sandi asked, as she cuddled it close.

"Yes! Let me see it!" I stretched out my hands. Victoria leaned over and looked at the doll. Her nose wrinkled up but she did not say anything. So often, she did not say anything; although, sometimes I could read her face. This was one of those times—she definitely did not like the doll.

Sandi passed the doll to me. "They make them in a little room on this floor. If you want to check them out, I can take you there."

"Okay, I'd like to see them. I've seen them around—a lot of the Western women have them." I turned the doll over in my hands. It was a little, ten-inch long, chubby, brown-skinned doll. It was wearing a white sari and had its hair pulled back in a bun. It wore little, brown, pocked rudraksha beads about its wrists and neck—just like Cha Ma.

"It's a great way to keep a part of Cha Ma with you at all times," Sandi said, taking the doll back and nuzzling it against her face. "Come on! I'll take you to the doll shop and then you can decide whether or not you want to buy one." She stood to go. "Victoria, you coming?"

Victoria shook her head no. "You guys go and have fun," she urged.

"Okay! Namah shivaya!" I called as we stepped out of the room.

"See ya!" Victoria called back.

I followed Sandi, watching as she nuzzled and cuddled her little doll. *It really does look like Cha Ma.* Before we reached the narrow staircase that led to the meditation roof, she stopped. A door that I had never noticed before was open. Inside were two Western women sewing away.

"Namah shivaya!" Sandi sang hello. "I've brought another customer. Her name's Maya. She wants to see your Cha Ma dolls."

"Namah shivaya!" I peeked into the "shop" (actually, it was a little closet only big enough to fit two average-sized Western women). On the shelves were a few dolls. I saw several Cha Mas and one other. It looked like a soft, cute version of Kali—made of black cloth with a red sari.

"Namah shivaya," said one woman. "My name is Shivani." She stood and took one of the dolls off the shelf. She held it out to me. "Here's one of the Cha Ma dolls." The Kali doll remained on the shelf. I looked at the Cha Ma doll, but now for some reason, I did not want it. The Kali doll commanded my attention.

"Can I see that one?" I asked, pointing at it.

"Oh! That's our Kali doll…" She waved her hand toward it, but did not move to get it for me.

"Is it for sale?" I asked, growing increasingly desirous of it.

"Yes…" she said hesitatingly, "but, we don't make many Kali dolls. This is only our second one." She paused, weighing perhaps, what she was about to say. "You have to be careful when it comes to Kali…a Kali doll, a Kali mantra, Kali as your favorite deity—your ishta-deity. Kali is very destructive. If you take her for your ishta-deity, she will see to it that you are enlightened no matter the cost, even if it means death. So be careful about the Kali doll. I can't let it go to just *anyone*." She paused, again, looking me up and down. Perhaps to see what I was made of.

"I want it. I want the Kali doll!" I said, not giving it much speculation. I always did like to live life on the edge.

"It costs one hundred and sixty-five rupees."

"Okay, let me run downstairs to get my money and I'll be back for it. Hold onto it, okay?"

"Look," she said as she took the doll down from the shelf, "you can take her with you. Just make sure to bring the money back, okay?"

"Oh, you don't have to worry about that!" I could not imagine taking a Kali doll and not paying for it. *Talk about bad karma!* I took the doll and looked at the other woman sitting there who had yet to say anything. She simply sat there sewing on another Cha Ma doll—looking at us from time to time.

"Namah shivaya," Shivani said.

"Namah shivaya!" Sandi and I responded. We headed downstairs to the women's dorm to get my money.

"Now you have a doll to hold too!" Sandi said, snuzzling her Cha Ma doll.

I nodded, not holding my doll anywhere near as close to me as she did hers. I had bought her so quickly I had not taken the time to examine her. I stared at her as we walked. She definitely looked like Kali. Her skin was made of jet-black cloth. She had on a blood-red sari with gold, embroidered edging, which reminded me of my first Kali Leela. About her neck was a plastic mala of skulls. Later when I counted, I found there were 108 skulls—the women had been very detailed in making her. She wore lots of gold-plated jewelry—necklaces, bracelets, and waistchains. Her blood-red tongue stuck out of her mouth. Her black hair was long and rope-like, almost like dreadlocks. The only thing about her that was similar to the Cha Ma doll was that she was chubby and soft; but for some reason, Kali was just not as cuddly as Cha Ma.

I thought to myself as I peered at her—*Are you my ishta-deity? Are you my god?* Right then, I purposed to get a Kali mantra from Cha Ma the first chance I could. *I'm going to get a Kali mantra. She is my god—the one who will get me to enlightenment...come what may! I don't care what happens to me. Let me die, let my world come crashing down, I don't care as long as I reach enlightenment.*

"Hello! My name is Jnani!" A dark-skinned woman who looked to be African approached me. Her accent was clearly British in its crispness and tone.

"Hi! I'm Maya!" Even in our introductions, I was aware of the laziness of my own American tongue in comparison to the lilting staccato of her British English.

"You're an American?" she said in a manner that hung between a question and a statement.

I nodded. "What about you? England?"

"Yes, London. How in the world did you ever arrive at Mata's?" she asked me as she sat upon my bunk, her British tongue drawing out "Mata's" so that it sounded like *maah-taahsss*.

"Oh! It's a long story. Maybe I will tell you..."

"It is so good to see you. I haven't seen another black person ever since I set foot here in India." She leaned forward and whispered, "Black meaning of African descent, of course."

I smiled and nodded. "How did you come to Cha Ma?"

"Oh! I had been traveling around India for a couple weeks when I came to Kerala. I heard about Cha Ma and decided to come visit. I've been here for many weeks now...months..." Her voice trailed off. I could tell she was trying to figure out just how long she had been at the ashram. However, it seemed that as I had, she too had lost touch with time. It seemed to happen to almost everyone who lived here. As the days flowed one into another and we lived the ashram life, time began to fuzz and have no meaning.

"Yes, I had heard about you. It's a wonder I hadn't met you until now." *That's curious. Where has she been hiding herself?* My mind went back to the conversation I had had with Radha when I first arrived. It seemed so long ago. *Radha did say that she's not always here.*

"I know, it's probably because I come and go. I use Cha Ma's as a base to travel all over southern India."

"Oh," was all I said.

"I am leaving soon though. Back to England."

Jnani and I got along well enough. We related well with the situation of being two of the few—*only?*—people of African descent in southern India. We were objects to be stared at and even touched. Because her hair was relaxed she did not get the same stares, comments, and surreptitious touches that I did, as I wore my hair in twisties.

One hot afternoon as we were hanging out in the dorm, she asked, "Why don't you relax your hair? It would be so much easier…"

"Oh no! I like wearing my hair natural. And then, the way they ration the water supply…I would hate to be in the middle of applying a relaxer and get the water shut off."

She laughed, "Oh! That would never happen!"

I merely smiled. *No thanks!*

While we were talking, Radha walked into the women's dorm. "Namah shivaya!"

"Namah shivaya," we echoed.

"What are you doing?" she asked. She noticed my Kali doll sitting on my bunk. "Whose Kali doll?"

"Mine. I got it a few days ago." I leaned over to pick up the doll.

"Well, I'll see you later, Maya," Jnani said, as she headed out the door.

"Okay, see you!" I hugged the doll to myself, none too tightly. Something about her kept me from squeezing too tightly or drawing her in too closely. "You want to hold her?" I held out my doll to Radha.

She shook her head. "No. Hey, do you know what you've gotten yourself into?" Her voice sounded worried, which worried me. *What could be so wrong?*

"What do you mean? What I've gotten myself into?" I put the doll back into her place on the bunk.

"To have a Kali doll...to have a Kali mantra." She halted as if she had just thought of something. "You haven't gotten a Kali mantra, have you?" She sounded alarmed.

"Not yet, but...I want one."

"Well, I'm going to warn you and then you can decide how far you want to go with Kali." She sat down on my bunk with me. "Just beware and know what you're getting yourself into. All I know, what I understand, is that it's dangerous to call on Kali, to have her mantra, to have a doll or murti of her, to do anything as a devotee of her because she is so ruthless about getting people to enlightenment.

"Sure, people around the ashram say that if you want to attain enlightenment quickly...really, really quickly...you need to plug into Kali as she will get you there fast...that what would normally take many lifetimes to burn off, with Kali, will go in one. However, the damage done to the person is another story altogether.

"I know of someone…you know her, too. She lives here in the ashram—Shasta." My thoughts shot to Shasta, a woman who could barely move her legs. "She got a Kali mantra and soon thereafter fell down. Now, she's partially paralyzed."

"I didn't know that's what happened to her."

Radha nodded gravely and continued, "And I know of a guy who chose Kali as his ishta-deity and then went crazy. They had to ship him back to the U.S." She leaned close, earnestly entreating me, "Oh, Maya! Be careful choosing a Kali mantra and in choosing Kali as your ishta-deity. You think you want enlightenment at *all* costs and as quickly as possible, but you don't know the price. Not really. Please be careful!" Her warning was making me nervous. "I don't want to see anything bad happen to you…"

"Come on!" I cut her off, changing the subject. "Let's go see how darshan's going." I needed to get away. I respected her opinion a lot. I knew, deep inside, that she told the truth. I just did not want to hear it.

She sighed, "Okay," giving me one last meaningful look.

We headed out the door that opened onto the temple.

Marie

United States

When am I going to fall asleep? Marie asked herself, in a strange state of half awake/half asleep. Her nights were growing worse. No rest. No respite. Worries, fears, and doubts slammed into her from without and swirled around in her mind. Dark shadows on the wall shifted and grew deeper. When she looked, it would be nothing, or so it seemed. One thought pounded through her head, night after night—*Maya's going to die!*

To combat it she prayed. And she prayed. And she prayed. Nothing happened except that finally she would drift off into a disturbed sleep, only to jolt awake to more shadows inching closer to her.

This night she felt as though something were in the house— something *not human.* Wisps of it touched her heart with fear. *I've got to get up!* She felt an urge, an unction, deep down inside that told her: *Get up! Go pray throughout the house!* Fear within her fought against the unction.

Slowly, she shifted her body to a sitting position on the side of the bed. She sat for a long time, listening to the measured breathing of Paul. *He seems so "unbothered" by all of this. But I know he is. He must be! Maya is his girl, his princess. I can tell he's hurting by how much he's withdrawing from me.* Her rapidly deteriorating relationship with her husband had turned into one of the major sources of angst in her life. He had grown so distant, so untalkative, so different. He no longer felt like her husband, just someone she knew from long ago, who needed a place to stay and this was the place.

She stood, hesitating, unwilling, afraid. She could feel the presence growing—not good. It made her cold, as if ice water were pouring through her veins, and fearful. Slowly she walked through the bedroom and down the hall, guided by the knowledge that comes with living in the same house for many years. The night lights emitted a soft glow that did not help her vision much because they cast long shadows on the walls. She tried to pray, but could not. The ice-cold water in her veins had frozen her mouth shut. No words even came to mind.

She shuffled to the threshold of the living room and stopped. Her heart froze. A white coffin. In the middle of the living room. She could see the profile of her daughter from where she stood.

Pray!

She could not. Her mouth was frozen shut. Nor could she move. She was mesmerized by the vision. Terrorized. *Maya! Dead? Dead!*

Pray! Echoed through her mind again. She felt deep in her being that she needed to...*had to*...pray; but it was as if her entire body, including her lungs, her voice box, her mouth were bound by strong, unyielding bands of *no!*

Pray!

She closed her eyes against the horrible sight.

Pray!

"Greater...is He..." she hushed out a tremulous whisper, "that is in me than he that is in the world. Satan is a liar...and the father of...all lies." She spoke hesitatingly, fearfully. But, spoke she did. "This is a...lie and I rebuke it. My Father...my God...is the Father...of Lights. With Him there is no variation or shadow of turning." She began to gather momentum. "Every lie of the enemy I curse, just as Jesus cursed the fig tree and by the Word of His mouth caused it to die. Just like Jesus, I curse this that I see and I know it is dead. My daughter is alive. My daughter will live through this. We will be victorious. I speak the name of Jesus over my daughter...Jesus, Jesus..." She continued to pray in this way. She kept her eyes clenched closed. Finally after some time, she opened her eyes. The living room was empty. The terrifying vision was gone. She let out a sigh of relief, noticing that the awful feeling in the house was gone, too.

"Thank You, God!" she said, three of the most heartfelt words she had ever spoken.

CHAPTER FIFTEEN

RAINING ON A PARADE

Maya

Kollam, India

"**W**ELL, what do you think, Maya?"

"What do you mean what do I think?" I asked Devi. I imagined that I looked as flushed and hot as she did. I *felt* hot and flushed, horribly so. And I was feeling irritable, too. We were on our way to Kollam. It was mid-morning and already it was hot and dusty. We had just finished riding one of the little boats over the backwaters and had walked through the village to the bus depot. It was crowded. Dusty. Hot. That sultry India smell was in the air.

I could hear the babble of the people around me. I could not understand them. I did not always want to. Today was one of those days. Men started pressing closer and closer around us, "Taxi! Taxi!" *Please, oh please, let it be a taxi. Or even a rickshaw.*

Devi shook her head, firmly. "No! No! Bus! Bus!"

Aw, no! Not the bus! Ugh! I have yet to ride on one but—my eyes scanned the buses in the parking lot—*I'm not ready to begin the bus-adventure.* I did not want to seem pampered or unwilling to rough it, but I did not want to get on a bus without giving a little resistance. "Bus? Are you sure? If not a taxi…maybe a rickshaw?"

"A rickshaw costs too much to go to Kollam. The bus is so much cheaper."

I took a deep breath and squared my shoulders. *I will see this through!* I sighed within. *Not that I have a choice now!* "Okay! Let's do this!" I set my jaw and followed behind her down the street, all the while hating the thought of the bus. I kept my eyes peeled because little cars and rickshaws were speeding by. I marveled once again on one of the oddities of India—drivers did not mind hitting people as long as they did not hit the cows. I had heard tales of plenty of casualties and fatalities caused by drivers hitting pedestrians, but never any reports of anyone striking a cow, let alone killing it.

The road was dusty; we were dusty; the people were dusty; the air was dusty! Reddish dust had given the air a molten cast. I felt as if I could not breathe…the dust, the heat, the humidity, the cars, rickshaws, bicycles, buses, and all the people and animals! I felt inundated!

Vrooom! I lunged forward in the direction we were walking in order to avoid being struck by a colorfully painted truck with a fringe hanging down on the inside of its windshield.

Why do they decorate their buses and trucks? The drivers painted them all kinds of bright, garish colors. All the ones I had seen had had a name scrawled across the top of the windshield—

names like "Manohari," "Durga," "Lakshmi." The vehicles were completely broken-down and beat-up looking, except for the screaming colors and vibrant pictures painted on the outside and the lavish decorations within. Inevitably, an altar was erected on the front dashboard—a tribute to the driver's ishta-deity. The dashboard-altars sported loud, colorful cloths, a few murtis, and a couple of pictures of the ishta-deity or guru, all of which, I figured, had to be glued down. Fringe, either cloth or beaded, framed the windshield. To complete the effect, the driver made certain to have music blaring—kimini *ka-ching-chinging* away, tablas *thom-thom-ming*, the voices weaving tunefully in and out of each other. Always, the music was contemporary and peculiarly Indian—an odd mixture of Hindu songs and chants melodically woven over a strong dance beat.

"Two tickets to Kollam," Devi said as she stopped short at the small, dusty ticket window. The ticket lady, who was doing nothing, continued doing nothing. Devi asked, slight exasperation rising in her voice, "How much, please?"

I did not hear the ticket lady's answer; I was too busy observing everything around me. And too busy trying pump myself up for the ride. *I can do this! It'll be fun! Everybody does it!*

"Excuse me," I heard Devi say, "but you didn't give me my change back."

"I'm sorry, Miss," the lady answered monotonously. She reached into her cash register, counted out six rupees and shoved them across the counter. She informed us with stilted English, "You hurry. Your bus is soon to leave. Number 17. You will find it."

"Thank you," Devi said, pocketing the money. She turned to me, "Let's go!" She grabbed my arm and pulled me toward the dusty, hazy bus parking lot. Buses were everywhere.

Number 17…you will find it, echoed through my head. *How in the world are we supposed to find it in all of this chaos?*

Everything was everywhere. Randomly the buses sat, engines idling. People milled about. Some were squatting anywhere they chose. Others were standing and talking in the middle of the parking lot. Vendors strolled through, pushing their carts. Cows and goats walked about freely. Luggage sat haphazardly in the parking lot. The dust. The haze. The noxious blue fumes from the buses. Visibility was minimal.

"Okay, Cha Ma, help us to find our bus quickly," Devi whispered. She began to walk in a diagonal across the parking lot, veering to the right, weaving in and out of the bus/human/animal/luggage obstacle course. I followed behind her. No luck. She headed in the other direction, exclaiming under her breath, "Cha Ma! We need to find our bus!" No luck. We zigzagged across the parking lot several times. I grew increasingly more irritable. We dodged a couple of buses as they were pulling out. Finally, I saw our bus in the midst of all the others.

"Thank You, Cha Ma," Devi said aloud. *She could have been a little faster with helping us,* I thought to myself but would not have admitted it to anyone.

We stopped a few feet away from the bus, dumbfounded. *Could it be any more packed?* People were hanging out of the bus, mainly men. Several bodies stuck precariously from the front and back doors, forced open because of the sheer density of the bodies. From every single window, heads, arms, and even torsos poked out. The bus looked as if it were spewing forth people.

"Okay," Devi sighed, "let's do this." She strode toward the front door of the bus. With her left hand, she grabbed the rail and hoisted herself in, allowing the weight of her body to force people out of the way. It was to her advantage that she was larger than most of the people—most Westerners were. I scrambled on behind her, displacing people as I went too. We positioned ourselves toward the front of the dangerously crowded bus to the audible dismay of those already there. The air was thick, hot, and wet. It felt like a dense, smelly blanket around us. All avenues of ventilation were blocked by human bodies. Two men who were sitting smiled at us and stood, gesturing to their seat, heads bobbling.

"Namah shivaya!" Devi and I exclaimed our thanks in unison as we hastily sat. *Wow! Talk about chivalry!*

Within a few minutes, the driver forced his way into the bus, pushed a young man out of his chair—*Was he expecting to drive?*—and revved up the engine. Immediately a radio blared. A well-known duo, a man and a woman, began singing a Lord Ram bhajan. She sang in a high, undulating voice, the trademark of female Indian singing, as he wove a mellow undertone beneath her. Their voices complemented each other…perhaps…it was hard to tell with the decibel level so high. Our singers were not singing; rather they were *belting* out an ode to Lord Ram. Competing with them was the kimini "ka-ching, ka-chinging" fluidly on top of the "doom-doom" sound of the tablas. The majority of the people on the bus decided to join the duo in bellowing an ode to Lord Ram. The driver mashed the gas pedal and the bus lurched out of the parking lot, unbelievably overfull. It seemed in danger of tipping over at any moment. We were on our way!

Brilliant and His Strength were traveling with Maya and Devi. They "sat" in the seats nearest the two—one in front, the other behind. (And yes, it would appear they were sitting on the bodies of humans, but the people felt nothing.) Each was so massive that his body took up the space of an entire seat—and then some—had he really needed a seat. They were every bit of their names. Brilliant was, well...Brilliant. His iridescence shot in every direction. And His Strength was the epitome of harnessed raw power. Oh! If the humans only could have seen the contrast of the angelic beings with...the others...they would have been mesmerized.

The others. At the moment, the bus teemed with them. A couple hundred demonic beings. They ranged in murky, muted colors—from a flat brown to a mustard yellow to a sallow, sickish pink hue resembling vomit. These angels were smaller than God's angels...evil had dissipated them in every way, including their stature. Their eyes— some had one, some had two, a few even had three—were sunken as though they were going to disappear in the misshapen eye holes, or they were bulbous as if they were about to pop out at any moment. A supernatural slime oozed from their bodies that could not be seen in the natural, although it could be felt. This slime smeared onto everything and was difficult to remove. Each evil angel had its own particular stench that was horrible enough to make the strongest of men gag. These stenches intermingled and wove their way in all directions, especially into the ground, where they seeped in and rotted the soil and vegetation.

The songs to Lord Ram drew them in. The demons roiled around the bus, oozing and smearing and stenching it up. As the people sang to Ram, the demons tried to whip themselves and the people into a frenzy.

However, there was one huge, glaring, unavoidable glitch! Sitting smack dab in the middle of it all were two angels of God—Brilliant and His Strength—and they were raining on the demoniacal parade. Brilliant and His Strength could not help that the very nature of who they were, and even more importantly, *Who* they worshiped and served made them more powerful, more full of light, more full of goodness. They could not help that by their simple act of being, they were the greater and more powerful. The power of who they were and who they worshiped proceeded unconsciously from them and destroyed anything the evil angels attempted.

Additionally, they had every legal right to be sitting in the midst of the bus, even in the midst of a demonic party. This right flowed from the fact that Maya had intercessors—her parents and their friends. The power of their prayers was so strong, it was as if God *Himself* were on the bus counteracting everything the demons tried. The superiority of their authority and power was apparent. The truth of transcendence of prayer was evident. Those prayers, spoken on the other side of the globe, nullified the effect of everything evil on this bus.

The evil angels tried to whip the people into a frenzy. They tried to whip themselves into an even greater frenzy. But something kept the "party" at bay and finally everything and everyone died down. The music continued blaring…loudly…irritatingly…until the driver turned it off in disgust. Ram was not to be sung to on this bus.

Brilliant and His Strength nodded in agreement as they looked around. All the evil angels had positioned themselves outside of the bus. They looked as though they were hanging on with claws, stubby misshapen fingers, and hands with digits missing. Their faces were turned away because they could not stand the light that emanated from the Lord's angels. Spiritually speaking, the inside of the bus was light and radiant, while the outside was muffled in a murky brown shroud. All was silent now, except Brilliant and His Strength talking to each other in the heavenly language—their celestial language, about which the evil angels were clueless, but which disturbed and agitated them profoundly. To them, hearing those voices was like having to listen to fingernails dragging down a chalkboard. Of course, the humans could not hear them.

"So, what is the game plan," His Strength asked Brilliant, a humorous grin flashing across his countenance, "now that we've rained on their parade?"

Brilliant beamed back at him—his delight causing waves of effusive light to flow from him, "We're going to thunderstorm on another…just give it time." He looked about the bus, amused by what he saw. "Just give it time!"

CHAPTER SIXTEEN

LAUNDRY, PICTURES, AND OPEN DOORWAYS

Maya

Alleppey, India

SIX o'clock in the morning. Archana was over. *C'mon, Maya! I said to myself. Time to do laundry…maybe I'll do it before I bathe.*

I headed back up to the women's dorm to gather the articles that needed washing. I stuffed them into my bucket along with some powdered detergent. *I'll wash my clothes over by the brahmacharini huts. They should be done by now.* I trotted down the back stairway and skirted around Cha Ma's garden and a huge pile of grayish-black rocks that lay on the sand. As I approached the brahmacharini huts, I noticed that only one girl was there. *Good! I hate fighting with them for space at the spigot.*

I set my bucket of laundry down beside the wash-rock/scrub-"thingie." To my right, the brahmacharini was scrubbing away. "Namah shivaya!" I smiled.

Her head bobbled as she namah shivayaed me with a responding smile. Like almost all the brahmacharinis, she was slim and beautiful. Surreally beautiful. Big almond eyes and perfect white teeth, set in flawless, toasted honey skin. Her thick, raven hair was wet and hung freely down her back, stopping about two inches shy of her waist. I figured it was loose in order to dry, as the brahmacharinis tended to wear their hair in low buns. I could not gauge her age—somewhere between late teens and early twenties. With the Indian brahmacharis and -charinis it was so hard to tell. Some were in their thirties and did not look it except for a little gray poking through their hair.

I took my clothes out of the bucket, set them on the sand, and began running water into the bucket. She snatched my bucket from under the water, dumped the water out, and turned off the spigot. My head whipped toward her quickly. I felt enraged. Indignant. *How dare she? Who does she think she is?*

"Namah shivaya," she said, head still bobbling and smiling, "do not wash your white clothes plain."

"Huh?" I tried to take my bucket back from her. *Do not wash my white clothes...plain.* "What do you mean?"

"No. Rust will ruin your clothes. See?" She pointed to a faded red splotch in her own sari. "Here!" She took a square piece of cloth that was hanging off the side of her bucket and put it over the spout. She wrapped the ends of the cloth around the neck of the spigot and tied it fast. "There!" she said, satisfaction in her voice. She put my bucket back under the spigot and turned it on.

"Thank you." I felt stupid for getting so angry with her. "My name is Maya. What's yours?" I asked by way of a roundabout apology.

"My name is Parvati." She smiled a sweet smile at me as she reached down, plucked up my packet of detergent, tore it open, and poured half its contents into my bucket.

"You are new here, yes?" she asked in the affirmative as her head waggled no.

"Fairly new...I came about three months ago, I think..." I squished my clothes up and down in the bucket and watched the suds build.

"Yes, I know. I have lived here most of my life. My mother is Calicut Amma." I recognized the name. It was pronounced *"Kaah-lee-cut-taahm-maah."* Her mother was one of the kitchen stalwarts.

I took out a petticoat and started beating it against the slanted surface of the wash-rock/scrub-thing. Water and suds flew everywhere.

"No! No! That is not right!" she exclaimed and took the petticoat out of my hands. "Let me show you." She folded the cloth in half, into a tight little bundle, and began slamming it against the wash-rock. *Pow! Pow!* On the downswing, she would twist the cloth just so, so that it would wring against itself.

Pow!...swing...Pow!...swing...Pow!...swing...Pow! She swung it down four times and then laid it against the ridges of the stone and scrubbed up and down. *Scrunk! Scrunk! Scrunk! Scrunk!* The sounds echoed off the palm trees and reverberated throughout the silent morning air. She did this several times and then handed the cloth to me.

"You try," she ordered.

I took the cloth and tried her technique. The cloth made a satisfying *Thunk! Thunk!* as I swung and wrung.

"See? Very good!" She smiled again. She continued to stand there.

217

I nodded. I marveled to myself—I've been washing my laundry all wrong all this time. No wonder it smelled and remained stained after I washed it…even after I soaked it!

"How old are you?" I asked after a few minutes since it was clear that she was not planning to leave.

"Seventeen. I hear you are the black American woman…?"

"Yes. I guess you could say that." My concentration was caught up in the scrunking and thunking of the cloth. I could feel beads of sweat forming on my brow.

"I have never seen a real black American person." Long pause. "On TV, yes." Another pause. "But, not in real life." She giggled and smiled a toothy smile.

"Hmm…" I did not know what to say. I was done with the petticoat. I picked up a choli. She reached into my bucket, took out a sari, and began to wash it.

"Oh! Thank you!" I smiled at her in appreciation.

"For Kali…" she replied. We scrubbed with great focus. "So," she said in between *thunks*, "do you know the rule for laundry?"

"Huh uh…" I answered distractedly.

"Well, you must know it. There is only one rule. Do not *ever* violate it. Cha Ma says, 'All laundry must be down before the sun sets!'"

I gave her a quizzical look.

"Take your laundry down before dusk," she said in reply to my look.

"Why?" *Scrunk! Scrunk!*

She did not answer. Instead, she renewed scrubbing with intense focus.

"Why?" I insisted. Curiosity was getting the better of me.

She responded in a subdued voice, "Because of doorways…"

I did not hear her well, "Because of what…?"

She shook her head, pursed her lips and quickly responded, "Cha Ma just says no. *So don't!*"

"But, why not?" I pressed.

She would not answer me; instead she grabbed another article of clothing and began scrubbing that.

I let it drop. *Easy enough. But I don't see what the problem is. I'll have to ask someone why.* After a while we eased back into chatting, and as we scrubbed and talked, I promptly forgot her warning.

Marie

United States

Jovial and Mighty, the two angels assigned to Paul and Marie, shook their heads in consternation.

"I can't believe she's going to do this," Jovial muttered. Even in an attitude of great seriousness, he still manifested his name. He was Jovial—the Joy of the Lord was etched upon his being. He was given to raucous outbursts of delight and laughter. Even while embroiled in fierce warfare he laughed from the pure bliss of serving the Lord. Nothing gave him greater joy. At the moment, watching Marie, his faced evinced about as much seriousness as was possible for him—it would not last for long. He crossed his arms over his chest as if he were trying to restrain himself.

"I can understand the draw though," Mighty said with empathy. "She wants to know why—Why did Maya leave? What is it about this…woman…that grabbed her?" Mighty drew himself up to his full height, as he did his muscles flexed, involuntarily. He was power and strength and might coiled in upon itself.

Jovial nodded, "I understand that, but still…she has no clue what doorways she's opening."

"I know. There's a reason the Lord says no false idols. Humans don't seem to understand that the essence of a spirit can pass through a created object."

"Not all humans—Hindus definitely understand the principle. Thus the reason for all the idols and pictures."

"True, true…" Mighty's voice faded away as he watched Marie. "Too bad we can't stop her…"

"No, we can't," Jovial responded strongly. He knew Mighty's penchant for wanting to save humans from demonic activity. Actually his deeper desire was to war against Satan's principalities—if the battling could be constant, he would be thrilled. "This is an action she's taking of her own free will. She will have to deal with the repercussions that come with opening doorways…"

I just want to see what Maya sees in this…Cha Ma. Marie took out a print copy of an image she had found of Cha Ma on the internet. She had done an extensive amount of research on the internet and elsewhere about Hinduism, gurus, and especially Cha Ma. Marie placed the picture on the dining room table and sat down. She looked at the picture—*she looks normal enough!*—and then looked away, quickly. Everything within her rebelled against the idea of looking at Cha Ma. She forced her eyes to stay put as she stared into Cha Ma's eyes. Several long seconds passed.

Nothing. She felt nothing—no draw, no pull. No understanding. She let out a lengthy exhalation. She had been holding her breath. *I wonder what it is she sees in her....* No answer. She pushed herself away from the table. *Time to get on with the rest of my day.* She crumpled up the picture and threw it away.

CHAPTER SEVENTEEN

DON'T DO IT!

Maya
Alleppey, India

"MAYA! You're just the person I need!" Jnani announced as she grabbed my hand and pulled me toward the back stairs. I was standing on the balcony of the women's dorm, peering out over the brahmachari huts, looking but not really seeing. I was thinking about my last darshan with Cha Ma, thinking about how I wanted enlightenment so desperately. Thinking that I had wanted to ask her for a Kali mantra but I could not get up the nerve. *Maybe next time.* I was disappointed with myself, although I did not want to admit it. I had passed up a good opportunity. Life with Cha Ma was so random and filled with unpredictabilities, I was worried that I would not get another chance to ask her for a long time.

"I need your help!" Jnani said, pulling me with more strength than was necessary, as I was quite obliging.

"What's up?"

She whispered conspiratorially, "I'm going to put a relaxer in my hair."

"A relaxer! How did you get a relaxer here in India? *Where* did you get a relaxer here?" I asked her dubiously.

"I brought it over with me."

"How old is it? You don't want it to mess up on your head!"

"I don't think I've met the expiration date on it. But, anyway, I'm desperate. I have oooodles (her British accent strung out the word "oodles") of new growth. Just look!" That was the truth. I could see almost two inches of tightly coiled hair at the root of the straight hair.

"You're right!" I followed along behind her as she hustled up the stairs. "Aren't you worried about doing a relaxer here in India though? The water is so gross and scummy, and what if they shut off the water while we're doing your hair? Do you even know if it's on right now?"

"Yes, it's on…and I'm desperate. My hair is coming out as it is—too much new growth."

We had arrived at the bathrooms that were on the fourth floor. I could feel myself frowning—I was leery—very, very leery—of doing a relaxer in a toilet stall in the middle of India with the only water supply coming from a spigot and bucket, with that meager water supply cut off at random times of the day—just too many variables.

I thought of my own "hair drama." When I first had gotten into Hinduism, I had shaved my hair off—all off. I had been one step away from being bald. I did it as my own sort of "Munda vow"—the act of shaving the hair when taking a vow of sannyasa. I had discovered the principle upon reading the Mundaka Upanishad, which taught that just as one cuts or shaves one's hair off, so too could a person cut all ties with this illusory, material world. Hence, in certain vows of brahmacharya and sannyasa, the initiate would shave off his hair in order to represent "a cutting off" of worldly attachments. It was a male thing to do, a very male thing to do; but, I had wanted to prove to myself the earnestness of my own commitment. So I had shaved my hair off and kept it off. I had promised myself and others that I would start growing it again when, and only when, I found my satguru.

Upon deciding to move to the ashram in India, I had started growing out my hair. For one, I believed Cha Ma to be my satguru. Two, way too many people had told me horror stories involving rationed or no water and capricious power supplies at best. As I planned my trip, I began having "visions" of shaving my head, the power going out and being stuck with a short Afro-Mohawk—that was just not for me! So, I began to grow out my hair. Now it was long enough to be in twisties—every week I retwisted my hair to keep it from dreading up. The twisties made me even more fascinating to the Indians.

My thoughts went back to the last time I had ridden the bus. I had gone to Ernakullam with Devi. We had climbed the crowded bus—like any other day. This time we had to sit in the back, the very back.

After we sat down, I looked around. Nothing unusual—they were all staring at Devi and me, particularly me.

I leaned over, "Devi, check out the people."

"I was wondering when you'd notice. They're a little over the top, aren't they?"

They ARE over the top! Just when I was getting used to some staring...but this is too much! What is going on here? I could not help but wonder as all of the people were turned around staring at me. Literally. I could not even guess how many people had turned around in the bus and were looking backward...at me. The bus was too full to make an accurate guess. It seemed the only ones who were not looking were the ones hanging out of the windows and doors. They were too busy trying to stay on the bus and not fly out when the driver sharply cut the wheel in order to avoid a cow or another vehicle.

"What is it that's so different? It couldn't be my hair?" I asked, desperately wishing I could slide underneath the seat. No matter how many times it happened, all the scrutiny unnerved me.

"I'll bet it's your hair. I mean, you've always been a novelty. But, now that your hair's grown out so much...and with the little twists...you're even prettier." She hesitated and stumbled around trying to explain herself, "Not that you weren't pretty before. You were...but, now that it's growing out, it frames your face so nicely..." I did not say anything. Her analysis did not ease my extreme discomfort.

"I know what!" She flashed a mischievous grin. "Let's do an experiment. Lean over and see if they'll touch your hair." I leaned over. Immediately I felt hands messing with my hair. I sat up quickly. Several faces were closer, smiling, heads bobbing, looking as though they did not realize that it was socially inappropriate to touch a stranger's hair.

"I'm just going to ignore it!" I said with finality.

"Okay! You do that!" Devi challenged me. "I think it's going to be hard."

"We'll see." But Devi was right. By the end of the ride I was beyond fed up with being stared at and touched. I felt like an animal at a petting zoo. *That* was my special brand of tapas—to be the unusual Black American woman with unusual hair.

"Maya!" Jnani's lilting voice interrupted my reverie. My attention shifted to Jnani and the reality of putting a relaxer on her head in the middle of the boondocks of India—prescription for disaster!

"Come on!" she demanded as she stepped into the stall. She set the relaxer box on the floor and began to go to work preparing the caustic concoction. *There's something all wrong with mixing relaxer goo on the floor of a dirty stall!* I stood in the stall with her, watching. Within a couple of minutes, it was mixed and she was ready to go.

"Do you think we need to get some extra buckets and fill them up with water? Just in case the water gets turned off?" I half-asked, half-suggested. I felt so nervous. Skittish. *Don't do it! Don't do it!*

"No, no. The water's been fine all day long," she replied. I countered in my mind—*Yeah, okay, but they have turned the water and the electricity off early in the day,* every day, *this month in order to conserve.* I did not say anything as it was apparent that she was determined to relax her hair.

"Well, at least let's check and make sure the water is on right now." I reached over and turned the spigot handle. Light-orangish water chortled out. *Ugh! I don't know what rust and dirt will do to the chemicals in a relaxer. Wow! She must be crazy!*

"See? It works!" announced she triumphantly. "Let's get this over with." She began to part her hair into four sections. I stifled a sigh and started globbing relaxer goo into her hair. We worked quickly, applying the goo to her hair and smoothing it through. Twenty minutes later, or thereabouts, as neither of us had thought to bring a clock, we felt it was time to wash the goo out of her hair.

I turned the handle of the spigot…Nothing came out…*Nothing came out!* Horrible pause. And then, Jnani screamed!

Oh! That's really helpful! I thought harshly. Hurriedly, my mind scrambled to find a solution. *We have to do something, and fast. That relaxer won't be able to sit on her head for very long before the chemicals start breaking down the hair strand!* I did not want to say my thoughts aloud to Jnani because she was frantic but not doing anything to help herself.

"I know what," I suggested, "let's take the buckets from here and run up to the water pools. We can scoop up some water and use it to rinse out your hair." The water pools were right above us, on the roof. They were like two huge, square swimming pools, 12 feet by 12 feet and about two feet deep (I would guess—although it was hard to tell the exact depth as the water was greenish-brown and full of scum). The pools were intended to catch rainwater (especially during the monsoon season) to be held in reserve for whenever the ashram needed it. As far as I was concerned, now was definitely one of those "need" times.

She and I sprinted out of the stall and grabbed the buckets from the other five stalls. We had a total of seven buckets. We ran up the stairs and scooped up the water. We could not carry all of the buckets at once so we had to make two trips.

In between the runs, Jnani cried, "It's burning, Maya! It's burning! Oh! Please hurry!" She looked comically tragic with a head full of relaxer goop. She looked like someone had squirted a can of whipped cream on her head in the shape of a soft-serve ice cream cone.

"I'm hurrying! I'm hurrying!" I exclaimed. I was not as worried about the burning sensation so much (although it could be incredibly painful) as I was concerned about the acidic chemicals burning the hair off her head. Now that would be awful. Within a couple of minutes we had all the buckets sitting haphazardly in the stall. She leaned over and I started pouring.

"Ohhh! This is a disaster!" she moaned. I could not have agreed with her more, but I said nothing. I kept pouring and swishing my free hand through her hair in an attempt to get the goo out. "What was I thinking? Why did I try to do this? This is going to take many more buckets...."

My sentiments exactly! The task at hand, of washing all of the relaxer out of Jnani's hair so that it would not eat it up, seemed impossible.

"I know what...I'm going to stick my head into the next bucket and swirl my hair around. Can you go get more water?"

"Yes!" I responded, taking the now empty buckets with me and shooting out the door.

Finally, 30 minutes later and innumerable trips up to the rain pools on my part, Jnani was done. We had rinsed, shampooed, and conditioned all residual traces of the relaxer goo out of her hair and off her scalp.

"Thank you, Maya," was all she said.

"Namah shivaya," I wearily said my "you're welcome." She could have said more, shown more appreciation, I suppose; but I was too tired to really care. We parted ways—me to my bunk and she to her room. Within a couple of days, she approached me and told me that she was leaving the ashram—she was going to continue traveling around India before returning to England. We said good-bye and that was the last I heard of Jnani. I cannot say I was not glad.

CHAPTER EIGHTEEN

A MANTRA
AND A NAME

SCRISH! *Scrish! Scrish!* I was standing in the center of one of the gargantuan rice pots, chappels off, the hem of my blue work-skirt undignifiedly and inappropriately tucked up into the waistband. My feet were nestled in an inch of murky, ricey, ashy water. Pot-washing duty! And I had the privilege of washing the huge pots. *There is something peculiarly satisfying about standing inside a pot, scrubbing away.* Even though the sun was waning, the heat was not dissipating. I was unbearably hot. Beads of sweat dripped off my fore-head and into the cleaning water. I was so engrossed in scrubbing away all the flecks of rice that I did not notice anyone approach me.

"Hi!" A woman's voice startled me. I turned around rapidly. Two Westerners, a woman and a man, were standing before me. I had for-gotten that I was in front of the Western canteen. The brahmacharinis had had us, the Westerners (ostensibly because we were larger and stronger), roll the rice pots to the front in order to clear the cooking area behind the kitchen. They wanted to clean up that area.

"Namah shivaya!" I said in greeting. "You must be new here?"

The woman nodded, "Yes, I'm Linda and this is Doug. We just got married. Six days ago." Her eyes sparkled with happiness. I looked at her husband. He, too, was smiling unabashedly. I could tell they were thrilled.

"Yes," he added. "We're on our honeymoon. Our parents bought us a trip through India."

"We had heard that the backwaters in this area are beautiful so we decided to come to Kerala for a couple of days. Then we're off to Madras." Linda picked up his trail. *They are so couple-y.* I could not help but smile at their happiness and excitement.

"Well, good luck now that you're here!" I teased good-naturedly. "They always say that once you get here, you'll never leave."

Linda and Doug laughed. "That's fine!" Doug said.

Linda gestured toward the pot I was standing in, "What are you doing?"

"Washing pots," I responded. She gave me a humorous look. "I know, I know, it's gross!"

Doug walked over and peered into my pot, "I don't see any suds."

"That's because there aren't any," I replied between giggles.

"Awww, noooo…" He gave a look of mock disgust.

"I know what! We've got to get you guys registered. C'mon, I'll take you to the Foreigners' Office." I climbed out of the pot and slid my feet into my chappels. I could feel the soggy rice that clung to my feet squish up against the plastic. *Ewww!* I led them through the ashram grounds, pointing out the canteen, the temple.

"Here is where Cha Ma gives darshan…"

"Who's Cha Ma?" Linda interrupted.

"You don't know who Cha Ma is?" I asked with feigned incredulity. "Well, you're in for a treat. Cha Ma is considered a guru…" I continued on in this vein as we walked through the ashram, punctuating my discourse about who Cha Ma was with descriptions of the ashram. Soon we arrived at the Foreigners' Office.

Of course Narayana was there, leaning back in his chair with his heels on the desk. He was humming a tune while lightly ka-ching-chinging his kimini.

"Namah shivaya, Narayana," I helloed.

"Namah shivaya, Maya," he responded, putting down the kimini. "So, you have brought me two new foreigners?"

Wow! He's being pleasant! It must be because of Doug and Linda.

"Yes, this is Doug and Linda. I'll leave them with you."

"Yes, excellent idea!" He smiled at me as I left the office. I heard him address them, "Namah shivaya, I'm Narayana. May I see your passports and visas?"

I headed back out to the kitchen to finish washing pots. My pot was waiting for me, as were two others. The job had grown in my absence. I sighed, kicked off my chappels and climbed in. My coco-brillo pad was sitting in the ricey murk where I had thrown it down. I picked it up and recommenced scrish-scrishing. My thoughts were full of Doug and Linda—*What would it be like to be married? They look so happy. I wonder how long they'll end up staying here…*

The sky darkened to indigo as I scrubbed. I could hear the other pot washers in the kitchen finishing up. Sandi and Victoria who were part of the permanent pot-washing crew—*They actually requested permanent pot-washing duty!*—came out to help me. With their help, we were done in no time. We rolled the pots around to the newly tidied back—*It doesn't look much different to me!*—and leaned them against the rickety bamboo fence. *I hope they don't make it fall.*

"Whew! Done!" Sandi said wiping her hands on her dirty, white sari. *I wonder if she wears the same sari for pot washing every time or does she have a different one. I'll have to remember to ask her.*

"Let's go!" Victoria said leading the way through the kitchen. As we walked through the canteen, whom did we encounter but Dirk, of course. By himself. Puttering about. Stringing up yards of twine and fastening clothespins to it.

"Good night, Dirk!"

"Yeah, good night…" he answered distractedly, as he strung string above his head throughout the canteen. "Oh, did you know? Cha Ma is meditating out by the brahmachari huts. Everyone is there."

"Everyone, that is, but you!" Sandi answered with a chuckle.

"Yeah, why aren't you out there?" I asked. Underneath the joking, I seriously wanted to know.

Dirk shrugged his shoulders, "I dunno." His German accent slipped through slightly. "I've been here for so many years. In the beginning I used to run behind her, trying hard to be wherever she was. However, with time…*everything* grows old. It's okay to meditate. However, I find myself useful and much more fulfilled here in the canteen."

"Oh. I see," I responded as I edged toward the exit of the canteen, several steps behind Victoria, who did not stop to chat. "Well, I'm off to go meditate, see what Cha Ma's up to."

"Me too!" Sandi echoed with great relish.

We walked from the Western canteen around the left corner of the ashram to the back where the brahmachari huts were. The moment I turned the corner, I could see—it looked to be close to 300 people sitting. A sea of white with splotches of yellow and orange here and there. In the center was Cha Ma and the swamis. None of the female swamis were with her, only the men. It looked like most of the ashramites were there. Everyone was pin-drop silent, in deep meditation. It was a "wild" image: the moon, this little lady in white sitting in deep meditation and over a couple hundred people sitting cramped up beside her (earlier having jockeyed hard for position around her). Now after finding their place, they were silent. Everyone was meditating. Hundreds of bodies, rock still. The white, barely-there light of the moon dusted everyone with an "otherworldly" glow. It all appeared so surreal and supernatural.

Victoria, Sandi, and I found places to sit on the edge of the circle, directly across from Cha Ma. That way we could observe whatever happened; but we were far enough away to have space. I made myself comfortable, sitting cross-legged with my hands arranged in a specific mudra meant to deepen my meditation. I closed my eyes. But I could not focus. I focused on my breathing—to no avail. I focused on my third eye—to no avail. I focused on the blue spot behind my eyelids— no luck. I felt like someone was watching me. *Hmmm, I wonder if a divine being, a spirit, is paying attention to me?* My mind wandered. I kept trying to meditate, but I just could not focus. I opened my eyes a miniscule crack. To my left, Sandi's hazel eyes were wide open, looking around. She was not bothered at all that she was not meditating.

I closed my eyes again. I gave it my best shot. Again I could not focus. I felt like the "itchies" were moving all over my body. *I will not scratch. I will not scratch.* My left hand crept out to scratch my right ankle that was sitting under my left leg. Then my back began to itch and I had to scratch it. I had to scratch here and then there. I felt hot. I felt uncomfortable. Sweat trickled down the middle of my back, which made my back itch all the more. In between the "itchies" I still felt like someone was watching me. Finally, after much struggling, I gave in and opened my eyes. Everyone seemed in deep meditation with the exception of me and Sandi and, of course, Alice, Anneshwari, and Rukmini who were sitting right beside Cha Ma. If Anneshwari and Rukmini moved any closer to Cha Ma, they would have been sitting on top of her. I watched the three of them (Alice, Anneshwari, and Rukmini) consume themselves with not meditating. Alice was busy looking at everyone else. Rukmini and Anneshwari were busy looking at Cha Ma, watching her every "not move" because she was deep in meditation and not stirring.

I noticed that one of the Indian men kept pushing at Rukmini. She just ignored him. I realized that he was pushing her because she was sitting on the men's side. It did not help that she was so much taller than almost all of the Indian men. For that matter, she was taller than most of the Western men. I wondered how long the men would put up with her violating their side. I figured their chauvinism would have to prevail at some point or another.

Above the meditators, swirled "visitors." Drawing them in. Further and further into meditation. Adding to the willing delusion in their minds. Some swooped down and whispered into the ears of the meditators—faint tendrils of brownish-yellow smoke appeared to waft from their mouths into the humans' ears. Others massaged the humans' temples or grabbed their heads and shook them from side-to-side. Their laughter and shrieks of glee echoed within the atmosphere. It appeared as though they lifted the humans—some part of them that was ethereal—up high into the sky and then, cackling with demonic delight, threw them back down into their bodies. The landing was not pretty—damage was done to their souls. Although it was imperceptible, over time it would wreak havoc upon their fragile human core.

I felt myself jolt to! I opened my eyes. I felt dazed. *I must've fallen into meditation.* I glanced at my watch. Over an hour had passed. I marveled at the fact that one minute I was busy looking around and then, bam! over an hour had gone by. I tried to recall my meditation. Nothing came to mind—just murkiness, almost like a deep sleep. *Did I hear someone laughing?* My mind continued grasping at my meditation—no luck. *What was that meditation? What was it? It was as if I were traveling with some beings and they were laughing...I don't feel too good...* I felt sick to my stomach.

"Oh, so you've come out?" Sandi leaned toward me. "Look! Cha Ma's giving darshan." I looked. Lines extended on either side of Cha Ma—the residents were getting a late night darshan. *Hey! There's Doug and Linda!* They were sitting on either side of Cha Ma, on the male and female sides, respectively. They were alternately gazing at her and watching the crowd. It was evident that they were completely fascinated.

"Look! There's the couple that I met earlier. They're touring the backwaters of Kerala." I watched them closely. "They had never heard of Cha Ma."

"Well, it sure does look like Cha Ma's giving them the special treatment," Sandi whispered.

"Now that's true!" Sure enough, Cha Ma was leaning over and whispering into Linda's ear. Whatever she said caused Linda to burst out in laughter.

"The lines look kinda thin," I noted.

"Oh yeah! I've already gotten darshan. So has most everyone else. She's been giving it for some time now. You need to go ahead and get into line if you're wanting it."

Hastily I stood and began to pick my way through the sea of women. "Namah shivaya…namah shivaya…" I said, excusing myself for leaning and stepping on so many bodies. *Hmm, maybe I can ask her for a Kali mantra…*

I plopped down in the women's queue, which had about ten women. She was going slowly—talking to the person getting darshan, chatting and laughing with the brahmacharis and –charinis near her. My breath caught involuntarily—Narayana was beside her, passing the men to her, being distractingly beautiful. I tried my hardest not to look at him or think about him as I waited. I did not want Cha Ma to read my mind and see my thoughts about him. I was afraid that, like so many other times when she read people's minds, she would tell the whole crowd what I was thinking. If she did I would be mortified. I worked hard to control my thoughts.

Within ten minutes, I was before her. She hugged me, chanting, "Ma…Ma…Ma…" into my ear. Her voice was low and gravelly. She lifted me up and stared into my eyes, smiling.

Here's my chance. Do it! Do it now! I launched forth into my purpose, "Cha Ma, I want a Kali mantra." Out of the corner of my eye I saw Narayana swiftly glance at Cha Ma, then me.

She looked at me quizzically for a long moment, her head cocked to the side. Then she nodded. "Kali mantra," she murmured. Her voice had dropped even deeper than normal and sounded almost inhuman.

I nodded. A flash of fear *(terror?)* tore through me. *Did her eyes just go gray?* I questioned what I saw. *No, I'm sure I was just imagining it.* She gave me a knowing smile as her eyes narrowed. It seemed as if she looked right through me. My heart clutched. I almost wished I had not asked her. She leaned forward and whispered into my ear, "…………………….."

She pulled back and stared into my eyes. Her face was dreadfully earnest. Her hands gripped my shoulders so tightly it hurt. "You tell no one Kali mantra," she said this clearly, unequivocally. *I didn't know she spoke such good English.*

Deep inside of me I felt more than heard a voice rumble: *It is yours and will take you to enlightenment. Great power in it. It will destroy all that hinders you.*

She pointed to my chest and stabbed me with her finger. "Your name…Premabhakti." She pulled me to her and hugged me again. I felt horribly confused and dazed. She whispered the Kali mantra into my ear twice more. Then she released me, almost shoving me off her.

I stumbled backward. I could barely see. I felt an odd sort of madness as though "stuff" were swirling viciously within me and before my eyes. I began slowly, painstakingly, heading back to where I had been sitting on the edge of the crowd. I struggled to focus against the uproar within me. A brahmacharini leaned forward and whispered to me, "Kali has blessed you. She has given you your name. It is Premabhakti."

I nodded. Her voice warbled to me from afar, but I noted what she said. The mantra chanted within me of its own accord, weaving its way insidiously through me, deeper and deeper still. I heard myself repeating it over and over. Already it was taking on a life all its own. Once uttered and released into the atmosphere—it grew and increased of its own volition. It was a living thing.

———————————

Brilliant shook his head. Beside him stood His Strength, Majesty, and Awe. They stood in the sky watching the scene below them unfold—although many of the key participants in the scene below swirled in the atmosphere. These, however, dared not come near the four angels of God.

Majesty made a sound of disgust, "A Kali mantra!" He swung at the air with a massive fist. The atmosphere undulated from the disturbance caused by his movement.

"And took a name…" His Strength added, shaking his head.

"We will still watch over her and protect her so that she will not die, but in accepting the mantra…and the name…she has opened herself to the enemy even more," Majesty said as he observed the scene below him. "She will meet much trouble now, much more than she has been encountering. He is not allowed to kill her. *That* is a direct order from the Lord. *That* cannot be countered or opposed. But much misery and suffering is in store for her."

"Why did she have to do that? Sometimes I don't understand humans…" Awe said, looking perplexed. "And yet it is my pleasure and joy to serve the Lord in fulfilling all His commands concerning them." His face for a moment demonstrated pure delight.

"I agree with you," Brilliant said. "Especially this family…this girl. Oh! How she has a place in my heart. It is my joy to take care of her."

He paused for a moment, deep in thought. "Although, you are right, Majesty. Now we will see much worse happen to her."

"Her mother and father must continue praying!" Awe added.

"They will," responded Majesty. "Their love for her is great and the Holy Spirit will prompt them, but their struggle is going to increase, too. They will continue to stand strong in the face of it all, but it will be at great cost. Especially now, because more will be coming at them." He paused and then continued with certainty. "Ahhh, so many things she will go through now because of this choice."

Awe shook his head in consternation and asked, "Why oh why did she have to take a mantra and a name?" The other angels, staring down at the scene below, shook their heads in a mixture of bewilderment and disgust in answer to the question.

Marie

United States

"Maybe you need to go home, Ms. Marie," said her assistant, Rita. "You look awful."

Marie tried to smile but her head hurt too much. "Thanks for the compliment." She paused for a moment. "I think I will go home. I'll stop by the drugstore on the way home to pick up some sinus medicine." She massaged her temples and closed her eyes. *I'll feel much better after I take some medicine.* The headaches had been growing stronger and stronger with each passing day. They were lasting longer too. What had started as a slight twinge behind her eyes had grown to a sharp, throbbing pain in the front portion of her head. At times the pain was so intense it made her nauseated. It was almost impossible to sleep.

Slowly with the headaches came something else that was disturbing—spots in her line of vision. They were growing larger—big splotches floating past her eyes, sometimes so numerous they obscured her vision. Other times, they seemed to grow tendrils, forming a sinister, black webbing across her field of vision. But as randomly as these spots and webs appeared, just as randomly did they disappear. It made her wonder if it was anything at all.

"Go home, Ms. Marie!" Rita interrupted her thoughts.

"Okay! I'm going. Just give me a moment. I need to clean up my desk a bit." She leaned over to pick up a wad of paper that had fallen on the floor. The downward movement caused her head to scream in agony. "Never mind! I'm going to take your advice and go home." *And lie down.* Within minutes, Marie was leaving the building. *I'll stop by the drugstore along the way and get something strong for my sinuses.*

As she climbed into the car, she began to pray, "Lord, please make this headache go away." That was her prayer. She repeated it to herself. The pain was so intense she could not think of much else.

"This is sooo good!" Sickness hissed to Despair. Sickness was a vile pinkish color. His form was decidedly different than most of the others, with the exception of Illness, Disease, and those of that "nature." Their particular brand of rebellion had caused their bodies to morph and shift into hideous monstrosities. Sickness had appendages that most closely resembled tentacles. With these he attached himself or stuck into a person to cause various illnesses. His face was no longer face-like, but more a pulpy, lumpy mess with holes that used to be the eyes, nose, and mouth. "You were so right! She won't, she can't, pray for the girl when she's preoccupied with her own issues. Now we've got to keep her in this state." He slowly inserted his finger, which had the appearance of a tentacle, into her head and moved it around. "This should keep her busy..."

Disease stepped in closer. "Too bad we can't kill her."

"No, that we cannot do. God has said no." Sickness hesitated, his mind circling around a possibility. He continued to move his tentacle around in Marie's head. "But...but...she opened a door to us...she's fair game."

"No, she's not! You know the Law!" Despair countered.

"But..." Sickness cackled, "if we catch her unaware..."

Despair, true to his nature, replied, "It will never work! You know God will not allow her to die if He has said no...I don't see how this is going to work..."

Sickness huffed in exasperation, "Ah, Despair! You're starting to sound like Doubt now!"

Disease interjected, "Stick to the plan! That is all there is to it. Satan has said to make this...woman...how I *hate* humans!" he shrieked this aside, overcome by his own abhorrence of humans. "We are to make her suffer and suffer horribly. I'm with Sickness—I think we may have an opportunity to kill her. But not yet. Let's stick with the plan that our lord gave us—make her suffer so much she cannot pray for that infernal girl. And then when the girl is destroyed, much, and many will die with her."

Sickness nodded his agreement. "For now I will continue my work on the mother. Speaking of Doubt...where is he? With the father?"

CHAPTER NINETEEN

DEATHLY ILL

Maya
Alleppey, India

"BLEEEEEEECH...BLEEEEECH..." *I feel absolutely awful.* I was too sick to think very cogently. What was supposed to be a thought process was more a disjointed flux of mental meanderings. *I wish I could get up off this floor! I hate kneeling here. No! Let me not lie to myself—I am lying here—sick as a dog and then some. I feel like I am going to die...I am going to die!* This I knew!

I lay with my head on the filthy bathroom floor. I could not pick it up. Honestly? I just did not care. I did not care that I was lying in one of the filthy third-floor bathroom stalls. I did not care that I could not distinguish whether the reddish-brown mess I was lying in was my own or that of the bathrooms. The nasty reddish-brown that stained the stalls could have come from the juice of the betel leaves that the Indians chewed and then spit out, from human feces that splashed about, or from a lack of good cleansers. Or...a putrid mix of the three.

245

It was probably the latter. I simply did not care—I just lay there. Face half-hanging into the hole in the floor.

Beyond chanting my mantra. Beyond praying to Cha Ma. Beyond calling Kali's name. Even in my horrifically sickened state, I had noted a correlation between calling Kali's name and being sick. It seemed that every single time I uttered Kali's name, I felt worse. However, what could I expect? Everyone had promised me...warned me...that Kali was ruthless in getting a person to enlightenment, even bringing death if she deemed it necessary. I clung to a hope—*if I die I will be either enlightened or very close. I want to...die...for enlightenment*—as I floated in and out of lucidity, in and out of a strange hallucinogenic state.

In my fleeting moments of lucidity, I could hear people coming and going, using the bathrooms to relieve themselves. I could hear them showering and dressing in the toilet stalls. I could hear people standing at the long sink-trough, brushing their teeth with tooth-brushes or with the more usual thing—fingers and small branches. Several times that I was aware of people banged on the door of my stall, yelling at me in the gibberish of their tongue to get out.

It did not matter. I wafted in and out of consciousness. The pain was unbearable. I was beyond any sense of humiliation and shame. Many hours ago I had stopped trying to get my expelled bodily mate-rial into either the toilet or the bucket. My shirt and skirt clung to me, all wet and soiled from my being sick. I did not care.

"Premabhakti? Premabhakti?" A pleasant and cheery female voice floated toward me over the toilet doors. I felt anything but pleasant and cheery. In fact, I felt so bad that moving my mouth made my head hurt worse and caused me to feel profoundly nauseated.

"Here...I...am..." I managed to whisper. On "am" I began to dry heave, having expelled all the food and liquids that were in my stomach hours ago. *Laundry bucket...throwing up...* My laundry bucket was supposed to be the vomit receptor. The problem was that I could not move my arm enough to actually grab the bucket that was a foot away from me. *Is that blood?* Thin, wavery strands of red extended from my mouth to the floor (I had missed the bucket). I felt it coming out the other end, too.

"What do you mean? I can torment her, but I cannot kill her?!" Death asked Chamunda Kali with an icy tone. "Why am I listening to you anyway? There is only one among us that I obey and that is Lucifer himself. But you? You are just a mere prince or should I say, *princess*, of a principality." Death spoke condescendingly to Chamunda Kali as they stood over Maya in the bathroom.

"I am a Queen!" Chamunda Kali shouted at Death.

"Oh! Queen of Heaven...that's right!" Death snorted in derision. "That's an archetype! A concept. A *notion*. You're not a female. You're not even male...by now, you are so misshapen and distorted and perverted that you are an 'it'!" Death laughed in Chamunda Kali's face.

Chamunda's face began to ooze a yellow, pus-like gooze in all her anger. "You..."

"Oh!" Death said airily, with a whimsical wave of his hand that was much too frivolous for the conversation and occasion. "Let's just let bygones be bygones! Our conversations always take this turn. We must be united, for a house divided will fall. We must bring Maya down!" He turned his attention back to the deathly ill woman lying on the floor in her own refuse. He stretched out his macabrely-unreal "hand."

"No! We cannot kill her." Quickly, Chamunda caught his hand with her own. "Don't you know? Satan wants to destroy the whole family and everyone connected to them. He has a plan that he is sure will work. And it seems God hasn't caught onto him!"

Death raised an eyebrow at that last comment and pulled his hand free, but Chamunda Kali did not seem to notice the eyebrow-raise of doubt nor that he had pulled his hand free.

"So, what are we to do?" Death asked resignedly. Although Death was her senior, here in this situation, given that this was Chamunda's territory—had been for hundreds of years—and given that Maya had a Kali mantra and a name, which opened her soul directly to Chamunda Kali, Chamunda had authority over her.

"We are to let Sickness and Disease have their way with her. You may too…as long as you can restrain yourself from killing her. Play! Play all you want with her. Bring her as close to death as you like, but she mustn't die! You can make her think she's going to die. You can make her wish for death. But you can't kill her. God said no!" With that, Chamunda stepped back through the wall of the stall and into the shadows of the main bathroom corridor, curling her fingers around the necks of people as they passed by.

"Where, oh where, is that Kartika?" Chamunda whispered to herself as she continued to caress necks hatefully. As if bidden, Kartika shuffled out of the darkest dark shadow. Chamunda pushed into her. "I need a little distraction." Kartika's body began to stagger and stumble as Chamunda tried to function within her.

"Ahhh! Why are you wasting your time?" Death hissed at Chamunda. "This is where the real fun is." He, Sickness, Illness, and Disease descended upon Maya.

Bang! Bang! Bang! Bang! "Premabhakti, let me in! The door's locked!" Whoever it was was rather insistent. The only problem was that I was too sick to move.

"I…" My voice dwindled away. I heaved again. *More red…blood?*

"Hold on! I'm going to get the nurse! She might have something she can give you!" The faceless voice ran away.

I was all alone, again, with my sickness. I did not realize I had wanted company so badly until the faceless voice had come by and then left and her departure had left an all-consuming awareness on my part that I was lonely and scared. I felt like I was close to death. *I don't want to die alone…*

I continued dry heaving thin, mucousy red stuff and having diarrhea. For how long? I had no idea. I felt as though I were trapped within my own body. I wondered whether I would live or not. I felt horrendous. I hurt so badly. *Kali help me!* I prayed to my ishta-deity over and over until it became simply—*Kali*. I did not care that her name seemed to make my condition worse.

Finally, I heard the faceless voice coming back, talking to me. It was in the bathroom stall but I could not "see" it. I could not place who it was. "So, what do you think?" asked the faceless voice with great concern. *How did they get into the stall when I had locked the stall door? Or had I?* I felt a vague sense of relief flood through me in knowing I was not alone.

"She's in very bad shape. I hate to see people as sick as this. We need to get her out of here, into a hospital or, at least, a clinic where she can be given proper medical attention, the attention she needs."

A cool hand lightly touched my forehead. It felt like my eyes were open, but I just could not see. I shook my head—I did not want to go away.

"I don't think she wants to go to a hospital or clinic," the faceless voice noted. I recognized the voice now as that of a woman named Karuna.

The nurse responded, "Well, let's just get her up to her room."

"She's in the dorm. Doesn't she need more privacy?" Karuna interjected.

"Yes, you're right! She needs to stay out of the dorm for now. In a room. I know where there's a vacant one off the balcony. We'll wipe her up a bit. I'm going to give her something…Cipro…Flagyl…I'm not sure yet. Judging by the smell, it's definitely dysentery. I just can't figure if it's amoebic or shigellosis…have to think…I hate to give doses as strong as I plan to give to her. She needs to be in the hospital when it's like this…. I'm also going to give her an antiemetic/diarrheal, which should stop the dry heaving and diarrhea." As she talked, she put my left arm around her shoulder and Karuna put my right arm around her shoulder. They began to half-pull, half-drag me out of the stall and up the stairs. "If she doesn't get better by the morning, I'm taking her to the hospital."

Once there, the nurse left to get the shots while Karuna proceeded to change my filthy clothes. Then she gave me a wash up, especially my face. It was filthy from where I had been throwing up on myself and from where I had been lying on the floor of the bathroom. I kept floating in and out of consciousness…hallucinating….

The nurse came back. How long did it take her? I could not fathom. I was so out of it. The medicine in the shots burned as it coursed through my veins. Karuna and the nurse positioned me on the cot with a bucket beside me should I need to throw up any more.

I went back to sleep and did not wake up for over 24 hours—or so they said.

Death, Sickness, Illness, and Disease were with Maya as the nurse and Karuna half-carried, half-pulled her to the room. However, the moment they reached the door, something entirely unexpected happened. They slammed into an invisible wall, as if it were made of spiritual bricks. The impact of their ethereal bodies against it hurt them. The nature of the wall burned. They pitched backward and tried again. It was as if the wall itself was a force that was on the offensive.

Death rattled off a string of purely demonic obscenities, never heard by human ears. "The prayers of the saints! Her *cursed* mother or father, one of them...or *both*...is praying again! How I *hate* them! How I *hate* that they pray! Even their weakest, stupidest, most thoughtless prayers *are effective!!*"

Death, Sickness, Illness, and Disease shrieked high-pitched screams as the continued prayers thousands of miles away burned into their supernatural nervous systems. The bravado of Death was gone. He scampered away. Sickness, Illness, and Disease scattered too. All whimpering. Instantaneously diminished.

"Come on in!" I called. Several days had passed since my bout with dysentery and I felt much better. Not so well that I could go anywhere, but well enough to sit up on the cot for a little while and chitchat with people.

"Namah shivaya!" Karuna said as she stuck her head through the door. "How are you feeling today? Do you need anything from the store? I'm about to go over there and get some nuts. Do you want anything?"

"No...I'm okay. I had the broth from the kanya this morning and also my first cup of chai." I was lying on the cot, lazily doing japa on my mala.

"Okay! I'll be right back. Are you up for a little company?"

"Oh yes!" I vigorously nodded my head. "I'll be here waiting. Ha! Ha!" I laughed hard at my own joke, so did Karuna. I closed my eyes and continued my japa as I waited. The tulasi wood flowed smoothly through my fingers as I chanted my Kali mantra. I started drifting off to sleep....

When I awakened it was dark, but an odd darkness, like the meager, gray light found in the midst of a hurricane.

———————————————

Chamunda Kali stood in the room. "Get her now!" she screeched. "Stupid, stupid girl! For chanting my mantra! Ohhh! All the hideous things I can do to her. And, whatever you do," Chamunda Kali contorted about the room, "don't kill her yet, Death!"

Torment and Death leapt forward upon Chamunda's orders. Death lay upon Maya, allowing his body to meld into hers. The weight of his evil affected her physical body. It began to shut down immediately in his presence.

Many a healthy body would have resisted; but hers was too weak. Even more powerful than her physical weakness was her spiritual weakness—she had given herself over to Chamunda. Further, through thoughts and conversations about suicide, through talking about wanting to die to reach enlightenment, she had wished death upon herself too often—she had flung wide a gaping doorway. She had opened herself to Death to do whatever he wanted (to a limit—God was still God and He had Death on a long, albeit invisible leash). Torment slid under the cot and pulled from beneath, wrapping his tormenting tentacles around her heart and mind.

Suddenly I felt something grab me, pushing and pulling me down into the cot. I tried to gasp for air. My nose and mouth were covered, blocked by something that was darker than the darkness, but it did not seem to have any form. I tried to move, flail about, anything to get free…all to no avail. It was as though I were straitjacketed to my bed by cords that went straight into the pit of hell. I lay there in a state of surreal, dream-like immobility. I could not scream. *I'm going to die! I'm going to die! I'm going to die!*—was the mantra that pulsed through my mind to the time of my rushing, panicked blood. However, I could not see by whom or what I was to die.

"You're going to die! You're going to die!" Death, Torment, Chamunda Kali, and her cronies chanted as they grabbed her and suffocated her and danced about her.

"Let's take her for a ride!" Chamunda suggested on a whim.

Immediately, Death and Torment let go of her soul. Chamunda grabbed it and pulled. The lesser demons grabbed at Maya's soul, just to be "devilish."

I felt my soul lift out of my body. I looked down and saw that my body was on the bed. I looked to either side of me but I could barely see. I was terrified. Horrified. Something had me. No! Many things held onto me. In fact, it was these "things" that had pulled me from my body. Whatever they were, they pulled at me with a great force. I feared that the part of me that was floating was going to be torn to pieces. Fear and terror gripped me. I felt intense evil emanating from whatever it was that was tugging at me. I felt myself grow colder and colder, freezing cold. Still, the mantra continued—*I'm going to die! I'm going to die! I'm going to die!* Underneath was yet another that thrummed and coursed through me—the Kali mantra. It was violently alive and threatened to take ownership of my soul, of my mind and heart.

"You're going to die! You're going to die!" the demons continued to chant. Suddenly, they stopped and shot backward. Instantaneously. As if they were pins hit by a bowling ball.

"Oh, no! Why didn't I think of *her* and her infernal *praise?*" Death bellowed.

"Whose praise?" Terror asked in confusion.

"The mother's! The mother's!" Death responded.

"We've got to go!" Torment sounded not a little bit tormented, "Her *praise* is burning me! And I can feel the presence of the angels of the Lord. I can feel their power. I don't want to face them!"

"But! We have legal right to be here. Premabhakti was using *my* mantra! She was calling *me!*" Chamunda shrieked, but none too convincingly.

"Okay! You tell that to the angels of the Lord," Death said, throwing Chamunda a dismissive look. "They are functioning under a greater authority…her mother prays. She has been a prayer warrior for so long. The power upon her… You know what the Bible says about the fervent, earnest prayers of a righteous person! We don't stand a chance with her. I'm leaving. Right now! Chamunda, choose your battles wisely!" With that, Death disappeared. The other demons did not have the same ability to make themselves "disappear"; instead, they shrank in upon themselves and scampered away.

Chamunda looked around and realized that her cronies were diminishing in size and vibrancy (if their hues could be considered "vibrant" in any way) as the angels of the Lord approached. "I'm leaving, too!" All demons, including Chamunda, fled.

Bang! Bang! Bang! I was awakened by knocking on the door. I was lying in my cot. Whole. Sound. But my body was wracked with intense pain.

"Premabhakti! Open up the door! Prema! Open up!" It was Karuna calling my name.

"Huh?" I asked in a daze, but she did not hear me as she was still outside the door.

Bang! Bang! Bang!

Karuna called through the door. "Open up! You're scaring me! Open up! I've been banging and banging. You have me worried. Are you sick again?"

Laboriously, I swung my feet over the side of the wooden cot and paused as I waited for the dizziness to dissipate. *When will this dizziness leave me?* "Coming…coming…" I could hear how worn out my own voice sounded. I could not believe I had been sleeping all day and no one had come to awaken me. Finally, I shoved myself up and shuffled to the door. *When had I locked the door?* I unlocked the door and let Karuna in.

"Premabhakti! What in the world took you so long?" she asked me.

"What do you mean? What took *me* so long? I guess I am not as recovered as I'd like to think. I didn't mean to sleep all day. And then when I heard you banging on the door…it took me a long time to pull myself out of such a deep sleep and wake up enough to get it."

Karuna peered at me with a strange look in her eyes, "Sleep all day? Prema, I haven't been gone but five minutes, tops."

"Uh uhhh!" I shook my head in disbelief, at an utter loss for words. Wisps of the vivid dream stung my mind. Its icy-cold clutches were wrapped tightly about me, gripping my heart, slipping its tendrils into my mind.

"What do you mean, 'Uh uhhh'?" Karuna pressed. I could literally *feel* her eyes piercing through me. "Why don't you go lie back down?" She said as she gently prodded me back onto the cot. "And tell me why you think you've been sleeping all day."

I lay back down feeling incredibly sleepy. I gave a big yawn as I mumbled, "I don't know. I just feel like I had been sleeping and sleeping. What woke me up was this horrifically bad dream in which something, or some *things*, were trying to kill me. I was so afraid. I have never in my entire life felt so afraid. It felt like *something* was trying to suffocate me…and it was doing a pretty good job of it."

"Wow!" Karuna sat on the floor and leaned against my cot. "What do you think about it?"

"About…what…?" I asked. I could feel myself fading away.

"Ahh, don't worry about it. Go to sleep. Get the rest you need. I'm just going to sit here for awhile."

Karuna sounded far away. I was almost asleep. And then I heard from an even greater distance what sounded like a foreign language, a beautiful, melodious foreign language.

"What…are…you speaking? What language?" I asked from a half-asleep state. *My! I feel so good. I can't believe I can go back to sleep so easily. It's like the fear I felt earlier just disappeared. Wow! How crazy! What to do now?*

"Nothing," Brilliant responded as he sat down beside Maya to keep an eye on her. He touched her head. Light flowed from his hand into her. "I'm speaking into your body God's Will in our language—the language of Heaven, the language of the Lord's angels. And His Spirit has allowed you to hear me." Brilliant smiled down at her. Maya was already asleep. He continued to speak into her. The heavenly language flowed from him into her—pure, golden light.

On the other side of the world, her mother prayed in the Spirit. Driven. Compelled. She gave herself to the prayer, trusting God to do what He willed.

CHAPTER TWENTY

BHOPI THE LEPER

OKAY, *Prema…today you're going to get up.* I sighed as I half-heartedly admonished myself. *You need to get up…* I had improved enough to return to the dorm, but not enough to get out of bed for long. I only journeyed from my bunk in order to go to the bathroom or to walk around the dorm a bit. *This dysentery has taken something out of me. I feel so wasted, so exhausted. I have never felt so exhausted in my life. I have never been so sick in my life. I don't know how many times I can go through something like this before it kills me…dysentery's no joke…* I considered these thoughts as I lay on my bunk. The ashram was bustling as usual. I just could not get myself going enough to join it. I lay there for I do not know how long, watching the comings and goings of everyone from the window by my bunk.

Alice came in munching on peanuts of course. "He's here!" she announced as if I should know who "he" was.

"Who's here? Who's he?" I asked listlessly.

"Bhopi...Bhopi the Leper," she replied as she peeked out the window by Anneshwari's bunk. She had a clear view of Cha Ma's apartment from there.

"Bhopi the Leper? Who's he?" My curiosity was stoked, but only a little.

"You've never heard of *Bhopi* the *Leper*?" she asked incredulously, overemphasizing "Bhopi" and "Leper." "Come on, let's go to the stairs and watch him. I'll tell you all about him."

I was intrigued and repelled. A leper? Not that lepers were unusual in India. They were everywhere. Because of their physical condition, they were relegated to the position of being an "untouchable," a dalit. They existed at the very bottom of the caste system, which many denied even existed. Every leper I had seen appeared homeless. Most sat on the sidewalk or on the side of the road begging. They often sat together.

They had a distinctly unpleasant smell of rotting, putrid flesh. The disease made their flesh look like melted candle wax...sliding...oozing...over an eye, over a nose. Goozy. Pus-y. Or if the eye or nose had been consumed, over the vacuous hole. Sometimes, the leprosy disfigured their ears and noses so that they sat in unnatural places to the side or below where they were supposed to be. And occasionally, I saw lepers without ears and noses altogether, only a yellow, pus-riddled orifice. As for their extremities, they would wind pieces of cloth around the diseased parts. Or if the disease was advanced, the pieces of cloth were wrapped around the stumps of fingers, hands, toes, and feet.

I tried not to look at them. But if I could not avoid it, I would not look them in the face. I could not bear to. I hated to admit it—they repulsed me. They frightened me horribly. I did not understand leprosy. I did not know what caused it or why. I had always understood it to be incurable and contagious, highly contagious. That was what I was afraid of—that I would contract the disease, that it would consume me and that I would be deemed an untouchable. All three fears competed equally and irrationally within me.

I wanted to see this Bhopi. But I was afraid of what I would see. In the end, my nosiness won out. I slowly pulled myself up from my bunk. *Man, my energy's just not the same.* I joined Alice on the spiral steps as she was peeking around the corner, trying to hide herself behind the wall, not that anyone cared about two Western women standing on the stairs.

"There he is!" she whispered. I saw a man standing alone in the garden by Cha Ma's quarters. I studied him—"Bhopi the Leper." I did not see anything remarkable—he was a dark-skinned Indian guy. Slim. Tall. Alice began telling his story in a hushed voice, "Everyone knows about Bhopi. He was a leper. He came to Cha Ma many years ago when people first started coming to her. He had a bad, bad case of leprosy—his skin was sliding off his face, big, ugly holes in his face where the leprosy was eating through. When he came to get darshan from Cha Ma, they did not want him to get close to her—being that it's contagious and all. But she said to let him come."

I stared at him, fascinated, enwrapped in the story. "When he got to her, they say that the swamis...but they weren't swamis back then. They were still brahmacharis...you know, Swami and Swami Shivaramananda. Hey! Do you know Swami Shivaramananda?" I could only squeeze in a head shake, no. "Well, he's one of Cha Ma's swamis. Like Swami, he's been with her from the beginning...way before they were swamis..."

Okay, she's all over the place! I was interested in the story, but I wanted her to get to the meat of it. Alice had a tendency to follow mental rabbit trails. My patience was fast dissipating. "And so what happened?" I urged her along.

"Well, the swamis ran behind the building to throw up. They say he smelled horrible, and on top of it he looked disgusting. They say that she hugged him and then started licking him…"

My stomach turned in acute repugnance, "Started…licking him? Yuck! You're lying!"

"No!" She shook her head emphatically. "I'm not! It's true. Or rather, that's what they told me. And they say that after she licked him that his leprosy healed. All except one spot…"

"One spot?" I asked incredulously, staring in half-awe, half-disgust at Bhopi the Leper.

"Yes, one spot on his back remains unhealed. She says so that he will keep coming back to her." She finished the story satisfied.

I continued staring at him. *He did have those weird blotches on his skin. Sort of like pock marks or some sort of light and dark spots. Maybe its true…but licking him? Yuck! Yuck! Yuck! And why not heal him completely? Why keep him dependent like that? It's kind of cruel to not heal him completely…* I stopped myself from that critical line of thinking. I shouldn't be criticizing the guru! Who am I to know what's best?

Marie and Paul
United States

"It's a job, Mare…" Paul said, his voice trailing off. He had anticipated resistance to the idea from his wife and he was right. He sat down at the table. *I have to deal with this. Face her.*

"But Paul! It's beneath you!" Marie shot back. "You were an officer in the Army with twenty-seven years of service. You should be doing something with more responsibility, more pay, and more meaning than this. We don't need the income that badly. Why don't you just wait?" Her tone softened as she spoke. She placed her hand on his shoulder and quickly removed it when she felt him flinch. *What is that from?* She went and sat down across from him.

He stared down at his hands. "Mare, I'm tired of looking. I've sent out over fifty applications. It's been over a year. And still nothing. At least with this, I'm doing something. And the money will help."

We don't need the money. We're fine. But Marie knew. He needed the work. He defined himself in great part by his ability to work and to work well. It seemed God was allowing him to be stripped of everything that gave him his identity and value—starting with his work. She knew that not working, not finding work, had been and still was excruciating for him. But, this?

"Just hold on, Paul!" she urged. "Something more must be coming. A security guard at a department store for a dollar over minimum wage? Why do this to yourself? And what about your feet?"

I know, I know, he thought to himself. He agreed with his wife 100 percent. And he knew that she knew. Nothing really needed to be said. He did not need the work that badly. But they both knew he hated sitting idle. And even more than sitting idle, he hated the rejection. He needed to work; it helped him feel better about life, about himself, about how things had changed.

After the Army, so much of his life had changed, starting with his health. Somehow, he was not sure how it happened or when during his stint in the Army, severe gout and arthritis had set into his feet. To make matters worse, during the same time and in much the same way, he had gradually lost vision in his left eye—to the point that he was considered legally blind in that eye. This put a strain on his right eye so that he suffered intense headaches and blurred vision when he had to look at anything intently for any amount of time. These disabilities, apparently nonexistent while he was in active duty, had attacked him with a vengeance as soon as he had left the military.

Now over a year after retiring, he could not stand for longer than ten minutes, let alone walk the length of a football field. This made it nearly impossible for him to take a standing or walking job. Nor could he do much vision-intensive work such as working with computers or reading without horrible headaches and impaired vision. So, yes, deep down inside, he wondered how he would be able to work the long hours on his feet. But he *needed* the work—he *needed* to do something with himself.

At least if he were working he would not have time to sit and think. *That* was the worst of it. Having ample time in which to sit and think. He hated, absolutely hated, being still because then he sat and pondered and examined and criticized his life—all he had done, and *not done*, the choices he had made. The worst choices being, in his mind, those he had made concerning his own children.

He found himself to be a failure with his children. His son lived in California, as far away as could be—literally a thousand miles away from him in body and in heart. And his daughter had run even farther away and had gotten herself caught up in a God-cursed religion in a God-forsaken place on the other side of the world. Constantly his mind badgered and condemned him—criticizing his treatment of his children. *You are an awful father! It would have been better if they had* been born to anyone but you. *You don't deserve children. You never knew how to treat them.* On and on it went.

The demons enthusiastically helped in his self-condemnation.

"You are a horrible father!"

"You are a pathetic man! You should never have been born."

"Of course they would leave you. You were never there for them when they were growing up. They're just following your example." Condemnation, Hate, Deception, and many others opportunistically slithered in and worked on him.

And then, the worst—Despair would come and hiss, "You will never see your children again. They want to have nothing to do with you. You will die all alone! And they will die far away from you!"

Every day, almost every hour of the day, they came and spoke his worst thoughts and fears. They assailed his days with accusations and condemnation and assaulted his nights with heart-gripping, fearful nightmares. He wanted to work. He *had* to work. He had to get away from his own mind!

All of this sat between Marie and Paul as they discussed the new job. Marie studied him. Finally, she conceded, "Okay. Whatever you feel is best. I will support you in it." She voiced strong support of her husband; but her heart was not in it.

He nodded and rose from the table. In silence he went and sat in his armchair, falling quickly into his doubts and fears. His wife stared at his empty chair, her heart sinking even further. *Oh God! What can I do? He doesn't need this job. He shouldn't do it.* She felt no confirmation within her from the Holy Spirit. All she felt was fear and a coldness seeping in from without. A random, though not unrelated, thought drifted by—*I'm losing him.*

CHAPTER TWENTY-ONE

I WISH UPON...MANY STARS

Maya

Alleppey, India

KALI Leela—a very long night as the crowds numbered into the thousands. I washed pots, which took almost three hours. It was fun though. We played and splashed and just had a grand time. Later I hung out in the Western canteen with Dirk, Devi, Radha, Karuna, and a new girl, Chandy, from Australia. Doug and Linda (they had decided to stay—Cha Ma was too arresting to leave) stopped by to chat for a while, joining in easily with the ashram banter and gossip. When we had exhausted all conversation, I headed to my bunk in the dorm to get a little bit of shut-eye before the end of Kali Leela.

It did not last long. The music was as it always was—too loud. Being in the women's dorm did not help as we sat above the temple.

The amplified music was deafening. Further, all the people tromping through the women's dorm on their way to the inner temple was an incredible nuisance. And of course, I was an item of "stare-ation"—the black American woman with the unruly hair. It seemed that some came to the ashram just to see the oddity. *News of the unusual travels fast and wide. It never fails.* Sometimes I found their interest humorous, but usually I tired quickly of being a spectacle—and this was one of those times. I decided to go to the roof and meditate the rest of the night away until the bhajans signaled the end of the program, which would not be until very, very late (or very, very early depending upon how one looked at it) considering the size of the crowd. Easily, several thousand were present to pay homage to and receive darshan from Kali disguised as Cha Ma.

No one was on the roof. I climbed to the highest place of the temple, the uppermost deck, which was a little 7-by-12-foot platform that sat over 12 feet above the regular meditation roof. This was my favorite place because of its solitude. Few people climbed so high, preferring, instead, to sit on the meditation roof below. It afforded a breathtaking, panoramic view of the surrounding area. During the day, the lush, deep green of the palm trees stretched far into the horizon, spanning out for miles and miles on three sides to meet the vast Indian Ocean which stretched dark and beckoning. At night, the diamond-laden sky met the rippling currents of the ocean and whispered dark, unseeable mysteries.

I sat on my asana facing the Indian Ocean, shawl about my body. The light of the moon, a thin sliver of moon, shone delicately on the water, making the water appear fragile and weak. I settled my hands in my lap, closed my eyes and "went away"—I would like to say that I went into a deep, blissful meditation; but truth be told, I was whisked away to the land of sleep. I awakened after a while (however long it was) sitting hunched over, listing to one side like a ship whose sails had no wind and whose wheel no captain. I roused myself and sat staring out at the ocean.

Then, I saw it...a falling star. I made a wish upon the star: *May I be enlightened in this lifetime!* Right behind it, another fell and another and another...on and on they fell—sporadically and haphazardly. For each one, I cast the same wish: *May I be enlightened in this lifetime!* They created a beautiful, ethereal light show—streaking across the sky, one after another. I could not believe my "good luck"—or was it luck at all? *Twenty-seven falling stars!* I counted! *Twenty-seven! Perhaps it is a sign from the universe?* I wondered. *I'll take it for that...a sign from the universe! How auspicious!* I sat spellbound by the magnificent show as it blazed across the sky above a delicately illumined ocean. "Have I ever seen a sight so beautiful?" I half-whispered, half-thought this last question, lost in deep wonderment.

"Oh, Maya!" murmured Brilliant who sat, unperceived, beside her. He waved his hand across the sky in a gesture of extravagant pleasure, "The earth, the heavens, the very universe cannot help but proclaim love and adoration for the Lord with their entire being. Hard to imagine, hmmm, that these things demonstrate love and worship?" He smiled and placed his hand upon her head. A peace and calm descended upon her. She took in a deep draught of air and slowly exhaled it. She stared out at the ocean—all was quiet and still.

After some time, she began to chant her Kali mantra. "Oh my dear child, why must you do that?" Brilliant whispered into her ear. "You invite a curse and you remove our immediate protection." He paused and hugged her, "I will watch over you, thank God for your parents' prayers, but I must step back…"

Even as he said this, Chamunda began to creep forward, having been waiting in the shadows. "I knew she would call for me," she cackled, sounding not at all joyful.

"That is okay!" Brilliant laughed. As he laughed shimmery sparkles showered from his mouth and eyes, "We win in the end!"

"Yes, I know…" Chamunda Kali circled slowly around them. "but it's not yet the end."

"And we win with her, too!" he said, laughter sliding in on his voice, as he stepped back. He felt Chamunda's frown, even though he was looking at Maya and not the evil being. "You know that, too, don't you? You just can't admit it? You can't even allow yourself to see it!" He laughed again. "No, it's not that you can't *allow* yourself…no, *you* and *your kind* are no longer *capable*." His words spoke of a deeper mystery among the angels. Chamunda's frown deepened.

After a moment's pause, Chamunda stepped closer to Maya who unconsciously wrapped her shawl about herself a little more tightly. Maya felt a chill to her bones as she sank into a deep, sepia-colored meditation that soon blocked out any feeling at all.

Hours passed as Chamunda played with her mind. She was roused out of her meditation by the exuberant singing that announced that Cha Ma was almost finished with Kali Leela.

Wow! That was strange! Did I really see a meteor shower with twenty-seven meteors? That is so auspicious! And then, a meditation of a light being talking with Kali. Did it really happen? Or was it just my imagination? Realization startled me—I wasn't meditating then! I was looking at the ocean, thinking about the falling stars. I was lucid! So…no, it couldn't have been my imagination. What were they saying? I wish I could remember.... The music began to take me away. I left the roof to finish the Kali Leela dancing out by the brahmacharini huts.

Deep in the shadows between Cha Ma's room, the brahmacharini huts and the black rocks upon which the brahmacharinis dried their laundry was an open clearing. It was perfect for dancing—sandy, level, and large enough for free movement. Pale tendrils of light reached out to the huts from the temple, not enough illumination to really be observed by anyone but enough so that I could see and not run into anything. I had "discovered" the place a few weeks back. Since then, I had taken it for my own—dancing there often. I preferred it to the crowds, the pushing and squishing of the temple, the being sat upon and stared at, the being touched and the hair-pulling.

Quietly, I sang along with everyone inside the temple—a song to Devi—as I walked my way over to the huts. I was completely alone. All of the brahmacharinis were inside with Cha Ma, and it was forbidden for a man to enter the brahmacharinis' area. I could not even imagine a man coming near and violating the sanctity of the brahmacharini side. So much of Cha Ma's reputation hung on her keeping her unwed brahmacharinis virginal, safe, and pure. Once there, I began to dance—confident of being unseen in the shadows, assured that every-one was inside.

After a while, the music crescendoed madly from one song to the next, building to a wild, crazy climax. The night was almost over. The voices of thousands of Kali worshipers rolled stridently, passionately, out of the open windows and doors of the temple. I danced to match the intensity of the music and singing. At one point, I scanned the ashram building—all was dark except for the temple itself, which was brightly lit and festive.

Then I saw toward the front of the building on the third floor, the tall, slim silhouette of a man standing on a darkened balcony. It did not seem he was hiding so much as he had stopped whatever he was doing and just happened to be in the shadows. *How long has he been there? Is he watching me?* And then—*he's probably not even looking at me.* However, I could tell, from the angle of his head that he was and it seemed he was transfixed because he did not move at all.

There was something about him. Perhaps it was his posture, his stance, or maybe the tilt of his head that spoke of...an aloneness...a loneliness. It seemed odd—the two of us so far from each other, yet connected and similar—both of us were on the outside of the Kali Leela, in the dark, so many people around and yet so alone. I kept dancing—he was too far away to stop me and it did not seem that he desired to. Later when I looked he was gone. *Who was he?* echoed through my mind like a refrain. *Who would watch me so?*

CHAPTER TWENTY-TWO

FREAKS

NARAYANA popped his head around the corner of my little workspace. "Premaaaabhaaaaktiiiiiii, what are you doing?" he singsonged in his thick-accented voice. *I love how he says my Kali name!* I sighed, (thankfully) not aloud. His eyes, his beautiful eyes, were aglitter with merriment. His mouth expressed a playful smirk that spoke of a hidden joke.

Immediately, unsolicited by me and woefully uncontrolled, thoughts flew through my head. *He is so beautiful. I wonder what it would be like to kiss him. I wonder what it would be like to marry him.* Mindbogglingly fast, my desires grew wings and flew away. I struggled to rid myself of the subversive thoughts. *Focus! Focus!* I admonished myself. *Pay attention to him and what he's saying. Go figure!* I pulled myself out of my daydream. He was still standing there. Smiling at me.

I was working my new job at the seva desk, which was in a small, narrow "half-room" right next to the Foreigners' Office. The "room" was no bigger than five feet wide and ten feet long. I had been "promoted" from pot washing to working the seva desk and cooking for the Westerners. Granted it was more work, but according to Radha, Narayana had made the changes. He had decided that somebody was needed in the Western canteen to help with the cooking (and any ole' -body could wash pots). Additionally, he felt that I would be useful at the seva desk, or so Radha said he said. I should have been offended that he would assign me extra work. I should have been...but Radha teased that he just wanted me closer...and that was all I needed. Today it seemed that way, considering his behavior.

In response to his joking, I caught myself smiling. I could not help it. *What am I doing, you ask? Nothing. Just sitting here, getting all distracted by you.* "Nothing. Just sitting here," I answered. "What about you? What are you doing outside of the Foreigners' Office?" I asked knowing full well that he would just as soon not tell me as tell me. But I wanted him to talk to me, listen to me, interact with me; so I rapidly snatched at some sort, any sort, of conversation.

Without saying another word, he stepped back into the Foreigners' Office. I felt my heart take a downward turn. *No! Don't you go doing that!* I chastened my emotions. *You know how he's a...freak!* I snapped myself in line and continued working. After a couple of minutes, his head popped around the corner again. His eyes were still glittering. A boyish grin played on his face.

"Preee*maaaa*—bhaaak*tiiiiii*! Preee*maaaa*—bhaaak*tiiiiii*!" He singsonged more vigorously this time, emphasizing the second sylla-ble. He began tapping on the wall. He had a penchant for doing that...tapping on anything in order to make a percussive tune. "I was thinking..." His voice trailed off as he stared at me, a strange, but beautiful look in his eyes. His eyes looked almost...and for a few sec-onds...full of—*could it really be? Desire? For me?*

He continued tapping a staccato rhythm that sounded vaguely familiar. "To serve Cha Ma is such a joy. I have known her since…since…for many years. She is my everything." Narayana was actually talking to, not barking at, me—now that was something wholly and completely new. *Strange.*

"What would you have done had you not come to the ashram?" I asked, wanting to know as much as I could about him.

"I don't know." He sat down at the desk next to me and continued tapping out his rhythm on its top. I was too aware of his close proximity, whereas he did not seem to notice at all. *Is a brahmachari allowed to sit this close to a woman?* I asked myself, although I already knew the answer—no. Resoundingly no. "I don't like to think on what life would have been like if…that's a great way to be miserable!" he said, smiling at me. "I love helping Cha Ma—passing people to her, serving her during Kali Leela, playing the kimini." He paused. "Soon I will be taking the vow of sannyasa. I will wear the yellow robes."

"Wow! I didn't know. I'm happy for you!" I lied. Disappointment washed through me. *So much for my daydreams of anything ever happening between us.* On the heels of that thought—*I shouldn't be thinking about him like that, anyway! He's Cha Ma's, through and through.* I felt a pang of jealousy. *I wish I were that close to Cha Ma. I wish I were an Indian and I could take a full vow of sannyasa. What I wouldn't do to be a brahmacharini, a real brahmacharini, not just a renunciate…Wow! Narayana in yellow…Cha Ma doesn't give sannyasa to many. That's such a high place, a great honor. He must be so dedicated! But then, he's always with her…* I felt another deeper, stronger pang of jealousy. I looked up. I was not aware that I had looked down in the midst of my musings. Narayana was watching me closely—too closely. *Why is he looking at me so hard?*

"Yes, during the next puja, I will take up sannyasa." Narayana continued to stare at me. I did not say anything. I did not know what to say. In fact I was starting to lose my focus—he was staring so intently.

Suddenly, as inexplicably as it had appeared, his mood changed. His affability and kindness disappeared. His face hardened into its usual look of disdain, hatefulness, and suppressed anger. He jumped up and walked away. At that moment, four Westerners climbed up the steps. He strode over to them and greeted them pleasantly, in marked contrast to the unnerving, hateful look he had just given me. After speaking with them for a few minutes, he led them toward the Foreigners' Office.

"Premabhakti!" he barked out my name. "Get four buckets and two mattresses for our new Westerners. Make sure the mattresses are clean." He flicked his hand at me negligently without even looking back as he walked off. My heart sank to the ground. *Every time! He does this to me!*

I turned and grabbed two mattresses from the jumbled, dirty pile that was sitting in the corner. No one ever bothered to clean the mattresses. Actually, it was impossible for them to be cleaned. Radha and I often joked that the whole lot of them needed to be burned. People used them over and over without their being sprayed with germicide or treated with any sort of disinfecting agent. By now they had to be a cesspool of germs, bacteria, fungi, you name it. I carried them at arm's length to the door of the Foreigners' Office, which was now closed, and dumped them there. *I'm so stupid! Stupid! Stupid!*

As I bent over to grab the buckets that sat by the seva desk, I felt the tears come. Hot. Burning. One spattered on the ground in front of me. *Ah! Great! Now on top of it, I'm crying! I am such a wimp! Narayana is the rock that I am smashing myself up against. Why do I like him? Why, oh why? He's rude and mean.* I grabbed four buckets, swallowing back the rest of the tears that burned in my throat. *But there's just something about him.* That familiar tight, painful lump usually associated with Narayana rose. I set the buckets beside the mattresses and went back to my post at the seva desk.

Thirty minutes later I still struggled against the lump in my throat. The new Westerners had come and gone, taking their buckets and mattresses with them. The door of the Foreigners' Office remained closed. Finally my duty was over. I went to sit on the balcony facing Cha Ma. I watched her give darshan and listened to one of Cha Ma's swamis, Funeral Swami, sing. He was called Funeral Swami because he sang only sad, mournful tunes to Devi. My heart felt as low as he sounded. I leaned my forehead against the wrought iron lattice of the balcony. Finally I let the lump in my throat have its way. Tears fell as I sat feeling forlorn and lonely. I listened to Funeral Swami sing bhajan after bhajan—my heart pained with the depth of his songs.

And then, I turned my head and there…was Narayana staring at me, his eyes full of yearning and desire. He quickly turned his head and walked back into the Foreigners' Office, shutting the door behind him. *How long had he been standing there watching me?* I felt myself sigh involuntarily. My heart twisted again as I wanted to hate him. *He is such a freak!* I needed to hate him. It was best if I could; but I could not.

Marie
United States

Paul's right—I really do need to go to the doctor. I need some antibi-otics for my sinuses. I don't think I've ever had such bad headaches. And they're getting worse. Marie thought to herself. She had stopped telling Paul. They were firm believers that if something was wrong, go take care of it. She had no real excuse for not going to the doctor, except maybe being overworked and busy.

She had been praying to God to heal her sinuses; but they seemed to only get worse. Her headaches had grown in duration and intensity. Now they were constant and steady. And the spots and webbing before her eyes were worse too. In fact, just last night she had caught herself waving her hand in front of her face in order to clear the cobwebs. She had thought that there was an actual cobweb in the bathroom. *I'll go. I've got to go…soon, too.* She took some over-the-counter sinus medicine with a pain reliever and went to lie down.

Maya

Alleppey, India

"How's Doug doing?" I asked Alice as we walked away from the Indian canteen. It was time for morning chai and we had just received ours. *Of all people, Alice would know.*

"Oh, he's not doing too well," Alice replied as she took a sip. This was the first time I had ever seen her put anything to her mouth other than peanuts. I stared strangely fascinated. I did not realize how accustomed I had grown to seeing her eat peanuts until now. "He still has the boils and they've grown. They're so gross."

Doug, within a few weeks of arriving with Linda, had come down with a hideous case of boils. They covered his entire body, even the soles of his feet and the palms of his hands. He could barely walk because the weight of his body upon his feet caused great pain and made the boils explode.

I had seen him two nights ago. I had passed him in the hallway on the fourth floor. He was on his way to his room from the bathroom. He was walking flinchingly on crutches because the movement caused intense pain. I had seen firsthand just how desperate his condition had become—he was a mass of large, oozing, yellow, sick-looking boils—his face, his torso, his arms and legs. He had been wearing a loosely tied dhoti, the ends tucked into the waist, to allow for as little touching of his body as possible. He could not put his weight down on his feet because of the boils there. He could not put his arms around anyone for support because of the pain and because of the nastiness of exploding boils upon the other person (no one knew whether or not he was contagious and even if he was not, no one wanted to touch him anyway). He struggled with the crutches because they assaulted the boils under his armpits and on his palms. I felt so sorry for him.

"What are you going to do?" I had asked him, teetering between extreme repugnance and pity. *Poor guy! Even his eyes look pus-y and weepy.* As I looked in his face, his eyes swollen almost shut by the many boils on his eyelids, a boil popped. *Eww! Nasty!* I stepped away. I did not mean to, I did so involuntarily.

"I don't know..." his entire demeanor spoke of defeat. "You know, sometimes I feel like such a freak." His brutal honesty unnerved me. To tell the truth—he did look like a freak. I decided to go in a different direction with my questions.

"Have you talked to Cha Ma?" I asked.

He nodded, barely. One burst under his chin (from the movement I surmised) and began dripping goop that looked like watery mustard mixed with mayonnaise. My meager dinner of kanya and curry of two hours ago threatened to erupt from within me. I clamped my mouth tight. *That would not be good! To throw up on him!*

"Yes." He peered at me from his hideous mask. A look of fear and something else sneaked out.

"What did she say?" I urged him as he had fallen silent.

"She said that I have to stay with her. That I'm under a death star and that if I leave her, I will die. As it is now, she's keeping the effects of the death star at bay, but that's why I am like I am. She says that I'm burning karma and that it must take its course. When all is done, which will be soon, I'll be enlightened."

"Wow!" I was amazed and I felt another sensation totally opposite to what his condition should have engendered—jealousy. "Enlightenment in this life!" I exclaimed. *What I wouldn't do for enlightenment in this lifetime! And to have the reassurance of it from an avatar of Kali?*

"Yes, she says that all I have to do is let these run their course and not leave her." A boil popped. I could almost hear them when they exploded. "In the end, I will be enlightened."

"You are so blessed! So blessed by Kali, indeed!" I started walking away, lost in my own envious thoughts.

"Namah shivaya, Premabhakti!" he called behind me.

"Namah shivaya, Doug!" I meandered off. *Enlightenment! To know in this lifetime that I would be enlightened! What I wouldn't give for that! Oh, please Kali! Make me enlightened! Make me enlightened! I'd willingly die for enlightenment. To get out of this cycle—once and for all!*

———————————

"Oh yes! You will be enlightened all right!" Chamunda whispered as she pointed her bony finger at Doug. Her jab in the spiritual realm caused one of the boils to explode. "Ha! Ha!"

Disease spat on his hands and rubbed them over Doug's face. Immediately, three more boils began to grow. Chamunda jabbed at them. They cackled hysterically at their grotesque game.

CHAPTER TWENTY-THREE

NO WASTE

"**P**REMABHAKTI, do we have to use these tomatoes? So many of them are rotten!" Karla, a German woman visiting the ashram, asked. A look of poorly disguised disgust was evident upon her face. The clipped staccato of her accented voice added to the effect.

"Yes, we do." *I hate when people who are visiting the ashram challenge me about how to cook stuff,* I thought as I answered Karla's question. I had been cooking in the kitchen for a little over a month and felt like an old-timer. Perhaps I was a bit too confident in my position.

"But…shouldn't we throw these away? They're bad. They smell!" With the "uggy" look still on her face, she leaned over to throw a couple of soft, overripe tomatoes into the garbage bucket.

I walked over and looked into the bucket. *Hey! There's nothing wrong with those! There's no white mold or black rot!* "No. We'll salvage all we can from the tomatoes. We—*in the ashram*—," I added with a particularly condescending emphasis to let her know *she* was *not* one of the ashramites, "can't afford the luxury of throwing away food just because it's rotten, it's gone bad, or it's sour." I walked over to Dirk's cupboard for some spices. "There's always some use for it. And then if it's boiled long enough, it will be just fine," I said as I rooted around in his cupboard for more mustard seed. Because my back was to the "cutters," I could not see their expressions of disgust and dismay. "Ah! That's what I'm looking for! Mustard seed and cumin…." *Great spices for drowning out the smell and taste of food that is not yet too bad, but is bad enough.*

I turned around. Everyone's face was turned toward me, the disgust and dismay morphing into looks that were indescribable and disturbing. *Uh oh! I think I said something wrong! What did I say wrong?*

"Uh, excuse me," said a little Western guy. Kinda mousy looking. I had not bothered to learn his name because he did not strike me as someone I really wanted to get to know.

"Uh huh?" I answered distractedly, not even bothering to look him in the face as I went to grab another bucket of tomatoes for them to chop up.

"You're really planning to use rotten tomatoes?" he asked incredulously.

"Oh yeah!" I responded, still not thinking. "As long as they haven't turned completely black or white with mildew or mold, we're good to go." *Even with the mildew and mold, I'd use them. I just wouldn't let you all know.* I set the bucket of tomatoes down on the floor beside them. "What I need you to do is chop these up too. I've looked them over a little and I don't see any mold or mildew."

No one moved. They sat there staring at me. I repeated myself, "Just chop them up. I'll cook them really well so that no one will know, and all the germs will die," I added. *That should reassure them.*

Karla pushed away her knife and cutting board with a look of grim resolution, "I'm NOT cutting any rotten tomatoes for us to eat, whether they're cooked *really well so that no one will know and all the germs die* or not!" she mimicked me nastily. *Not* the thing to do—we ashramites were a feisty group, not given to backing down in an altercation. Some of the other Westerners followed her lead. It looked like it could turn into a culinary insurrection in the Western canteen. I decided to back down.

"Okay! Okay! Let me have that bucket of rotten tomatoes. We'll just use the other ones; they're good." I capitulated, taking the bucket of tomatoes. I peered down into them. *They don't look all that bad to me. There's no white or black spots on them.* I carried them over to the cupboard and hid them in the little corner that was between the cupboard and the wall. I figured I would get them later and put them in the soup or give them to the cows. *Do cows eat tomatoes? Are they good enough for Rukmini's beloved cows? Would she even let me close to them?* Next to Cha Ma, Rukmini loved the ashram cows that she took care of. Aside from them and Cha Ma, nothing mattered to her. *Oh well, I'll do something with them.*

As I walked back, I saw Karla, no-name-guy, and several of the other Westerners cutting the "good" tomatoes with a smug look on their faces: They had won the battle. *No worries...I just might stick those tomatoes in the soup after you're gone.* A smile played on my lips with that thought. I headed out to the "fry kitchen" to sauté some garlic, onions, and spices to go into the soup. Within a couple of minutes I had forgotten all about the tomatoes sitting, hidden, in the corner.

Later that evening, after bhajans and dinner, everyone dispersed. Cha Ma headed into her apartment. The rest of the ashramites scattered—some to get ready for the next day, others to meditate, others to just hang out and talk, still others to sleep. I climbed up to the uppermost deck of the temple to meditate. I settled onto my asana to keep my vibrations from going into the cement and to keep the chill of the cement from traveling into my joints. I arranged my blue woolen prayer shawl around my shoulders and over my head.

After I was comfortable, I stared at the Indian Ocean. It was always lovely this time of night. The air was so still that I could hear the waves as they gently rolled toward the shore. The moon was almost full and shone bright white—its light dancing delicately over the surface of the ocean. A few clouds scudded by drowsily, the light of the moon playing off their tops. The air was warm and moist, touched with that distinctly "Indian" smell—sweet and fragrant.

I sat for a long time by myself in the dark and in the silence watching the scenery—the moon, the ocean, the slowly drifting clouds. I closed my eyes to adjust to the beginnings of meditation. I chanted my Kali mantra for a while to get myself centered. Then I left it off and felt myself drift into meditation. After some time, I came to with a start.

The sky was cloudier now. The moon was obscured by the clouds. *Get down. Go to the kitchen.* It was as though I had heard someone speak to me, commanding me. I felt so *prompted*, so *compelled*. I stood up, shawl draped over my head and shoulders. I grabbed my asana and climbed down from the deck.

On the meditation roof a few people were meditating. All were facing the ocean. Most had shawls over their head—possibly to keep out distractions, make them feel enclosed, ensconced, in meditation. *How strange! At this time of night, there should be a few more people than this.* I continued down the inner stairs of the temple from floor to floor. The main lights were off, so the temple was dark with only a dim light burning here or there. A few Indian families were camping out for the night on the balcony and on the temple floor, in preparation for seeing Cha Ma tomorrow. They were talking quietly among themselves, lying on threadbare blankets or on the bare floor.

I walked out the temple door and ran into one of the brahmacharinis. I did not know her name (honestly they all looked alike to me). She was intensely beautiful with keen features, big eyes, a small frame, and clothed in white. "Cha Ma is in the kitchen," she said, out of breath as she ran-walked from the brahmacharini huts to their room in the kitchen.

When I heard her, a dead-weight hit my stomach. However I did not put two and two together. I trotted behind her to see what the hullaballoo was about, for wherever Cha Ma went, there a "show" would be. I entered the brahmacharini kitchen. In the dim light of the single bulb hanging from the ceiling, Cha Ma was talking and joking animatedly causing everyone to laugh. The crowd of ashramites surrounding her was easily over 50 people. The Indians were laughing and joking with her (the Westerners, too, although they could not have understood what was being said). I stood on the periphery, watching and enjoying the boisterous, lively scene—the "Cha Ma sighting"—it was always such a big event when Cha Ma came out of her quarters for the evening. Inevitably, a large crowd would appear.

Suddenly Cha Ma, in the midst of talking to a brahmachari, turned and stared at me with an odd look. Just as abruptly as she looked over the heads of all the ashramites clamoring at her and fixed her eyes on me, she about-faced and headed toward the inner kitchen. She threaded her way through the pots and pans and huge cooking gear—the company of ashramites in tow behind her. I pulled up the rear, alternately curious and disinclined toward the madness of the crowd. I considered going up to the dorm in order to get some sleep; instead, I strolled behind everyone as she headed to the Western canteen. *Why is she going there?* Curiosity pulled me along.

As I walked into the Western canteen straggling behind the last, a couple of brahmacharinis turned to me, "Premabhakti! Premabhakti! Cha Ma is calling for you!" they said with a thick Indian accent making the words barely recognizable. They grabbed my arms and pulled me along, "Come quickly! You mustn't keep Cha Ma waiting."

I lurched and stumbled behind them, stepping on people's toes as I went—so many people were milling about. "Namah shivaya! Namah shivaya!" I kept exclaiming as my "I'm sorry." I could not regain my balance as they were gripping my arms and pulling me along.

Finally, I made it to the front of the crowd. Cha Ma was standing there, waiting. Her face was not its usual cappuccino color, rather it had turned ominously dark, almost black—a look of pure fury upon it. *What could make her* that *angry? Does it have something to do with me?* I did not have time to wonder.

When she saw me, she bellowed, "Tomatoes! Tomatoes! No waste!" She turned around and grabbed a bucket—*the* bucket—the *rotten tomato* bucket that I had hid in the corner. *How in the world did she find it? She's never in the Western canteen!* Her eyes blazed. Her face was stony hard in anger. She turned back toward me, glaring. "No waste! *No waste!*" she bellowed at me again, her voice deep and strong, fearsome. I nodded my head rapidly out of terror. My heart was pounding. I felt my body shaking. "Why you waste?" she boomed at me. I could find no answer. I just stood there shaking my head from side to side. I felt my body trembling even more. Pure, raw fright raced through me!

"No more waste!" she thundered. And then she let it fly in Malayalam. I should not have been able to understand what she was saying, but it was as if the words were being typed across my mind as she spoke. *You stupid, stupid girl! How did you ever become a kitchen girl? You are so stupid. You are useless. A nothing! A nobody! You don't think. You waste everything. You stupid, ignorant girl!* She shook her head back and forth…in a definitive way that was very different from the "normal" Indian "bobble." This was a fierce back and forth motion that emphasized words in a language that I did not know but understood.

I felt as though I were in a gigantic kaleidoscope that whirled around and around as she spoke—flashing, bold, nauseatingly bright colors slid from one mad, chaotic pattern to the next. My vision narrowed myopically as I could not see or even notice anyone or anything but her. Her. The satguru. The *avatar* in all her fierce, bellicose anger. Kali. *Chamunda Kali!* One uncontrollable sensation after another assaulted me. Her words alternately pummeled me viciously and burned into my being. I felt myself clench tight inside, folding in upon myself. Searing heat rose through my body—burning through the soles of my feet, stabbing up through my bowels and gripping viselike upon my heart, my throat, and up into my face. Tears began to stream down my face. I was *beyond horrified!* I turned heel and did the one thing I could think to do—I ran.

I ran for the temple, up the inner stairs all the way to the meditation roof. Her words resounded in my ears and pinged around in my head. I yearned desperately for the meditation roof. No one was up there. More than likely, everyone who was awake was down in the kitchen with Cha Ma. I thought to climb to the upper platform. I decided not. I dropped my shawl and asana and stumbled in the dark to the edge of the roof.

With my toes hanging over the edge, I looked at the brahmacharini huts, thinking, *What would it be like if I threw myself down? Right now?* I thought of stories I had heard of people who "chose" death, and in exchange for "losing" their lives, received enlightenment.

I burned for enlightenment. *I just want to get away! I want to be done with this stupid cycle of reincarnation once and for all! Merge into* the ultimate Brahman. *What would it be like if I threw myself over the edge? I should...if I really wanted enlightenment I would jump. Give it up. Right now!* A contrary thought arose: *What if I didn't die, but I ended up a paraplegic or something? What if I injured myself horribly and I couldn't walk or do anything and I didn't die either?* I stood on the edge crying, wavering in doubt, fear, horrification, humiliation. I stood there a long time, sobbing.

Jump!

I felt...heard...the command from within and without me. Standing there with my toes hanging off the edge, tears streaming down my face, I thought about how wonderful it would be if I jumped. I was utterly overwrought.

Jump!

Many of the "divine beings" and "enlightened masters" taught that if we truly wanted enlightenment, we would not value our lives in any way. When we came to a place where we would gladly forfeit our lives, then and only then would we be on the brink of enlightenment. The moment we took the "leap" to die we would enter into the realm of the enlightened. *Did I desire enlightenment enough?* I stood there crying.

Jump!

The breeze blew the fragrant, humid Indian air into my face, ever so slightly drying my tears, although I was unaware of it. All I could think about, all I could see, was myself dead. I wanted to die. I burned to be free of the cycle of rebirth, of having to be reincarnated over and over. *I want to die! I want to be gone from here!* The words ran like a litany through my mind. *I want to die! I want to be gone from here! I want to die! I want to be gone from here!*

Finally, my mind and an awareness of my surroundings came to me enough so that I noticed that all the lights were out in the brahmacharini huts. All of the lights of the ashram were out. No one was stirring at all. Still, I was all alone on the meditation roof.

My emotions took a decided downshift. Gone was the vociferous madness and shrieking insanity; instead, an aching emptiness and insatiable void surfaced. I felt all alone. Miniscule and inconsequential in a huge and vicious world. I looked out over the ocean. *What would it be like to drown in the ocean? In the Indian Ocean? To just be lost forever in that vast expanse of water?* I longed to be lost in the silvery blackness of the ocean.

Jump!

How I *ached* to, but I just could not. Simply…I could not. Toes hanging over the edge, my weight shifted harrowingly forward on the balls of my feet. I yearned to jump, but something…*something*…kept me from jumping. I stood there—suspended on the balls of my feet, more off the roof than on—for I do not know how long. Slowly another thought wove into my consciousness, definite and uncompromising—*No.*

Simply…

No.

Finally, I drew back from the edge. I turned around, picked up my asana and shawl, and headed over to the uppermost deck. I climbed up and sat down on my asana. I wrapped my shawl around my shoulders and continued to cry. I felt alone and profoundly *lonely*. Full of yearning. I stared at the ocean, its inky blackness interrupted by the reflected moonlight on its surface. Its beauty undimmed by the chaos and storminess within me. Perhaps the chaos and storminess within me were beautiful in their own respect—I could not see that, though. Weeping, I watched the moon dance from one end of the ocean to another. Gradually the tears erased themselves as the sun began to rise behind me.

All around Maya sat angels, bidden by the Lord upon the distant, ceaseless prayers of her parents. One, Brilliant, sat beside her and stroked her head. He placed his other hand over her heart—pinkish light diffused from his hand. Another, His Strength, sat on the other side of her, whispering words of solace and peace into her. The words of pure, white light flowed fluidly into her being and comforted her. Strengthened her. The pink and white light spread throughout her, dispelling the pain and loneliness.

A few feet out a group of hulking, warring angels formed a circle about her, standing shoulder to shoulder, facing outward. They peered into the darkness and saw much. Their shields were lifted on their left forearms. Their swords were drawn and shone brilliantly, only slightly less than the brilliance of the angels themselves. Standing nearby (and if one looked closely to see—standing in the air) were two angels, Majesty and Awe, looking on.

Majesty, Awe, Brilliant, and His Strength had been present the entire evening. They had observed the scene in the Western canteen. They had been with her as she teetered for so long on the edge of the roof. In fact, it had been Brilliant who had pressed against her—it had not taken much force—and had kept her body from toppling over the edge. They would be with her until the very end. The evil ones had slithered into the background, ashamed of their own inability to withstand and defeat the Lord's angels. Their humiliation egged them on—they would not, *could not*, give up. No, they would redouble their efforts.

"Soon..." Suicide hissed as it slunk halfway into the floor and away from the radiant light of the angels. It did not go too far—it still had squatters' rights on Maya. She had flung wide the supernatural door-way to the evil ones. "It shan't be long before she...*Premabhakti*..." Suicide stabbed with diabolical intent at her choice. In response, Majesty blew at Suicide, his breath flowing from his mouth like a glittering ice shower. Suicide staggered backward as if on an invisible staircase. After he had found a place of partial safety, he rasped in sinister promise, "...beckons us...yet again!" Majesty snorted in reply and rolled his angelic eyes. A spark of fierce light shot from them—a solitary bolt of lightning. A whimper escaped from Suicide as he scampered away.

Awe turned to Majesty, "How long must it be like this? I hate seeing her anguished and agonizing on the brink of suicide!" A frown threatened to find its way upon his face. How his heart hurt for her!

Majesty turned and smiled at Awe, "It will be many times that she will find herself here. Almost every night. She has given herself to so much evil. That is the nature of man's free will—they can choose as they like." He surveyed the area rapidly, his eyes honing in more upon things invisible than visible. He continued, "If it were not for the prayers of her parents, she would die very soon. In fact, she would already be dead. Ah! The power of the prayers of the saints! If only they knew!" He smiled again and the joy evidenced in the smile caused a radiation of glorious, incandescent light to pulse from him, almost tangibly so—it was so thick in its purity, it could have been touched by a human hand—almost. Awe smiled with him, glowing too. They were silent, smiling, lost in the pure joy of what they were and Who they served. They watched Brilliant and His Strength pour into her.

"Yes," Majesty drew their minds back to the conversation, "she will have many, many nights of this. But...and it is a *great* 'but'...her parents' prayers are and will be unfailing. She will not succumb. We will fight every night on this roof for her. We will not tire. And we will prevail!"

Even in the midst of the Lord's angels, after Maya had regained possession of her senses a bit, she began to chant, "Ommm Kali…" As she began to invoke the evil, the Lord's angels stepped back. Suicide returned, sliding in, hoping that the Lord's angels would not stop him. They did not. They could not—she had made her choice. Suicide brought Depression and Despair with him. They sat down on either side of her, draped their putrid arms about her, and began to hiss into her ears.

The Lord's angels—Majesty, Awe, Brilliant, His Strength, and the legion prayed for by her parents—stepped back…waiting…

"In time, my dear Maya," Majesty promised, "in time…"

GLOSSARY

Alleppey (Alappuzha)—one of the districts of Kerala. It sits on the Indian Ocean and boasts innumerable canals and waterways (called backwaters). It is often said to be the "Venice of the East."

Archana—a session of focused chanting of the names of, and to, a god or goddess. It is believed to purify the chanter, burn off karma, bring great spiritual power, and take one to extraordinary heights.

Asana—meditational sit mat, usually made of cotton or wool, or in special cases, animal hide.

Ashram—Hindu version of a monastery where many spiritual seekers live, usually as monks (brahmacharis, sannyasis, and swamis) and/or nuns (brahmacharinis and swaminis). The ashram life is centered around the worship of, and service to, a particular deity or guru. In India, men are usually the ones who take on brahmacharya and the vow of sannyasa, which is avowed celibacy and lifelong dedication to the guru. However, in the case of Cha Ma's ashram, women also vowed celibacy and a life dedicated to the guru or deity.

Avatar—a human incarnation of a god or goddess. Hindus believe that gods and goddesses take on a human form in order to come down and help humanity when humanity is most in need.

Betel leaves—a type of leaf chewed in India.

Bhajans—Hindu religious songs usually of and to various gods, goddesses, and their consorts (i.e., Shiva, Kali, Ram, Sita, etc.).

Bhakti—intense love and devotion to a god or goddess, guru or satguru.

Brahmachari—a devout, unmarried, celibate boy or young man who lives in an ashram (brahmacharini is the female counterpart). His life is dedicated to whatever deity he worships. Our Western equivalent would be a junior monk or nun. After the stage of brahmacharya, the next step a brahmachari would make, if he was dedicated enough and progressed far enough, would be to take the vow of sannyasa. The vow of sannyasa is a formal vow of celibacy and service to the deity or guru for the rest of his life.

Brahmacharini—female brahmacharis.

Brahmin—the highest rank in India's caste system; a position usually held by kings and priests.

Chai—spiced tea. In India, it is often called masala chai. It is made of black tea, lots of cream and sugar (honey), peppermint, cinnamon, cloves, ginger, cardamom, black pepper, and masala tea spice.

Chakras—seven energy centers that are believed to be along the length of the spine.

Chapati—a thin, round, unleavened flat bread cooked on a stove.

Chappels—sandals, usually made of thin, cheap plastic.

Choli—a little half-top worn underneath a sari. It is usually formfitting, with buttons up the front. It is made in a fabric that complements the sari. However, in the ashram, cholis were usually big and baggy so that little was revealed.

Dalit—the untouchables. In India's caste system, they are considered the lowest. Unemployable and unwanted, they often live on the streets and are social outcasts.

Darshan—the viewing of a guru, satguru, god, or goddess. It is considered a very great blessing.

Devi—another name for goddess. It is a general term used for all female deities (Durga, Kali, Lakshmi, etc.).

Dhoti—a form of traditional dress for Indian males and is worn instead of pants. It is a long, rectangular piece of cloth that is wrapped around one time and tucked into itself at the waist in order to stay on.

Durga—one of the goddesses of Hinduism.

Enlightenment—when a person is free from the cycle of reincarnation. One is bound to the cycle of reincarnation, to be born over and over and over again for eons, until one's karma, whether good or bad, is completely exhausted or burnt off.

Ghee—highly clarified butter used in religious rituals.

Guru—spiritual teacher. (It is believed that the satguru will take a person to moksha, enlightenment.)

Hindi—an Indo-European language; one of the official languages of India. It is spoken throughout India, especially north and east India.

Householder—a person who follows a guru or devotedly worships a deity but lives a family life. He/she marries, has children, etc.

Iddly—An iddly is a food native to Southern India. It is made of ground rice that is fermented overnight. The resulting batter is put into an iddly tray and steamed. Cooked, it is approximately four inches in diameter and one inch thick. It is eaten with many things, particularly sambars, chutneys, curries, dahls, and curd (yogurt).

Ishta-deity—favorite deity or god.

Japa—repetition of a mantra or a name of a deity. It is believed to increase spiritual power, purify the chanter, and remove karma. Different mantras have differing effects.

Kali—one of the Hindu goddesses. She is considered the most malevolent of all the gods and goddesses. She is usually depicted as jet-black, with dreadlock-like hair and her tongue sticking out. She has four or more arms (the more arms the more malevolent). The arms hold different weapons (machete, sickle, sword, etc.). One of the arms holds a severed head. Another arm holds a bowl with which to catch the blood. Kali has different names and personalities. Bhadra Kali is a favorite and is considered sweet and cute. Chamunda Kali is the most pernicious of all her forms. She is thin and emaciated. She looks perpetually hungry and is depicted as living in a cemetery.

Kanya—rice and water gruel that is usually used as a base to curries and pickles; of a thin, soupy consistency; salted to taste.

Karma—According to Hindu philosophy, it is the thoughts and actions that a human accumulates over many lifetimes. All karma, whether good or bad, must be depleted (or burned off) before one can attain moksha.

Kimini—small hand cymbals. One cymbal is held in each hand and is banged against the other. They make a high, *ka-ching ka-ching* sound.

Kitchen ammas—kitchen mothers, the older women who work in the kitchen and oversee all the food preparation.

Krishna—one of Hinduism's major gods.

Kriyas—spontaneous, uncontrollable movements and behaviors that manifest due to the movement of kundalini energy through the chakras up and down the spine—jerking, slithering on the floor, rolling, rocking, etc.

Kundalini (energy or shakti)—the Sanskrit word for "coiled (like a serpent)." Hindus believe that it is a dormant spiritual energy that lodges in the root, muladhara, chakra. Once it is awakened and then energized through spiritual practices and/or contact with the guru, it will move upward along the seven chakras. The final state, enlightenment, is when the kundalini shakti passes through the sahasrara chakra, the last chakra at the crown of the head, and merges back into Brahman. Kundalini shakti is often viewed as a goddess.

Lakshmi—one of the goddesses of Hinduism.

Loka—world, realm, or dimension on planes or in dimensions different than our own. The Puranas (Hinduism's main texts) state that seven lokas exist. While in the ashram, I was taught there were nine.

Lorry—British word for truck, often used in India.

Mala (Japa mala)—a string of beads used for keeping count of the number of repetitions when doing japa (repetition of a mantra or name); usually made with 108 beads or some numeric derivative thereof.

Malayalam—a Dravidian language; one of the predominant languages spoken in Kerala.

Moksha—enlightenment. It is the Sanskrit word for freedom from the cycle of rebirth (reincarnation).

Mudra—hand positions, movements, and gestures used in Hindu religious ceremonies and in meditation. They are believed to have differing spiritual effects given the particular mudra used.

Munda—"shaven head"—The principle thought of the Mundaka Upanishad is that just as one cuts or shaves one's hair off, so too can a person cut off all ties with this illusory, material world. Hence, with certain vows of brahmacharya and sannyasa, the initiate will shave off his hair to represent "a cutting off" of worldly attachments.

Murti—a replica or three-dimensional, physical representation (statue) of a god or goddess that is used in worship to that deity. It can be made of metal, porcelain, sandstone, or any other material.

Namah shivaya—is derived from one of Hinduism's fundamental mantras: "Om namah shivaya." Namah shivaya means salutations to, I bow to, I salute the Shiva in you. It is a way to say hello, good-bye, thank you, excuse me, you're welcome, what did you say, etc., depending upon the context of the phrase.

Om chamundayai namaha—salutations to Chamunda Kali. One of the many phrases chanted during archana.

Om maha kalyai namaha—salutations to the great goddess Kali. One of the many phrases chanted during archana.

Om para shaktyai namaha—salutations to the ultimate primordial energy of the universe. One of the many phrases chanted during archana.

Om shiva shaktyaikya rupinyai namaha—salutations to the union of Shiva and Shakti. The refrain chanted during archana.

Peetham—a low bench, usually only a few inches off the ground.

Pranam (half and full)—to bow. A full-pranam is to lay prostrate on the stomach, forehead touching the floor. A half-pranam is to get on one's knees and bend over, touching one's forehead to the floor. Both gestures are a sign of reverence for and honor to the deity, guru, satguru, or teacher. Sometimes children pranam (bow) to their parents as a sign of respect. Another version, but not really pranaming, is to touch the feet of the guru, satguru, teacher, parent, etc. with the hands. This too is a gesture of respect and reverence.

Premabhakti—divine love. *Prema* means "ultimate, divine." *Bhakti* means "love."

Poona (Pune)—one of India's largest cities; located approximately 95 miles to the southwest of Bombay (Mumbai).

Puja—a ceremony of worship to a god, goddess, or guru.

Punjabi—traditional Indian clothing for females, particularly favored by girls and young women. It is a two-piece set with baggy pants and a matching top that extends to the knees or calves.

Radha—Krishna's consort.

Ram (Lord Ram)—one of the gods of Hinduism.

Ramancheri Tura (Taraikadavu Tura)—small village in Alleppey (Alappuzha).

Rudraksha (Tears of Shiva) beads—often called the "Tears of Shiva" and are round, dark brown, pocked seeds. They are believed to purify the wearer and give spiritual power. Hindus believe the beads have particular characteristics, which are determined by the number (one, two, seven, etc.) of sides, also called faces.

Samsara—the karmic cycle of death and rebirth.

Sanskrit—an ancient Dravidian language. It is the basis of much of Hinduism's foundational texts, chants, mantras, and songs.

Sannyasa—stage of religious devotion in Hinduism where the person takes a formal, solemn vow of life-long celibacy and a life lived solely for the guru or deity. It comes after the stage of brahmacharya. The sannyasi wears yellow and is considered a true and earnest Brahmachari or Brahmacharini. The next and highest stage is that of swami. At that stage the clothing is orange.

Sannyasi—one who has made a vow of sannyasa.

Sari—traditional Indian dress for women. One piece of cloth, usually several yards, is wrapped around and around a woman's body. The trailing edge is hung over the shoulder and down the back, most of the time (Gujarati style is tucked into the front). Underneath is a petticoat and choli.

Satguru—the "ultimate" spiritual teacher. Hindus believe that out of all the teachers, in all the lifetimes, the satguru is the one who will definitely take the person to enlightenment.

Seva—volunteer work; selfless service that is offered up to the guru or deity. It is believed that seva purifies the person (leaving only the higher nature) and burns off karma.

Shakti—the underlying force, the fundamental power, the ultimate energy of the universe. This forced is seen as feminine.

Shiva—considered one of "the three" major gods—Brahma, Vishnu, and Shiva, respectively the creator, the sustainer, and the destroyer.

Shudra—the servant class. They are second to the lowest on the class scale. They are one step higher than the dalits, the untouchables. They are treated much more poorly and are significantly more impoverished than the servant class in many other nations.

Siddhis—thought to be spiritual powers that are attained as one progresses and garners spiritual power and knowledge. Included in them are mind reading, astral projection/travel, levitating, etc. It is believed that it takes many years of intense, single-minded effort to attain them and that most people never will.

Sita—Ram's wife in Hindu lore.

Swami—a high position and a great honor. It means that the man has mastered his lower nature and is free from all karma. In the hierarchy of brahmacharya, sannyasa, and swami, swami is by far the highest honor and position. Only a few ever attain this level.

Swamini—female swamis.

Tapas—spiritual disciplines or disciplines meant to subdue the lower nature so that the higher nature will dominate; also meant to increase one's spiritual power and/or burn off karma.

Trivandrum (Thiruvananthapuram)—the capital of the Indian state of Kerala. It is located far southwest on the Indian subcontinent.

Vibhuti—sacred ash, often from a puja. It is believed to have spiritual power.

Author Contact Information

Website: www.jovanjones.com

Mail: Jovan Jones
P.O. Box 58302
Fayetteville, North Carolina 28305

Email: jj@jovanjones.com

Additional copies of this book and other
book titles from DESTINY IMAGE are
available at your local bookstore.

Call toll-free: 1-800-722-6774.

Send a request for a catalog to:

Destiny Image® Publishers, Inc.
P.O. Box 310
Shippensburg, PA 17257-0310

*"Speaking to the Purposes of God for This
Generation and for the Generations to Come."*

**For a complete list of our titles,
visit us at www.destinyimage.com.**